UNCLE DANNY

a novel

W.F. WALSH

Palmetto Publishing Group
Charleston, SC

UNCLE DANNY

First Edition

Printed in the United States

Paperback: 978-1-64111-437-0
Hardcover: 978-1-64111-438-7
eBook ISBN-13: 978-1-64111-439-4

FOR DAD

ACKNOWLEDGMENTS

There are always many people to thank when working on a book project. First and foremost, Janet Walsh, my wife and editor. Writing is a great pleasure. Editing is a major, meticulous process that takes weeks. She is an incredible editor between being a great radio personality and mom.

I would also like to thank my Dad's family for their information about Danny and some the stories that helped make up this book. Also a giant thanks to our daughter/artist/gemologist Amy Walsh for her black duck design and consulting on cover design.

Our video trailer was by voice actor Ed Reynolds and the Reynolds Media Group who do a superb job.

Great thanks also to Jack Joseph and the team at Palmetto Publishing who have been super to work and really know how to produce a novel and my Los Angeles agent Burt Shapiro.

FORWARD

PRESENT DAY RHODE ISLAND

The headlines in local papers and on the television news stations were that human remains had been found in South Kingstown, Rhode Island. According to the reporting, a developer was breaking ground on a new housing project when construction workers uncovered what they thought were human bones. State Police were quickly called and secured the scene. Officials planned to use an anthropologist to help identify the remains. The property in question belonged to the Catholic Church at one time before being sold for development. Before the church held the deed, it was owned by a famous bootlegger and gangster of the prohibition era who went missing in the 1930s and was never found. The legend of what happened to one of the most famous gangsters in Rhode Island and bootlegging history was still mystery. Could the remains found be those of Danny Walsh, aka "Uncle Danny," who disappeared with $40,000 cash ($767,000 value today) in his pocket after having dinner at the Bank Cafe in Pawtuxet Village? Could the mystery dating back to 1933 finally be solved?

CHAPTER 1
NOVEMBER 1929

The snow was starting to fall heavier as the cold Chicago wind was whipping off the lake across Michigan Avenue down to Dearborn Street in the Loop District. At ten o'clock in the morning most people were already at work, but the street was still bustling with crowds dressed in heavy coats and hats. It was that bone chilling cold that no amount of clothing could keep out.

Patrick McDuffy was glad to be wearing a long, black coat as he stood watch at the door of what appeared to be a jewelry store. The coat covered the "Tommy" that his right hand gripped underneath as the empty jacket sleeve dangled in the cold. His weapon of choice had been developed by John Thompson eleven years before in 1918 when Patrick was just a kid. At six foot two, the 28-year-old redhead wasn't a kid anymore. He was all muscle and a respected member of the Bristol Gang. Bristol was just one of a number of gangs in an organization called the "Big Seven" that ran booze up and down the east coast. The Big Seven was feared by just about anyone who knew who they were including politicians and even law enforcement. The Big Seven made their own rules. Four Irish Americans, two

Italian Americans and one Jewish American were the Big Seven. Along with making all the rules, they also broke all the rules.

Money was the name of the game, and moving illegal booze was how the Big Seven was winning big at it. Just months earlier, Black Friday brought the crash of the stock market. For most, it was devastating. Some people were left dead broke. Others were so downtrodden with their life savings gone they committed suicide. For members of the Big Seven, the crash equaled opportunity. Their product was depression-proof. In fact, they sold more after the crash than before. It seemed a lot of people felt they needed the numbing effects of illegal alcohol.

"You're late," Patrick said to the two men also wearing heavy overcoats and hats approaching from across the busy Chicago street after being dropped off by car.

"Traffic," replied the taller of the two. "We got caught down by---"

"No excuse, Marky," Patrick interrupted with his thick New England accent, clearly agitated with his second in command.

The three men all checked their watches again waiting for the exact time to enter the store.

"Two minutes," Marky said as Patrick and his number three, Joey, stomped their feet to stay warm.

At exactly 10:15, the men walked into the store where three customers were standing at glass counters looking at possible Christmas gifts for loved ones. The store was decorated for the holidays which tended to be the busiest time of the year in the jewelry business. In the back corner, the store manager looked up from his desk, and with a surprised grin on his face, he immediately put his hand under the desk feeling around for and finding a button, which he pushed.

The door to the back room was to the right of and just behind the manager's desk. It was brown with no windows and secured with three bolt locks.

Patrick walked directly to the manager, lifted his arm from inside the long coat exposing the Thompson submachine gun, pointed it and pulled the trigger firing a short burst expelling three .45 caliber cartridges from the 50-round drum. The force of the rounds entering the manager's chest pushed him backwards breaking the chair as his body fell against the wall, and the smell of gunpowder filled the chilly air. For a moment there was silence in the room except for the sound of Christmas music playing on the RCA radio in the background.

A split second later, customers screamed in fear for their lives as Patrick shot the locks off the backroom door, and the acrid odor of gunpowder started to engulf the entire building. He and Marky kicked the shot-up door open and entered the backroom while Joey locked the front door. He then held the hysterical customers and two clerks at gunpoint.

Two gunshots came from just behind a large curtain that split the back room in half missing Marky by just a few inches. Marky turned toward the sound of the shots and fired his Thompson. A loud scream followed as his bullets found their target. Then there was another moment of silence.

"Curtain," Patrick barked. Marky took the barrel of his weapon and used it to push the curtain aside exposing the second half of the room filled with cases of what appeared to be bottles of religious wine. The man who had shot at Marky was dead, slumped over a row of ruined cases of bottles shattered by the impact of bullets. The liquid ran down the wooden boxes and onto the floor as the sound of dripping whisky lingered in the background.

"Smell that?" Patrick asked. "That don't smell like no wine."

"You were right," Marky replied while looking around for anyone else who might be in the room and pose a threat. "I think he was alone."

Sacramental wine was one of the only alcoholic beverages allowed in the United States under the Volstead Act. These cases of communion wine bottles were filled with 80 proof whisky, part of a large stash produced in Canada by the Big Seven but stolen in a grand heist weeks earlier and shipped to Chicago.

"One guy or two ain't going to send a message to these Chicago assholes," Patrick said. "Joey, bring those people in here," he ordered.

Marky got excited. He loved this stuff.

It only took a few moments for the terrified customers and clerks to be herded into the backroom. "You all line up over there. Face the wall." Patrick said pointing to the concrete back wall of the room.

"Don't kill the civilians," Joey said to Patrick who was clearly angry and wanted to send a message. "It's goddamn Christmas."

Patrick McDuffy's Catholic upbringing in New England did little to temper his hatred of the Chicago Drucci Gang.

"Remember who they're connected with," Joey said also not too excited about executing bystanders. "We've already sent them a message. How about we destroy all the product?"

"Joey, don't fucking tell me what to do," Patrick snapped while his trigger finger tickled the bottom of the gun he was pointing at the five people standing just feet away. A car could be heard pulling up to the front of the store.

"Waste them all. Fuck 'em," Marky yelled with a kind of excitement most people reserve for sporting events.

"Jimmy's here," Joey said to Patrick.

All was quiet for a minute except the sobbing of one female customer who clearly didn't know whether she would live or die.

"Did you get the money out of the safe under the desk?" Patrick asked quietly with an eerie, calm tone.

Joey held up the three white pillowcases filled with money showing their take for the day.

"Get in the car, you two," Patrick ordered.

"Patrick, waste 'em---" Marky tried saying before being cut off.

"In the fucking car, now!"

The two lieutenants looked at each other and then over at the five innocent people standing facing the wall before walking back to the front of the store and out to the waiting get-away car.

Patrick looked at the five and put his finger on the trigger. "Today's your lucky day. Merry Christmas," he said and then pulled the trigger emptying the bullets from the drum into the cases of liquor sitting lined up in rows on the floor sparing the civilians. As he headed for the door the five were heard crying as the smell of whisky and more gunpowder filled the air.

Just before he went out of the store, he paused then cleaned out some of the jewelry on display for good measure. Two minutes later he was out the door and into the Chicago cold to the waiting car.

"Let's go," he ordered with a shout while getting into the back seat of the black, snow covered four-door Packard. The car slipped away into the busy Chicago traffic. It was time to get out of Chicago fast and head back home to New England. Their message had clearly been sent.

———————

The line for tickets stretched from the box office of the famous New Amsterdam Theater, down 42nd Street all the way to 8th Avenue. *Ripples* had opened back in February to rave reviews and was the hottest Broadway show so far in 1930. Dorothy Stone starred in the show and was sitting in the 3rd row of the empty orchestra section which would be filled with a sold-out audience in a matter of hours. Her schedule typically didn't include time to mingle with the patrons, but this was a special group of VIPs, and *Ripples* producer Charles Dillingham made sure they were given a private audience with his star.

Sitting with Stone were William "Big Bill" Dwyer, Owney "The Killer" Madden and "Uncle Danny" Walsh, three members of the Big Seven. Dwyer and Madden were New Yorkers while Walsh was a Rhode Islander in town for more than a social call and night at the theater.

"I hope you boys enjoy the show," Stone said as she finished her visit with the men and got up to take her leave heading backstage.

"Bye, doll," Madden replied. "Maybe we'll see you after." This was a thought she didn't want to contemplate, trying to keep these powerful men at a distance.

"What a dame," Big Bill Dwyer muttered while deep inside he had the same dirty thoughts the others had in their minds about the beautiful starlet. "Chuck, you got our tickets?" he asked changing back to a business tone in his booming voice.

"Three front row seats," the producer replied while pointing two rows in front of where they were currently sitting in the theater. Even with the economic mess the country was in, these seats were still hard to come by.

"Good, now get lost." Big Bill ordered.

Dillingham knew he wasn't wanted for the conversation about to begin in the empty theater. He nodded and took his leave as the three Big Seven members gathered closer together for the real reason they had come to the theater on this cold Saturday night in February.

"The *Black Duck* is moving next Friday along with the *Goose*," Walsh said, starting the business of the evening. Newspapers speculated that his trips to New York were more than just shopping trips and theater visits. The men he was talking to ran New York. He ran Rhode Island, Massachusetts and most of New England. Together with the other four members of the Big Seven, they supplied outlawed liquor to people up and down the east coast while making millions of dollars.

"We were screwed in South Boston last month," Madden said. "I think it's a direct result of the Atlantic City Conference."

"No doubt we took a hit. Whether it was because of the conference last year can be debated," Walsh said.

The Atlantic City Conference had been held in May of 1929, and some said it was one of the first organized crime summits ever held in America. Bootlegging had become extremely profitable and at the same time extremely violent, especially in New York and Chicago.

"The wops got the shipment and the money, and the Feds let them do it," Madden said with anger now in his voice. "End of story."

"Goddamn Feds tipped them off. They have someone on the arm," Walsh countered. "But so do we, and our guy heard nothing about it. None of our Fed informants did."

Madden reached over and tugged on Walsh's sleeve pulling him closer. "That's the problem, Danny. That's a problem in your organization up there. Was this guy just asleep at the wheel? Why didn't he know the wops were going to be there? I blame your mole in the Feds. And maybe you should, too."

Walsh was never one to walk away from a good fight, but he wanted to keep the peace within the Big Seven knowing that their bigger enemy was the Italian mafia who were making inroads to their once exclusive business and doing it in a violent way.

"I'll take care of it," the 36-year-old Walsh said. Born in Valley Falls, Rhode Island, Walsh was making a mint on the constitutionally outlawed product he sold at 7 dollars a gallon after paying 66 cents for the same gallon in Canada. He had started small, moving liquor for other bootleggers when prohibition started in 1919 and in the eleven years since, created a small empire. Even now after the crash, business was booming.

Madden respected Walsh and knew it would be taken care of. Walsh was now one of the Big Seven and viewed as an equal member of the syndicate. He let it go at that while turning to the operation at hand.

"Supply is down in New London, Providence, Hartford and Bridgeport," Dwyer said. "No booze, no money. These are company tigers."

Blind tigers, also known as speakeasys, were where the product met the customer. The Big Seven supplied thousands of them all the way down the east coast to Florida totaling over 2000. "Company" or Big Seven-owned blind tigers brought them even more money because they took out the middleman.

"My trucks are coming up to Stonington on Thursday. They will meet your people at 9 p.m. and get things underway," Madden said to Walsh. "Your trucks will go north, mine south, after the transfer."

"Agreed. If there's a delay because of weather or Coast Guard or Treasury patrol, we'll use the standard communications code," Walsh said.

Ironically, the men sipped some Canadian Club poured from an unmarked bottle Dillingham had brought over for their quality time with Dorothy Stone. The shipment they were discussing was almost 200 thousand dollars' worth of the same Hiram Walker produced product arriving on two ships sailing from the French island of Saint-Pierre just south of Newfoundland. Saint-Pierre and sister island Miquelon were the two main hubs the Big Seven used to move booze out of Canada. This time of the year, the weather could be hazardous if not fatal, but it was worth the risk they would take given the payday that waited on the other end.

"The *Goose* and *Black Duck* will set up along the rum line, and your boats will need to be ready and in place," Madden said to Big Bill Dwyer. Dwyer ran the smaller boats used to ferry the cases of liquor from the ocean-going ships set up along what was known as the rum line twelve miles offshore marking the edge of U.S. jurisdiction.

"Our four flat boats will be in place. Usual light signals," Dwyer replied confidently. Dwyer had no love for the U.S. Coast Guard. He had lost his son in a firefight with a Coast Guard patrol boat while running rum from Bimini in the Bahamas to the Florida Keys. All hands on that rumrunner were lost, and the Coast Guard touted the bust in all the papers to the extent of even showing pictures of the dead. Big Bill Dwyer had vowed revenge and stepped up his operations, never wasting an opportunity to screw the federal government. He was a big man of 42 years with a balding head and scar on his nose from a knife fight when he was a teenager. He had worked his way up on the streets building a small criminal empire which he folded into the Big Seven, as did the others.

Madden nodded in agreement and took a sip of his Canadian whisky. Madden's story was also one of growing up in a tough New York neighborhood without a father. A German soldier killed his dad just before the Great War ended twelve years earlier in 1918. He had a particular dislike for Germans and anything that had to do with the federal government, blaming them for sending his father off to war.

"Let's not fuck this one up. I don't have to tell you what the price tag was for all of us after what happened in Boston," Madden said referring once again to their loss of product weeks before at the hands of the Italians. It was all about supply and demand. There was a lot of demand, and these men made damn sure there was enough supply. Madden was married. His 35-year-old wife of three years looked much younger. Sally Madden had played the field quite a bit before meeting up with Owney one night at a club in Green Point, Brooklyn. She had grown accustomed to the rich mobster lifestyle he delivered to her but still wanted to be independent.

The men finished their drinks and business before settling down and enjoying the show. Not only was it a good front for a meeting place, but the theater made for a nice evening out.

---

12 hours later, Grand Central Terminal was loud and busy as thousands of people came and went from New York City. Inside and outside the famous terminal, homeless people huddled where they could, some begging for food or money to buy some. Others held up makeshift signs asking for work. The smell was a mix of locomotive diesel fumes and bread baking from locals trying to make a buck from the commuters. Danny Walsh and Patrick McDuffy boarded the first-class car on the 7 a.m. northbound New Haven Railroad train ending in Boston, but they would be getting off in Providence.

"We've got work to do," Danny said to his top lieutenant who had stood outside the theater the night before. Patrick's main duty on this trip was to look out for his boss. Both men were armed, and Danny almost never went anywhere alone.

"So, you said last night," replied Patrick feeling hung over from consuming half a bottle of Scotch before turning in the night before. "Where's the score point on this run?"

"Stonington," Danny said without much emotion. "Then we have another job to take care of." The train's whistle blew as it started jerking forward beginning the four-hour trek north back into their territory.

CHAPTER 2

ONE SCOLLAY SQUARE

The mood was cheery at number One Scollay Square on a very cold February day just after the New Year. 1930 was starting off right for these law enforcement personnel assigned to the Boston office whose charge was to break up and disrupt the movement of illegal liquor in the city and other parts of New England. A number of high-profile raids had just been conducted over the holidays landing some of them on the front page of the *Boston Globe*.

"Don't you look sharp?" joked Sergeant Jeff Howard as he commented on his partner's bright flowered tie.

"I'm in a good mood," replied Agent Ted Connelly walking in after taking the stairs up five floors rather than the elevator, just for the exercise. "Third raid was the charm to finally get some decent press."

"I'd rather not have the press, just the praise," Howard said with a half-joking tone to his voice.

Sergeant Howard had fifteen years in federal law enforcement, and hitting age 40 this year had made him realize that it would not be too long until he would qualify for retirement. His was a risky business these days, and he looked forward to changing careers when his time was up. Tall and thin with jet-black hair, he looked all the part of what was known as a "G-Man."

Ted was Irish. Born and raised in the Boston area, he had wanted to be a cop since he could remember. Once a Boston Police Officer, he had been accepted into the federal law enforcement ranks when Uncle Sam started filling newly created positions after the Volstead Act went into law. At 28 years old, he was always wanting more and fought hard to keep up with his contemporaries on material things. With dirty blond hair and a short stature, most of his friends could outplay him in sports. He was working to outplay them in life.

"Who's going to brief today?" asked Sergeant Howard as others gathered and the familiar smell of bad coffee filled the room.

"Don't know and don't care," Ted said with a smart-ass tone.

Mondays were always longer for these and the other agents working the Boston metro area. The term "metro area" was misleading seeing that their territory was actually made up of most of the six New England states. They focused mainly on Boston and the coastal areas of southern New England including Rhode Island, Cape Cod and Connecticut.

"I'm sure the North End crew will come up and maybe the Big Seven," Jeff said while making a coffee for himself.

At precisely nine o'clock, the agents gathered in the packed conference room for the weekly all call. Special Agent in Charge of the Boston office James Warren walked in and called the meeting to order. Warren was not liked by most in the Boston Field Office because of his management style and lack of people skills. He was quick to take credit for other people's ideas and just as quick to tear someone down who showed some initiative. Short, stocky and with a receding hairline, Warren was trying his best to climb the chain of command to compensate for what he lacked as a person. Some of the men called him by the nick name "Reverse" behind his back because he would sometimes just look at them in a mirror he had on the wall near his desk rather than turn around and look them in the eye.

"Pipe down, people," Warren said calling the meeting to order. "Today we'll talk about the Big Seven, North End Gang and this new crew up in Maine I suspect are actually Canadians," he started off.

Ted looked over at his sergeant who returned the look with the classic "I told you so" expression on his face.

Special Agent Eric Thompson was also in the room. He was credited with a number of raids over the last couple of years thanks to his confidential informants, better known as CI's.

"This Maine crew has slowly been working down the coast toward Portland opening gin-mills sometimes within a mile of Big Seven owned or supplied speakeasys. We've sat back and watched some of these just for sport to see how the Big Seven would react. So far, nothing," Warren explained.

"If they're Canucks, they'll figure it out fast that's it not good for their health to be setting up in competition to the Big Seven," one of the agents joked as the room laughed out loud.

"Special Agent Jennings has a CI working way up there in the sticks giving us some of our intel. They are definitely Canadians, and the money goes back to up to the mother ship in Montréal. I'd like nothing more than to shut down their little places, but it's more sporting to see what the Big Seven is going to do about it," Warren said. He took a sip of his coffee and continued. "Any intel you might have on these people, be sure to share with the unit."

He rambled on for a little longer before coming to an item of interest for Ted. "North End Gang scored big before we could get to them," Warren went on. "When we arrived, there wasn't even a pint of booze in the warehouse. In fact, this---"

"Word on the street is that the Big Seven is pissed," Ted said interrupting the boss who hated being interrupted, which everyone in the room could clearly see from the look on his face. "I think they would rather have it busted by us than robbed by the wops," Ted finished, disregarding that the term "wop" was not welcomed by all. He was the recipient of some dirty looks from other Italian American agents in the room.

"Clearly they were tipped off by someone. They knew we were going to conduct a raid and got there first. They also knew that the Big Seven's M.O. was large warehousing of stock," continued Warren. "They found out where the giant supply was and stole it in order to sell themselves while at the same time ruining our little party. Worse for them, the Italians robbed from the Big Seven. Probably not a good idea."

He pulled down a map that was rolled up hanging above the chalkboard. This week the agents of the Boston Field Office were looking at trying to get inside a possible new booze warehouse the Big Seven might be operating near the small coastal town of Ipswich. "It's about here on Plum Island," Warren pointed. " I want a couple of agents dressed as construction workers to go up there and check it out Wednesday. If it's a score, we'll take it Thursday."

"Do we still have the construction van?" asked Sergeant Howard. Jeff was tasked with logistics on many of these raids and intel sweeps.

"Yeah, and it will be you, Connelly and Thompson for the intel sweep," Warren ordered.

Jeff nodded in agreement. He enjoyed the excitement of the job, but as a new father, he would also measure risk more carefully. If they found a booze stash, Jeff was sure the raid would be a major operation the next day with Warren in command and taking full credit, especially if the papers showed up after being alerted to the bust. Jeff knew one thing for sure: they would not be wearing ties on Wednesday.

After a few more housekeeping items, the meeting broke up. Most of the men walked back to their offices or the squad room. Agent Connelly stepped outside into the ice-cold Boston air and walked over to a favorite street vendor for a hot chocolate. He handed the man twenty cents for the drink. The street vendor put the money in the cash box. The tightly folded note Connelly had secretly slipped him went into his pocket.

CHAPTER 3

FAMILY

Bingo was always on Tuesday nights in the basement hall at St. Mary's Catholic Church in Seekonk, Massachusetts. It was a weekly social gathering for the parishioners, but even more than that, a big boost to the operating capital of the church. With the crash, money was hard to come by for most. Bingo at the church, even for pennies, was a way to relax and maybe go home with a few more cents than they had arrived with.

Sister Judy Ann ran the bingo and prided herself on the increased attendance over the last couple of years. She was quite mature for her relatively young age of 28 and devoted to her religion and calling in life. Born in upstate New York, she had entered the convent at 25 after college and had been a driving force of good in the St. Mary's parish since being assigned there by the Bishop of Fall River. If not for the Religious Sisters of Mercy habit she wore, she would have had plenty of male company. At 5 feet 9 inches with long legs and natural sandy blond hair, the good sister could easily have had a career in Hollywood and possibly been one of those pin-up girls.

"Damn it," said one of the older ladies playing eight bingo cards at once when a number was called.

"Now-now, Ruth," Sister Judy Ann said with a bit of a cautious tone while walking by. "This is still God's house."

"I hope God gives me some better luck," Ruth remarked returning fire.

"Patience, my child," Sister Judy Ann replied.

The crowd was bigger than the week before as cigarette smoke rose to the ceiling of the small basement hall. Father Ralph always stopped by to give a prayer at the start of bingo and mingle with some of his flock. Tonight was no different.

"How are you, Father?" Asked Abby who was a bingo regular.

"I'm well. How are you doing this week? How's your mom?" asked Father Ralph. He knew most parishioners by name and made it his business to know their families, jobs and more. He was a tall man of almost six two and towered over Abby as she played her cards.

"She's having a tough week, Father. Please say a prayer," Abby said in a diminished tone.

"I will. I will also make sure she's on my list for Holy Communion."

"Thank you, Father. How's your brother, the policeman?"

"He's a federal agent at the Bureau of Prohibition and doing well, thanks. Still up in Boston," he said while correcting her facts. Father Ralph's last name was Connelly. His brother was Special Agent Ted Connelly. He continued to make his rounds and spotted Sister Judy Ann in the back of the room. It was important for his parishioners to see him at the bingo night where he could spend some time with them outside of the usual Sunday mass. He had another, much deeper reason to check on Sister Judy Ann's bingo operation. Their eyes met as the rest of the flock looked to the heavens for luck to win at tonight's St. Mary's Bingo. Father Ralph wanted to win at something else.

———

The body was covered with snow when the kids came upon it. They were out doing what most kids in the Boston suburbs did after a winter storm, sledding. It didn't take long for the police to arrive and secure the scene.

With at least twenty bullets spread across the torso, it was clear that this was no accident.

"Whoever this was, they wanted him dead," said one of the local Mansfield police officers.

"Definitely a hit," said his partner. "Oh shit," he said a few minutes later after searching the pockets and finding a wallet with a badge inside.

"What?" asked the other officer.

"A Fed."

"Jesus, that's what we need today," the officer said sarcastically knowing that this was not just a lost life, but a lost fellow law enforcement officer. He also knew mounds of paperwork awaited him after they processed the scene. The body was frozen solid, and he estimated it had been dumped sometime over the last couple of days given the condition.

"Robert Simpson, Bureau of Prohibition," said the officer as he read from the credentials. "What do you bet there's a card in the other pocket?"

"You think?" asked his partner.

The officer felt inside the opposite side of the jacket and pulled out a playing card.

"No shit!" the younger, less experienced officer said while looking at the card his partner was holding. "Big Seven?" he asked having heard stories of bodies found around New England with the telltale calling card of the Big Seven placed in pockets of dead people. The playing cards, usually the ace of spades, were used to send a message to anyone willing to go against them. Robert had been one of their informants on the inside of the FBI. He had worked closely with the Bureau of Prohibition and sold information back to the Big Seven. The Big Seven's stash location and the Bureau of Prohibition's planned raid leaked to the North End gang somehow missed him. It would not happen again.

The leading officer paused and then with more of a sigh, looked up and gave his answer. "Yeah. Big Seven job," he said to his young colleague.

———

CHAPTER 4
SUPPLY CHAIN

Cold was just a basic word to describe the state of the climate one was feeling. On this dark February night off the coast of Connecticut, the men aboard the *Goose* and her sister ship *Black Duck* had more colorful words to describe how it felt. The wind was blowing around twenty knots and the seas grew to a mean seven feet for the last part of their journey down from Canada. Some of the men spent time on the rails overcome by the motion of the ship as seasickness set in. The wind chill made it feel like well below zero. It was pitch dark and the navigator on the *Black Duck* double-checked his chart and navigation to make sure they were arriving at the correct place.

The two ships slowly closed in on the coast, but the closest they could get was twelve miles before the United States Coast Guard had jurisdiction. Transferring hundreds of cases of illegal alcohol to smaller boats always proved to be a good way to test the abilities of these not-so-legal sailors.

"Two long flashes followed by two short flashes," Captain Rick St. Pierre said to his first officer standing watch on the bridge of the old retrofitted tanker ship waiting for the correct recognition and rendezvous signal.

St. Pierre was from a long line of Canadian sailors who made a living on these waters. For St. Pierre, the risk of this type of merchant mariner work came with great reward.

"Aye," said the first officer whose beard was now frozen from the combination of wet salt air and below freezing temperatures. Both men had been operating the *Black Duck* for almost ten years. He looked back over his right shoulder making sure the lights of their sister ship were still in sight as they awaited the signal from small boats launched nearby to meet them at the rum line.

"There!" Captain St. Pierre yelled so all could hear him. The signal lights from the lead small boat appeared on the horizon and were approaching fast. "Be ready," he ordered to his crew of six other men. Being ready meant they would stand by to tie off the smaller boats and begin to transfer the cases of liquor. It also meant that two of the men stood ready with their Tommys should it be the Coast Guard or people wishing them harm.

The four smaller and faster boats slowed as the cold wind blew them side-to-side in the ocean swell. Two would head to the *Goose* and the other two would tie up to the *Black Duck*. The ice-cold spray of the ocean covered the men in the smaller boats as they slowed, bobbing up and down in the rolling sea.

"The black duck migrates in the winter," one of the men on the lead small boat yelled out to Captain St. Pierre looking down from the bridge.

"And returns in the summer," he yelled back the corresponding signal code. "Thanks for coming out in this weather!"

"Didn't have much choice," the man driving the lead boat yelled back as the sailors on *Black Duck* took lines to tie them alongside best they could in the heavy swell. "Dwyer sends his regards."

"Send mine back. Wish I could come ashore and sip some of this stuff with you, but time is ticking," Captain St. Pierre said. Big Bill Dwyer was in charge of the small boats that operated out to the rum line from shore. These men worked for him.

"We're secure," yelled one of the deckhands up to Captain St. Pierre who tried to sip a hot cup of Joe without spilling as the boats tossed back and forth on the turbulent Atlantic. That in itself was the telltale sign of an experienced skipper.

"Let's get the boxes moving," he said to his second in command who quickly relayed it to the men below. With that order, the transfer of illegal booze began just as it had hundreds of times before in many different kinds of weather.

In all, 535 cases of liquor were transferred from the larger ocean-going vessels to the four smaller boats making three trips back to shore with the stash.

The darkness of night was only a couple of hours from giving way to daylight, as the sun would soon rise over a cloudy, cold and mean looking sea. Captain St. Pierre wanted to be well underway headed north before that to avoid any detection by the Coast Guard.

"Release all lines," the captain ordered as the last of the fast boats drifted away from the *Black Duck* and the small fleet started the daredevil run back toward the Connecticut shoreline. "Full ahead make your course 055," he ordered the helmsman as both the *Goose* and *Black Duck* started the slow trek northeastward headed to Canada.

—————

Back on shore, the last boat approached the weathered and worn dock that served as an offloading point thanks to the generous bribe money Big Bill Dwyer paid to its owner. They had used this dock and farm many times over the last two plus years. There were many other rendezvous points and docks up and down the New England coast. The last "deuce," as the booze boys called them, was standing by ready to loaded up before heading north toward U.S. Route 1. Each truck was around two and a half tons, hence the full nickname "deuce and a half." They were old army trucks with canvas tops over the cargo areas bought at auction after the Great War.

Parts were sometimes hard to get, but Big Bill Dwyer's men kept them in running condition and labeled their canvas sides as moving vans.

The trucks spread out with some heading north and the others south. Each truck driver would go to a designated staging area, usually a farm or other off-road meeting place where local men with smaller vehicles would take their allotted number of cases to the speakeasys and blind tigers. Most of this was done late at night or early in the morning around dawn.

"We're headed to Rhody," Steve Fischer said to the truck driver as he walked over from the car after parking at the rendezvous point.

"Good for you," the driver replied with a tone that clearly showed he didn't give a shit.

Steve, the deuce driver and Steve's assistant in the matter, George, transferred the cases from the deuce to the waiting car. George was a skinny young guy of 19 and not really made for this kind of heavy lifting. Steve, tall and all muscle, was in it for the thrill of breaking the law and earning money.

"Let's go," Steve said to George after they put the last box into the back seat of the 1927 four door black Buick sedan sporting wood spoke wheels. "Cover the goddamn boxes, George," Steve yelled after he climbed into the driver's seat and looked back over his shoulder.

"I did," George answered as he opened the front door ready to climb in for the ride back to Rhode Island.

"I can see the fucking side of the case," Steve said with a disgusted tone. "Cover the whole thing for Christ's sake."

George quickly opened the back door once again and adjusted the tarp draped over the liquor so that it would cover the entire ten boxes sitting on the seat and floor weighing down the Buick.

"Good," Steve said as George finished and shut the back door before getting into the front seat. The sun was just coming up on a cold, windy and gray morning along the Connecticut shoreline.

They weren't half a mile away from the entrance to the farm when Steve noticed a police car following behind them. Before he could even say anything to George, he saw the bright red light and heard the siren of the officer's car.

"Goddamn it," Steve said as he slowly pulled to the side of the road. "I'll bet this is a shake." Shakedowns were nothing new to Steve and the others who moved the booze around the six New England states. Most of the time they would pay off the officer and give him a bottle for the house.

"Moving someone from the farm back there?" asked the officer as he walked up to the Buick.

"Yeah, and they've got a lot of shit," Steve said back using his usual mix of colorful language and curse words.

"I'll bet that's expensive," the officer said, which was code for his payoff.

"C note and a bottle," Steve said as he handed the officer a one-hundred-dollar bill. "George, grab a fifth back there." George quickly got out of the front seat and opened one of the boxes under the tarp in the back seat extracting a fifth of Canadian Club.

"Two bottles," the officer ordered.

"Two, George," Steve said to his partner. For them, it was just the cost of doing business.

"Have a fine day, officer," Steve said after George handed him two bottles.

"Drive safe," the officer replied with a smirk on his face. Both knew this was how the game was played.

Steve put the car back in gear and continued his trek north toward Rhode Island where the "company" speakeasys were getting low on product while the demand from their customers seemed to always be on the rise.

———————

CHAPTER 5

EASY COME...EASY GO

Plum Island was mostly a bunch of dirt roads and a place not too far from Boston where summer vacationers would flock to the beach to get away from the city heat and crowds. Large dunes filled with beach plum shrubs stretched up and down the waterfront giving the island its iconic name. In the winter, those shrubs were covered with snow and ice while only a few yearlong islanders lived in broken-down beach houses with potbellied stoves for heat. If someone wanted to hide something, this was the place to do it, but only during winter.

The wind was blowing cold and hard for the second day in a row that three of the men in the lead car had been on the island. For the others sitting in the second car of the take down team, they were used to these New England winters. The sun had come up just about two hours before, but it clearly was doing little to overcome the cold winter sea air.

"Pull up just over there," Special Agent Ted Connelly said to Sgt. Jeff Howard with his hand extended across the dashboard of the black 1925 government issued Marmon sedan.

Special Agent in Charge James Warren followed Howard's lead as both vehicles pulled to the side of the old dirt road covered with a dusting of snow. The building was around two hundred yards further up at the end of the road.

"Not a lot of cover," Connelly said to the others as they assembled around the hood of the first car. "We're going to have to split up and go across the dunes then come back in." The dunes ran parallel to the street giving them a least a little cover. Once they were across from the building, they would have no choice but to cross a field out in the open.

"Three and three," Connelly ordered as steam from his breath rose in the 27-degree air. Technically Warren was the highest-ranking member of the team, but Connelly was in tactical command.

"Check your weapons," James Warren said to the men in a tone reminding them who the overall boss was. "Take them down if you have to."

Ted looked over at Warren. "I'm not sure how many will be there. Yesterday it was locked and no one was around."

"Well, just in case," Warren said. "Let's go."

The men split into two groups of three with one group moving toward the dunes on the right while the others made their way to the dunes on the left.

Ted led his group quietly and slowly along while carefully ducking below the dunes until they were perpendicular to the old farmhouse. Warren did the same on the opposite side. The two men made eye contact and simultaneously began closing in on the building that was about the size of a cow barn. It was wooden and black in color with only two small windows on each side. The entrance door was on the end facing the ocean, and the snow-covered road leading to the building. All six men approached the building with weapons drawn then spread out around it should someone try to escape out a window. Just the day before, Connelly and his team had been on surveillance posing as construction workers. They observed through one of the windows cases of liquor lined up and stacked almost to the ceiling. They also noted in their report the day before that no other people were around the booze stash.

Each man doubled checked his weapon as Connelly used a crow bar to breach the door. His experience with this sort of thing along with his strength cracked the door in short order. Once it began to break, he and Jeff Howard used their shoulders, and the door quickly gave way giving the agents access to the musty smelling building.

"What the fuck?" Warren asked while walking into the empty building knowing that the newspaper headlines he was hoping for had just disappeared in front of his eyes as had the liquor, apparently over the last 24 hours.

Jeff Howard, Connelly, Warren and the others were stunned. "Jesus, Mary and Joseph," Connelly cried out.

"How the fuck could they move all that booze in one day, and how the hell did they know we were coming?" asked Warren clearly shaken up by the fact that he now had an empty barn to show for all the grand-standing he had done with the higher command about this big bust today. "I want a full investigation on how this leaked out."

The other men in the raiding party didn't say a word knowing that Warren would lash out at them. Some of the men knew they could even get the blame, understanding the history of Warren who was quick to take credit and even faster to point fingers.

"Let's go," Connelly said to his team knowing that the embarrassment of the failed raid would continue to haunt Warren while putting a smile on the faces of Danny Walsh, Big Bill Dwyer and the other members of the Big Seven. They might have lost one stash to the North End Gang weeks before, but they would not lose another.

———

"Don't leave anything," Sally Madden said to the man who was ten years her junior as he put his pants back on in the bedroom of her New York townhouse.

"Fuck no," Kevin said as he continued to gather up his clothes and drink the beer he started but hadn't finished before seducing the wife of one of the biggest crime bosses in New York. "That's the last thing I want to do."

"I love it when you come over to help with shoveling the walkway," she said with a twinkle in her eye. "Want to help me again tomorrow?"

"I can't, Mrs. Madden. If your husband found out about this or any of the other times, I would have a bullet my head," he said.

Sally couldn't really argue that point because she knew from past experience that it was a true statement. Owney "The Killer" Madden had earned his nickname and didn't suffer fools gladly.

"Well, I really enjoy your company," she said as he was just about to walk out of the bedroom and head downstairs and to his car parked about a block away on 2nd Avenue. "Owney is out of town until at least tomorrow."

"I've got to go. Take care, and thanks for the beer," he said in a bit of an innocent tone like nothing actually happened. He gave her a kiss on the cheek and disappeared down the stairs and out the door. She grabbed her bra and blouse to finish getting dressed before heading out the door herself.

Fifteen minutes later, she put on her warm wool coat to battle the 20-degree February afternoon and walked down the path Kevin had shoveled before their little encounter upstairs. Two blocks away at the corner of East 1st Street was a small diner called Mel's. With Owney out of town, she felt it was an okay place for her next meeting of the day. This one she hadn't arranged but knew it was to her benefit to take.

Always in the third booth on the right, he sat and waited. She walked through the door and saw him while stomping the snow off her boots. Putting on her best neutral face, she walked over and sat across from him.

"Good afternoon, Mrs. Madden," Special Agent Kent Davis of the Federal Bureau of Investigation said as he picked up his coffee cup to take a sip. "It's been awhile."

She just shook off the cold and worked at getting her jacket off as a waitress approached.

"Just a coffee," she said to the waitress without looking at her directly. Her eyes were on Special Agent Davis sitting across from her.

"So, how are you?" he started.

"Fine."

"Killer out of town again?" Davis asked knowing the answer, but he had to make some small talk.

"Why do you ask me that when you already know the answer? Do you think I'm stupid?" she asked with an annoyed tone in her voice.

"Just making conversation," he admitted.

She just sat there as the waitress returned with her coffee.

"So now there are these photos," he said sliding a manila envelope across the table with five 8x10 pictures inside.

She opened the envelope and pulled out the pictures. It was hard to keep a poker face when she saw her image in all the photos.

"So?" she said with a stone-cold tone.

"Now we've got conspiracy to sell in violation of the Volstead Act and conspiracy to commit murder. The last one is my favorite. By the way, what's his name? Kevin?"

"These don't prove a goddamn thing, Kent, and you know it," she answered.

"Is this not you with cases of liquor, with known felons, with Jimmy Johnson in the last known picture of him alive?" Davis asked.

"What do you want from me? You know this is my husband's business," she said with a tired tone.

"If he goes, you go. You know that, Sally. And you know what I'm looking for."

"That last picture also doesn't mean a thing, you bastard," she countered.

Special Agent Davis took a sip of his coffee then spoke again. "I don't give a shit about what you have going on the side. I do give a shit about making a case against the Big Seven and your husband. If you want to go down with him, be my guest, but we're going to take him and the rest of that crew down."

"Do I have any guarantees?"

Davis had been working on Mrs. Owney Madden for months now, but it was time to put the squeeze on.

"Not at the moment, but we might be able to work something out depending on what you can do for us."

"I hate Feds."

"Thank you."

"And if I walk away?" she asked once again.

"I've answered this since the day we met. You're going to jail, too."

"He'll kill me. You know that."

"We will make sure he and any of his people can't and won't get to you. I've been over this," he answered growing more and more impatient.

"I want a guarantee in writing," she demanded in a tense whisper so that no one would hear them.

"I need records and ledgers," he said back.

"It's possible, but only when I get something in writing. Something that says I walk and that you're going to keep me safe."

Special Agent Davis knew he had finally hooked his fish and sat back to take another sip of his now cold coffee. Moments like this were one of the reasons he had gotten into law enforcement.

"Done. I will have something within a week or two. Until then, no communications, and I will reach out in the usual way when it's time to talk again," he explained.

A chill rushed in from the door opening to the cold winter that awaited the two of them outside. Ironically, Sally had had a dream the night before that cold air from outside gave her a chill just as a bullet penetrated the back of her head. The weather wasn't the only thing giving her chills at this meeting. He paid for both of their coffees then got up out of the booth to leave. Looking down at her still seated Kent said, "I'll be in touch."

She didn't say another word while sitting and waiting for his exit in order not to be seen together.

CHAPTER 6

BUSINESS UNITS

Patrick pulled up in front of the textile factory that sat on the Blackstone River near Pawtucket, Rhode Island. The Big Seven used it for stashing liquor among other things they would sell on the black market. "Big Bill" Dwyer had invested in the textile company just to be able to use the facility for various projects. Danny Walsh had also bought in. They each owned 40 percent in order to have control of the property. A police captain named Larry Lynch owned the other twenty percent. On the outside it looked like a typical mill built of red brick with thick windows which now had long icicles hanging off of them. Inside it was a different story altogether.

Patrick opened the door and walked in from the cold. The reception area was completely legit as the young woman looked up and welcomed him to the factory, which, during working hours, produced yarn for clothing. There were two doors that led from the reception area. One was to the right of the reception desk and the other to the left. Both doors were locked. She buzzed him through the door on the right. He thanked her without saying anything else and walked from reception through the door which led to stairs taking him up one flight. At the top was another locked door, but this time he had to knock. A small box built into the door slid sideways as a man looked out and saw the visitor. Instantly the door opened.

"Which room?" Patrick asked.

"Three."

Patrick looked to the left and down the narrow hall where there were five rooms on each side, much like a hotel. The rooms were numbered, and when he got to the third he opened the door and went inside.

"It took you long enough," said the half-naked girl sitting on the bed with two fingers of whisky left in the glass her right hand held.

Patrick shut the door behind him and went to the table by the other side of the bed where the liquor bottle was sitting and poured himself a drink.

"You going to say anything?" asked the girl.

He took a sip of the drink and looked back at her.

"You're short this month," he said with a business tone to his voice.

"You're short every month," she said sarcastically.

Patrick picked up one of the leather straps sitting at the end of the bed, walked over to her side and cracked it across her legs, which were bare, making a snapping, almost whipping sound as it impacted her pale skin.

"You bastard," she screamed knowing that even if someone heard her, they would not interfere.

"I'm not in the mood. You're short this month," he continued.

"It's been slow," she said while getting up off the bed and fetching a towel out of the bathroom to wet down and put across the fresh mark on her legs. The rooms were set up like a motel. Each had a bed, a small bathroom and a couple of end tables. "I'm not magic, you know."

"You need to be," he said while unbuttoning his shirt. "You need to be more proactive."

"What the hell? What do you want me to do, stand out on the corner with a sign saying 'half price fucks upstairs, come right in?'"

Patrick stopped and considered his options for this girl. She was one of his biggest earners and ran this side of the business with the other girls who were working just down the hall. "You know what you're doing, Valentine."

Patrick played rough with both his day job and this enterprise. He took off his shoes and socks then picked up the leather straps once again. This time he had both.

"Now, it's time to play nice. Tie me up," he ordered.

"The usual?"

"Yeah."

He stretched out on the bed and she took the straps and tied each of his wrists to the wooden dowels that were on the headboard. "Tight," he ordered.

"You'll get what you want," she said after she tied him to the bed. She then took her drink and poured a little of the whisky on his chest and began to lick it. Next, she unbuttoned his pants and pulled them down to his ankles. On the bedside table there was a black blindfold which she reached for and put over his head to cover his eyes. Over the next three hours she pleasured her boss knowing he had no time limit unlike the one-hour tricks they pulled daily in this part of the building.

The cold air was biting, and gusty winds whipped later that evening as Patrick got out of his car and walked up the driveway of the old Victorian tenement house in which he and his family occupied the larger, first floor. He kicked the snow from his boots as he climbed the three steps to open the door to the mudroom.

"Take off your shoes, Patrick," Jeannie, his wife of three years yelled from down the hall. She was pregnant with their third child. "Tell Daddy hello," she ordered Patrick Junior who was about to turn seven and, like his little sister, born before they were married. Coming from a large Irish Catholic family, this had been a bit of a problem, which they solved by moving to Rhode Island from their hometown of Portsmouth, New Hampshire. Their marriage was a private affair arranged by one of the Bristol Gang's enforcers who had a brother who was a judge and willing to do it on a quiet Saturday afternoon. The judge had no idea what Patrick did for a living and also thought his brother worked in the cleaning business.

"What's for supper?" Patrick asked with his thick New England accent.

"Pot roast," Jeannie said as she greeted him with a kiss when he walked into the kitchen from the mudroom. "Can't you smell it?"

"Smells good, honey," he answered. "How's my boy?"

Young Patrick ran up and gave his dad a hug. "How's work, Daddy?"

"Busy. How was your day?" Patrick asked.

"Good. We made snow angels outside. Did you see them?"

"It's too dark. I'll see them in the morning."

Jeannie interrupted. "Wash your hands for supper, and tell your sister to come down."

"How are you feeling?" he asked pointing to her large mid-section.

"Good. Lots of movement."

"About four weeks away?" he asked while sitting down at the kitchen table. She had a hot tea waiting on him after hearing the car pull up. The smell on his breath of the midday whisky had been replaced by coffee at the office just before leaving work.

"It's a girl," Patrick Jr. said while walking into the room with his younger five-year-old sister Mary.

"You don't know that," Jeannie said as the kids sat in their appropriate chairs.

"I want a brother. That's what I asked God for," Patrick Jr. explained.

"We'll see. Let's say grace," Jeannie said changing the subject as the kids bowed their heads and she led the family in the dinner prayer.

"How was the office today?" she asked her husband.

"Busy. Trying to get the hospital contract," he said. Continental Cleaners was a good commercial laundry business he had a piece of with his brother Stan and of course Danny. It was also a legit enterprise giving them cover for the monies coming from the not so legit enterprises. "We shall see."

The family continued with supper as the cold air of a Rhode Island winter pushed against and rattled some of the windows. Number two heating oil kept them warm inside as the furnace worked overtime in the cold basement. To the family who occupied the third-floor apartment, the McDuffy's were just a nice Catholic couple. To Patrick's other family, his "work" family, they were watched over and untouchable.

———

Owney Madden and Big Bill Dwyer sat in the back seat of the warm car smoking cigars while their bodyguards stood outside after the almost four hour drive north from New York City. The farm was used to raise thoroughbreds, which was really the only passion Danny had except for bootlegging and making money. Lots of money. Danny had bought the farm because it was out in the country and he could appear to be a farmer and horse breeder. It was actually his second house in the Charlestown area of southern Rhode Island. A couple of years earlier, he had purchased a large mansion on the water, also in Charlestown, which he considered his main residence. In Providence, he had a couple of luxury apartments used for both business and pleasure.

The farm was big enough that a makeshift airfield had been built on the east side to look like horse paddocks in a row.

"Tell the old man that they should be here anytime," Marky said to Owney and Dwyer's driver who then opened the door to inform the bosses.

"There it is," Patrick yelled when he heard the telltale sound of an airplane engine now spotted and approaching in the northern sky. The snow had been plowed off the makeshift runway earlier in the day, and Patrick prayed the strip was long enough for the pilot and his boss to land.

The Ford built Trimotor aircraft descended to about three hundred feet for a flyover as the pilot measured up the field. There was no guarantee going into this trip that he could land on the farm, but he assured Danny he would give it his best shot.

As the plane passed overhead, both bosses jumped out of the car and excitement could be seen in place of their typical cold expressions.

"So far, so good. Now let's hope he can land it," Patrick said to Big Bill who had walked over to him.

"Damn well hope so," Big Bill said. "This is a risky investment."

The plane turned back downwind as the pilot lowered the flaps and slowed to landing speed. The wind was not an issue today as he carefully turned on a left base for the farm runway. Once on final, the engine sound dwindled as the pilot pulled the power back. The spectators held their collective breath and, except for the sound of the engine powering back, only an occasional horse could be heard in the background. Dropping a little lower than he wanted, the pilot added some power to the three radial engines holding his altitude until the moment he passed over the fence. With the field made, he pulled the power to idle and sat the Trimotor down on the well-groomed farm runway stopping with a hundred yards to spare.

Big Bill, Owney, Patrick and the others cheered and clapped, and they walked out to the aircraft. The engines were still steaming in the cold even after being shut down. The door cracked open and everyone could hear the booming voice of Danny from inside the airplane giving the crew congratulations. Then he appeared in the door and looked out to the men on the ground.

"We did it!" he yelled joyfully to the men walking toward the airplane. "It worked!"

Owney and Big Bill were clearly excited. "Great job, Danny!" Big Bill yelled back as they approached the airplane, and a crew member put the metal stairs out. "Damn," he said looking at the big old plane sitting on what was essentially a farm.

"This is going to change how we do business," Danny said as he came down the steps and gave each of the New York bosses a hug and kiss on each cheek. "We can carry a truck's worth in the back, and we're thinking about adding an internal tank for more, depending on weight."

Big Bill and Owney climbed up into the aircraft looking at the expansive area where cases of their precious product were strapped down.

"This will double or triple our movement from Canada further south all the way to Florida," Owney added. "We just need places to land down south."

Only the men assembled knew about this experiment that Danny had gone to great risk and expense to try. Flying a fully loaded cargo Trimotor from Canada to a farm in Rhode Island and successfully landing it was a big deal.

"We're working on that as we speak. Needless to say, this is a secret operation." Danny said mostly for the junior members of his crew and the Big Seven who were present.

"This was worth the drive," Big Bill said, clearly enjoying the moment. Big Bill was a man of few words but, along with Owney and the others, he could see that this could be a game changer.

The cost of doing business for the Big Seven was about to go up, but it was worth it for the speed and security they could use to expand their enterprise.

"The wops don't have anything like this," Owney said referring to their rivals in Boston.

"Chicago doesn't either," Big Bill added.

The men congratulated the pilot and copilot who were being paid very well for this new venture and charged with recruiting other aviators who may be interested in making some serious money while knowing they risked jail time along the way.

"Good work, Danny," Patrick said to his boss as he and the others started to unload the aircraft with product destined for customers who had a never-ending taste for more.

———

CHAPTER 7

HIGH OFFICE

The governor had suffered through two meetings back to back and was in a grumpy mood. Lunch was next on his agenda, followed by more meetings during the afternoon. Down the hill from the gleaming white marble state house was the Providence River, and just on the other side sat the Liberty Lunch diner. It was a favorite of Governor Peter Baker who had frequented the establishment long before he became governor of Rhode Island and even before he was a state senator. As a child, his dad had taken him to Liberty Lunch while making rounds delivering milk for Salois Diary.

Walking out of the State House's south entrance, the cold wind hit him like a slap in the face and a reminder that winter was still in full swing. The car with the state trooper sat waiting just at the bottom of the hill. As the governor approached, the trooper jumped out of the driver's seat and ran around to open the door.

"Thanks for warming it up, Jimmy," the governor said to his driver who was also his bodyguard.

"My pleasure, sir," Trooper Beck said. "Liberty?"

"Sounds good," Governor Baker replied.

A few short minutes later, the mile and a half drive ended just in front of the eatery. On a warm summer or spring day, the governor enjoyed the walk to lunch. At twelve degrees above, the warm car and driver came in handy. Parking was at a premium in this part of town, but this car with its special passenger pulled up right in front next to the no parking sign, which, in this case, didn't apply.

Out of the car and into the warm diner, the governor took his usual booth toward the back and away from the windows so that passersby wouldn't see him. He didn't have many moments of privacy, but having lunch while reading the paper was one of them, and it had become a daily ritual Governor Baker cherished.

"The usual, governor?" asked Frankie who was the second-generation owner of the Liberty Diner.

"You bet, Frankie."

The usual was a Providence classic of hot pastrami, olive loaf, melted Swiss cheese, onion and tomato on toast.

"Coke?" asked Frankie.

"Perfect," Governor Baker said back to the man he had known for years.

The diner was starting to get busy now that the factories just down the street were letting out for lunch. The smell of cooking food, coffee and the noise of clanking dishes filled the air. Frankie would also send a hamburger done up all the way to Governor Baker's driver sitting just outside in the running and warm Ford.

"Here you go. It's not cold yet, but then again you might not want it too cold today," Frankie said as he sat down a 12-ounce bottle of Coca Cola. He also put the *Providence Journal* newspaper on the table for him to read. Unknown to anyone else in the diner, this was the real reason he was eating there this day and at least once a week. Inside the paper, usually tucked into the sports section, was a plain manila envelope. Without batting an eyelash, the governor lifted the paper as if to read it in front of him with one hand and slipped the envelope into the inside pocket of his jacket with the other.

"Winter won't let up," Frankie said as he returned with the sandwich and chips.

"That's for damn sure, my friend," the governor said. "How's your son, Samuel, doing?"

"Getting along, thanks. Trying to get him through high school is not easy."

"I hear that," the governor replied. Both men had two kids about the same age and in the same grades. Frankie's son had a tough time adjusting to high school, as do many kids of that age. Governor Baker's son went to the local Catholic high school and also struggled. Except for their career paths, both men had a lot in common and enjoyed each other's company. The envelope containing ten one hundred-dollar bills in his jacket pocket was the other thing they had in common. Frankie was connected to the Big Seven and worked with Danny on various "projects." Governor Baker was one of many politicians who helped smooth things over when it came to doing business in the liquor trade.

After he finished his sandwich, the governor left his usual generous tip, thanked Frankie and headed for the waiting car just outside the door for his trip back up the hill to the state capitol building.

Shortly after the governor left, Jesse Young got up from the booth he occupied alone, paid for his coffee and also left the diner with his notebook in hand. Young was a reporter with the *Providence Journal* who had broken many investigative stories over the past few years and especially during this turbulent time when the Volstead Act was the law of the land. He had notes to take.

———

New England is cold in winter, but Maine's weather is especially brutal as seasonal nor'easters batter the coast with hurricane force winds all the while piling up snow across the state. Thankfully, this day was just dry and bitter cold after a storm days ago had dumped another foot of snow across the interior. The speakeasy was just outside Lewiston near a place called Poland Spring. Lewiston and its sister city, Auburn, were mill towns producing much of the material used for clothing by companies throughout the six New England states and beyond. The speakeasy was booming most nights serving up food and drink to the tired mill workers who would drive the extra distance from the sister cities, out into the country where local law enforcement turned a blind eye as the spirits flowed.

During the day, the owners would resupply and make things ready for their customers who would hurry in after work hours down in the city. Special Agent Ted Connelly and Special Agent Eric Thompson were assigned to keep an eye on this establishment along with a couple of other speakeasys in the state of Maine. This one in particular seemed to be a hub for illegal liquor deliveries and activity. Along with the booze, the place was an active sports book attracting gamblers from around the state and, in some cases, the entire region. They also suspected prostitution, but couldn't prove that as easily as the liquor sales and sports betting.

"There it is," Connelly said pointing to the panel van which arrived shortly after they did.

"Right on time," Thompson said making a note in his book. This was the fourth trip for the lawmen from Boston who continued to surveil the place while building a delivery pattern and timeline. This crew was different as they suspected. The supply line didn't have anything to do with the Big Seven. Instead of coming from the south, these men were coming directly from the north. Canada to be exact. The irony was that the Big Seven got their supply from Canada then distributed from points south of Maine. Bottom line was that someone else was doing business in the Big Seven's territory.

"Jennings' CI said it's coming from outside Montréal," Connelly said as the men watched from a distance. The small but busy speakeasy sat on a road that also serviced the Poland Spring Inn sitting at the end of a long driveway way up on a hill. The good news for these men was that the road was cleared of snow, probably because of the speakeasy and not the inn seeing that many of the local elected officials frequented the joint. This would be their last day on this surveillance before heading back to Boston.

Both men were looking forward to getting back, writing their reports and enjoying some home time. Connelly also had one other stop to make after their return to the city. That one he would do alone.

———————

The pool hall in Attleboro, just north of the Rhode Island border in Massachusetts, was filled with smoke and people as was the norm on a Friday night, especially in winter. Marky Flannigan, a second-generation Irish immigrant, had downed a few too many drinks and was itching to pick a fight. A couple of his associates also knew of his temper and wanted to get him out of there and safely home. They knew his family. Both of his families, as a matter of fact. There was the family back at the house in Foxboro and the other one that he worked for.

"One more game," Marky said to the younger man who had beaten him at pool three times in a row. "One more fucking game, you piece of shit little wop!"

"Come on, Marky," said his pal Alan.

Marky turned to Alan, who was actually bigger than he was, and got right up into his face. "Fuck you, Alan." Then he looked around the smoky room at the others who were starting to notice and feel the tension in the air.

"Come on, Marky. Let's head home. You've got to get up in the morning," Alan insisted.

"You afraid I'll beat you?" Marky asked as he turned his attention back to Anthony who was all of nineteen years old and a good pool player. He had no idea who Marky was or who he worked for.

"Any time, brother," Anthony said while holding the pool cue in one hand and the chalk in the other. "The Irish are easy to beat anyway."

Marky immediately lunged for Anthony only to be held back by the two friends he came with.

"Screw you," Marky shouted. Then he turned to his friends who now had him by one arm each. "Screw you guys, too."

"Why don't you go home and have some corned beef or something Irish. Maybe an Irish tea. Apparently, you can't handle anything stronger," Anthony joked loudly so everyone could hear while putting more gas on the fire.

The men holding Marky pulled him away and started heading for the door. Anthony went back to his own friends and started to rack up the pool balls for another round with anyone who would play.

Once outside, one of Marky's friends went to the parking lot to get his car.

"I've got to take a piss," Marky said to the other.

"Piss over there," his pal pointed to a tree on the dark side of the parking lot. The temperature was around ten degrees, and they wanted to get him home ASAP. Technically, these two didn't work for the Big Seven but were trying. They did some occasional work for Marky, connecting them to him but not the larger organization.

"I've got to shit, too," Marky said. "Be right back."

Marky walked from the parking lot back to the entrance of the pool hall. He opened the door and went inside. The table he had been playing was in the back corner near the restroom. He walked back toward the restroom and did not see Anthony. Knowing Anthony hadn't left through the front door and seeing his jacket still on the chair near the wall, Marky assumed his pool partner for the evening was in the bathroom. When Marky walked into the men's room, he smiled because he was right.

Anthony was in the first of only two stalls relieving himself. Marky looked around, and there was no one else in the restroom. He pulled out his Smith and Wesson M&P .38 Special and fired a single 158 grain bullet into the wooden stall's door lock, releasing it instantly.

Anthony stared through the now wide-open bathroom stall door at Marky standing a few feet away pointing the gun at him. The smell of gunpowder and some smoke from the discharged firearm hung in the air.

"You should have played another game," Marky said just before pulling the trigger three times. Anthony's face froze as the force of the bullets entered his body pushing him off the side of the toilet. His now lifeless eyes were wide open. Two people came running into the restroom seconds later. They could only see Marky standing just outside the stall, already having put the gun back into his jacket. He glared at them while walking out. "I would use the other stall," he said sarcastically pushing his way past.

Outside, his two pals waited in the cold not hearing the shots. Marky left the pool hall, which was now so quiet you could hear a pin drop in the building.

"Let's go," he ordered.

The three men got into the car and drove off to Marky's house. Ten minutes later they arrived. One of the guys jumped out of the car, opened the door and walked Marky to the entrance of the ground floor apartment. Without saying a word, Marky walked into the house and threw his keys on the table. The sound of the keys hitting the table this late at night put a knot in his young wife's stomach knowing he could pick a fight at any time. Marky Flannigan was not a happy drunk. He was a violent one. On this night his head hit the pillow, and he was down for the count. The next day he would go back to work for his boss Patrick who would most likely have to clean up the mess he had just made. What he didn't know was that the young man he killed in the bathroom was the nephew of the Foxboro police chief.

CHAPTER 8

ENTERPRISE

The industrial sized cooking pots donated by a restaurant supply company in Providence made all the difference in the world at the community soup kitchen St. Mary's Church ran when the weather got cold. People of little or no means from across the area relied on it. With thousands out of work and their fortunes lost, the church knew how important this operation was and started opening more often regardless of the weather. The soup kitchen was set up in the community hall the church owned a few blocks away on State Highway 152 in Seekonk. The building had a small kitchen, but it was better than nothing on these very cold days. Sister Judy Ann chopped onions while wiping the tears they caused from her face every few minutes.

"I can do that," Father Ralph offered as he watched her from the other side of the kitchen. "My eyes aren't that sensitive."

Despite the watering eyes, Sister Judy Ann looked forward to these days and her hours of service to the less fortunate. "It's the Lord's work, Father," she said.

"Yeah, but it's your eyes," he replied with a chuckle in his voice.

The two had started this venture a few years before, and it had been a success, even being written up once in the Boston newspaper. Father Ralph was not much of a cook, but he helped check in the "clients" as they arrived. On cold days like this, they would open at two o'clock in the afternoon.

"We're almost ready to open, and I'm not finished with the second batch," Sister said as she once again wiped her streaming eyes.

"That's fine. They'll wait and mingle," Father Ralph said as he gazed at her baby blue eyes while she mopped away the onion induced tears. He wasn't a big fan of the onion smell as the onions were chopped, but he could happily watch her cook for hours on end if given the chance.

The doorbell at the front door rang, and Father Ralph went to see who it was. Eastern Bakery donated much of the bread they used at the shelter and would deliver just before the doors opened. Usually the bakery brought unsold leftovers a day or two old, but being free made the price just right. As Father Ralph approached the door, he could already see a few clients waiting patiently in the thirty-degree air.

"Much appreciated, Glenn," Father Ralph said to the man holding two large boxes.

"Our pleasure, Father. There's more in the truck if you want to grab them."

Father Ralph nodded his head and walked through the biting cold air to the waiting bread truck. He looked back at one of the clients at the door and waved him over for some additional help. He knew some of the clients but not all. Two clients he knew would definitely be coming this evening. They always came on soup kitchen night, but not just for the food and warmth.

Three hours later, the kitchen was up and running. Sister Judy Ann and two other nuns from the parish along with two from nearby St. Leo's in Pawtucket served the food while Father Ralph checked people in and made his rounds. So far 22 people had arrived and were truly thankful for everything the church did.

A couple of the regulars were at the end of a table toward the back of the hall. It was a bit noisy with the heaters running, people talking and the usual clanking of dishes. Father Ralph made his way over to them and sat down.

"How are we doing, gentlemen?" Father Ralph asked the two.

"Great, Father. Thanks, as always," answered Todd Ellis.

"It's God's work, my son. We just carry it out."

Ironically, Father Ralph, Todd and the other man sitting at this end of the table, Rudy, were all the same age, yet they always felt a little awkward when he pulled out the "my son."

"It was God's work two weeks ago, too, Father," Rudy said chuckling then taking a sip of his soup. For the men sitting there, including Father Ralph, it was Rudy's way of sharing a little inside joke.

"We're on for Friday and Saturday at Aqueduct," Father Ralph said quietly changing his tone from sounding like a member of the clergy to a member of a secret gambling club. "These are the numbers," the good Father said while pulling out an envelope from the inside pocket of his black suit. He slid the envelope under Rudy's hat sitting on the table.

"How many races?" Rudy House asked after taking a bite of the bread.

"Seven each day," Father answered.

"Damn. That's good," Todd said.

"Where do you get this stuff, Father?" Rudy asked.

"The good Lord provides, Rudy."

"He's provided real good over the last couple months," Todd said while waiting for his soup to cool.

"Your bets were up again. Must be doing good on a priest's salary," Rudy stated knowing the answer but wanting to hear it again. Then he answered his own question. "Bingo's been busy, I'll bet," he said with another bit of a chuckle. Father didn't reply to that comment but knew what he was talking about.

"That Sister Ann is pretty cute for a nun," Todd said changing the subject and looking in her direction.

"Sister Judy Ann. Yeah, she's one of God's best servants," Father said.

"I see how you look at her, Father. Lead us not into temptation," Todd added with his best and only line from scripture.

"Gentlemen, thanks for coming, and I hope this was helpful in your lives," Father Ralph Connelly said as he rose from the table to tend to the other members of his flock. The men finished their soup and left the building with a few more things to do.

———

Never having enough product on hand can be a good thing if you're in business. When supplies can't keep up with demand, people work overtime to make their customers happy. Taking to the air in addition to their sea transport was starting to help with the continuing supply problem the Big Seven had. Occasionally there were also little extras.

"How much more can we put aboard?" asked the French-Canadian standing along the tied up *Black Duck* as Captain Rick St. Pierre looked over his manifest. Winters were exceptionally cold in Canada, and this evening was no different. The air temperature was around three degrees Fahrenheit with a wind chill of close to twenty below. The Port of Montréal was a very rare stop for the *Black Duck* which normally operated along the Canadian Maritimes. The ship was there to pick up a special shipment at the very end of the old Alpha pier. The cargo in question had originally been intended for a different destination.

"Thirty more cases in the forward storage," Captain St. Pierre answered.

"Thirty up front," the man yelled in French to the privately paid stevedores working their tails off in some nasty weather. The snow had finally ended, but the docks were wet, icy and very slippery. February was brutal.

"The soft package should be here anytime now," Frenchie, the nickname Rick's crew gave to the leader on the pier, said.

"That's the most important one," Rick said.

The last thirty cases of Canadian-made whisky were loaded into the forward hold down below. After finishing, the men working on the pier came aboard and warmed up in the ship's galley. The smell of fresh coffee and the warmth of steam-driven heat was welcomed by all.

"Does he know where to go?" asked Rick with a skeptical tone.

"He does. He's reliable," Frenchie answered confidently.

These were men of few words. Only the sound of the coffee percolating and an occasional banging of the steam pipes could be heard as they waited.

"He's here," one of the younger crew members shouted while catching his breath from running down stairs to the galley.

"Bring him down," Rick ordered.

A few minutes later, the crewmember returned with the special courier.

"Jacque?" Rick asked as the men walked into the galley which was now getting crowded.

"Oui."

Jacque had a last name, but none of these men knew it. He had one job to do, and that was to drop off the briefcase and key to unlock it to Captain St. Pierre. The captain would take it from there.

"Merci," Rick replied taking the case, handing over an envelope of cash and dismissing the courier. He then turned to the crewmembers. "We get underway at 1900." The men knew that they had been dismissed and quickly left to make all preparations for their departure. Rick took the small key and inserted it into the lock releasing it. He opened the case, looked inside, then closed and locked it. There was a safe in his quarters where the case would stay until they reached the Connecticut coast. There it would be transferred to a rumrunner and finally handed over to Big Bill Dwyer. Inside the case was close to three million U.S. dollars in stocks, bonds and cash.

The cash plus the liquor loaded onto the ship had originally been destined for the city of Chicago and Mr. Capone's family. The Big Seven had been tipped off that Capone's people were behind the hijacking of a major shipment they were driving out of Canada bound for New England. A Capone insider told one of Danny's boys the shipment had indeed ended up in Chicago. Today was payback and then some. Both Chicago and the

Big Seven had a working relationship, but occasionally mid-level enforcers made stupid decisions. This was the cost of doing business.

———————

"Where were you? I thought we were going out to dinner. Jesus!" Sally Madden said to her husband whose nickname "The Killer" didn't give her any pause to back off. "How many times, Owney?"

"I was working, for Christ's sake," he said removing his topcoat and shaking off the New York cold.

"I specifically said we were going to go to the club right after you got home. I said that yesterday and this morning before you left," she nagged.

"Not tonight, Sally. Just can't do it."

"What the hell have you been up to?"

"Don't ask me my business. You know better than that," he said pausing for a couple of minutes. Then he looked at her pissed off face and decided to continue. "I was moving some product. We can't keep up. The planes are starting to help, though."

"Planes?"

"Long story."

"I'll make you a drink, and you can explain. That's the least you can do now that we have no dinner plans and nothing to eat," she said with a sarcastic tone.

Owney knew his wife wanted to go out to the Polish club for supper. He had a little Polish in his background, but mainly they went there for friends they had made over the years. The club also served the very best kielbasa in the city of New York on Wednesday nights. The club served it on other nights as well, but it was always freshest on Wednesdays.

"Rocks?" she asked after she made her own Scotch and water. One of the bonuses of being in the bootlegging business was that the house was never dry.

"No, straight up," he answered.

The two took their usual seats near the radio facing the fireplace where the flames were about to go out.

"Put another log on," he ordered.

"Is your arm broken? You get your ass up and put one on," she countered.

He put his drink down, got up, took a large piece of wood from the pile next to the fireplace and placed it on the red-hot coals. Owney had the fireplace added to their brownstone because he liked a good fire in the winter and could use it to entice people to come around to his point of view when necessary.

"What planes are you talking about?" Sally asked.

"As far as you're concerned, they don't exist."

"Yeah, yeah, yeah. Jesus Christ, Owney. I'm your wife."

He sipped his Scotch for a few minutes and didn't say anything. The only sound was that of the fireplace and a siren outside off in the distance.

"Danny figured out a faster way to get product down," he finally said breaking the silence.

"With a plane?"

"Planes."

"Isn't that expensive? Not to mention dangerous?"

"We can afford it, but it's hard to get enough of them on the arm," he said and then took another sip. "Oh, the Chinaman is bringing supper. I called him before leaving."

"That's romantic," she said and then sipped her drink. "How many do you have?"

"Three for now. Trying to get more. Danny is leading that because it was his idea in the first place, but Big Bill asked me to see what I can do to help."

She stayed quiet for a few minutes as that bit of news sank in while the fire picked up thanks to the wood he had put on. Just then the doorbell rang as the Chinese food arrived from up the street. Most people paid a delivery fee, but the restaurant people knew who this customer was and never added a dime.

"How's Kevin doing?" she asked changing the subject.

"The same. Works hard. I'm moving him up. He's helping with the planes and has a good future. He's loyal."

"I'm sure he is," she said, knowing Kevin better than Owney thought she did.

They sat and ate their chop suey not saying another word with the fire crackling in the background. The two had grown apart over the last few years as his travel increased and the business of the Big Seven seemed to take up most of his time. She enjoyed the money, beauty treatments, parties and being Mrs. Owney Madden. Those were reasons enough to stay with him.

———

CHAPTER 9

COMPETITION

Writing reports was the worst part of his job. Special Agent Ted Connelly cursed silently as he slogged through the usual paperwork that came with a surveillance road trip. His coffee was cold, and he was only a couple hours into the morning after a tough, snowy Boston commute from the South Shore.

"Want a warm cup?" Special Agent Eric Thompson asked while sitting at his own desk, which faced his partner's. The two were close, and most of the work they did for the Bureau of Prohibition they did together as a team.

"Thanks, Eric, I'm good. Probably going to walk down and get a donut or something in a few minutes. You want anything?"

"I'm good."

Ted finished off his last report, pulled it out of the typewriter and sat it in the out box next to the picture of his wife. With that, he got up and put on his heavy overcoat before making his way downstairs to the first floor and out the door into Scollay Square. There were quite a few people milling about and some doing construction work on Congress Street. He was frozen just walking across the plaza to a coffee shop and wondered how those state workers spent all day outside working on the roads.

The coffee shop was busy with patrons trying to warm up for a few minutes while enjoying some piping hot Joe. He took a number in line and waited his turn. A few minutes later, the man with the baker's hat called his number.

"Large regular coffee with two sugars and an order of toast," he said.

"Butter?"

"Sure."

The man took the order, yelled to the back for the toast and started to pour the coffee. Ted took his right hand and put it into the deep pocket of his overcoat. A second later he pulled his hand out of the pocket holding a folded piece of paper hidden in his palm. Then he released his grip letting the paper fall to the floor next to his foot.

"Here's the coffee," the man said to Ted as he put it on the counter in front of him.

Ted looked down and picked up the folded paper off the floor. "I think someone dropped this. Looks like a receipt or something. Why don't you keep it in case they come back?" Ted told the man.

"Thanks. I'll see to it. Twenty cents for the toast and coffee," the man said as the place continued to bustle with more people coming in from the cold.

"Here you go. Thanks." Ted paid the man, took the small brown bag with toast and his coffee then left the shop heading back across the cold plaza to the warmth of his office.

The man at the counter quietly put the note in his pocket a few seconds later as the customer rush subsided a bit. Later that afternoon when the baker left the shop, he took a jitney cab a couple miles away to what appeared to be a barbershop. As he entered the shop, there was only one customer in a chair getting his hair cut. The other three chairs were empty. He proceeded to the back of the shop to find a door that was always kept securely locked. The barber reached under his counter and pushed a button signaling a man downstairs to come up and open the door. Once through the door and down the small staircase to the basement, the noise increased as the Park Street speakeasy was just getting busy.

Joey Cardin saw the man walk into the bar and approached. Without saying a word, the baker from the coffee shop handed Joey the note before taking a seat and ordering a Canadian-made whisky.

Patrick and Joey were in Boston checking on supply and on the operation as a whole. Joey showed Patrick the note. Patrick then got out of his seat and went toward the back of the bar where there was a makeshift office. He picked up the phone.

"Perry 2559," he said into the phone to the waiting operator who would connect him a few seconds later.

The ring tone was faint but only lasted a couple of seconds before the call was picked up.

"Yeah?" Danny answered at his office in Providence.

"Those people in Maine might have company in a couple of days. They are definitely stepping on our territory directly. Right from Canada," Patrick said to his boss about 50 miles south.

"Come on back. We've got work to do," Danny ordered and then hung up the phone. He finished counting the cash that was neatly stacked up in front of him. There were stacks of fifty-dollar bills and hundred dollar bills each bundle with a paper wrapper around it indicating its amount. *Looks like a small trip to Maine is in the immediate future*, he thought while putting the cash into a plain brown bag.

———

"There's just not enough here for a story, Jesse," barked Fred Rockwell as he picked up his Camel cigarette for a puff before knocking the ashes off the end. "Get another source," he ordered.

Having been executive editor for only a few months after working his whole career at the *Journal*, the 51-year-old balding newsman was not about to risk his neck for a story that could blow up in his face.

"This guy is a dish washer and overheard all these conversations," Jesse explained to his boss knowing full well that he would need to get more dirt on the governor before anything could be printed.

"You can't go and accuse the governor of the state of Rhode Island of collaborating with the mob without having a ton of rock-solid evidence. Look, I applaud the work so far, but it's too thin," explained Rockwell.

"The Big Seven," Jesse said, correcting his boss.

"The Big Seven, The Mob, Bootleggers...all the same," Rockwell countered.

Jesse wanted to get some pictures of the governor meeting with these folks that his sources said were members of the Big Seven or one of their local organizations. Pictures were hard to take because of the attention drew with those huge flash bulbs exploding.

"Also, I want you to go up to Attleboro and see about a possible murder up there. Someone said a guy was killed at The Blue Bonnet pool hall, but there's no police report, no body and it may be the work of some local bad guys. Of course, I thought of you immediately for this story," Rockwell said with a hint of sarcasm. He paused before proceeding. "Maybe that's the work of the Big Seven, too," he chuckled.

"You joke. This is bigger than you think, Fred. That's probably not the Big Seven, but who the hell knows these days?"

Fred took another drag from his Camel and waved Jesse out of his office as the smoke settled across the small room. Jesse had some contacts in the Attleboro area. It was an industrial town known for jewelry and fabric production. Jesse decided he would jump on U.S. Route 1 and head up there to get some lunch and snoop around to see if there was a story or not.

———————

There were a few exceptions, but, for the most part, Danny never carried a gun. He had Patrick, Marky and Joey to protect him when out doing business. The North End Gang wanted a sit down. He hated the Italians and knew they wanted to rub the hit on the Big Seven's booze stash in his face. Perhaps North End had other trivial business to go over, but the organization liked to gloat whenever they scored. The relationship between the two rival organizations had improved during the past few years when there was enough money to be made for everyone by running booze. Still, a few murders on both sides went unanswered, and each suspected the other of "disappearing" a member or two of their "family." The North End Gang and other Italians were slowly trying to eat away at the business the Irish had monopolized for years.

Hospitals were always great places to meet. Very public with lots of people around. The hospital in Braintree was just south of Boston and a favorite of the North End Gang because one of the board members was also a silent partner in their crime organization. It would always be arranged for an exam room to be made available.

Danny arrived thirty minutes before to stake out the entrance looking for anything that might be a trap or look even a little suspicious. He, Patrick and Marky sat in the black 1924 Chrysler Model B-70 parked across the street. All three men knew that this was an iffy exercise because there were multiple entrances to the hospital that anyone could use. Bottom line, this was a sit down, and no one would be at risk. Danny did, however, have his trusty walking cane. Not only did it play to the medical location as he walked in, but it also protected him. His cane was actually a cleverly disguised .410 shotgun made in Belgium by a master gunsmith. It was always loaded but had never been fired except for practice back on the farm in Charlestown.

The three men walked through the lobby of the hospital and down the first corridor to the right past one of the waiting rooms. The man at the end of the hall standing next to the last door on the left saw them coming.

"Just Danny," the man said to Marky and Patrick who would stay outside along with this guy who looked like an off-duty cop but wasn't. The man opened the door for Danny and closed it behind him.

Danny walked a few feet to where an exam room entrance was just to his right. The door was open and Angelo Bottelli walked forward to greet his colleague with the traditional kiss on each cheek.

"It's been awhile," Angelo said to Danny after their quick embrace.

"It has," Danny replied not exactly knowing the reason for the sit down.

"So, we have a mutual interest in what's going on up in Maine," Angelo said keeping the conversation all business.

"Are we going to talk about our product you and your pals hijacked?" Danny asked coldly.

"What are you talking about, Danny?"

"Fuck you. You know what I'm talking about. You and the Fed who sold us out."

Angelo just sat for a few seconds before speaking again. "I don't know what you're talking about, and if I did, I wouldn't tell you any of our business. There are good days and bad days. Maybe your people just had a bad day."

"Well, that little score for the North End Gang will go on account," Danny explained. The Big Seven's stash that had been stolen ahead of a federal raid months ago by the North End Gang thanks to a tip they had on the inside would not go unanswered.

"We heard a Fed met his demise in a pile of snow around that time. Probably just a coincidence, huh, Danny Boy?" Angelo loved to use the term "Danny Boy" knowing the Irishman standing across from him hated it.

"Probably," Danny paused for a few seconds before continuing. "So, what's this about Maine? You know damn well we control that territory. Hell, we've got places in Portland, Augusta, Bangor and in between. We've always kept to our business up there and nothing else. Everyone knows that. There's no 'mutual interest' up there between our operations."

"We don't have any of our people working that area but may have some interest with a third party trying to gain some of that territory," Angelo explained.

Danny gave this some thought for a minute or two. The last thing he wanted was to get the Big Seven into a skirmish with the North End Gang now that things were going so well in both their businesses. Plus, Dwyer and Madden in New York would not be happy.

"If someone is operating in our territory on their own, they do so at their own peril. That has nothing to do with the business between us."

Angelo knew double talk when he heard it. He'd been around the block many times.

Danny continued. "Just to be clear, you do not have anyone from your organization running booze down from the north or operating a speakeasy in the Poland Spring area, correct?"

"That is correct. But we may have some financial interest in such an operation."

Outside operators sometimes gave kickbacks to certain families for protection from any other organizations that may come along looking to do similar work. Danny could now see the picture pretty clearly. Apparently, this small group from Canada that was trying to carve out a little piece of the Maine business from the Big Seven had made a protection agreement with the North End Gang. These were loose arrangements at best and mostly benefited the protector, not the protected. The North End Gang promised influence and was not responsible if things happened outside their control.

"That's our territory. It's always been the Big Seven's territory, and New York will have something to say about it, I'm sure," Danny answered.

"Agreed. We just wanted it on the record with you that none of our people are working that operation," Angelo said. Translation: The North End Gang didn't give a shit what happened to the people or the operation. "They came to us and, we're happy to take their money."

"Understood," Danny said. "I will pass that on to Madden and Dwyer in New York."

The two shook hands and hugged before leaving five minutes apart. Danny was silent, as usual, walking out and didn't mention anything to Patrick or Marky until they were all back in the car.

"I'll call New York when we get back to the office," Danny said finally breaking the silence as Marky drove the car headed south. "We're straight."

"Did they admit the South Shore job and screwing us?" Marky asked with an edge to his tone. He would have liked nothing better than to shoot up those guys right there at the hospital. Danny knew he was a hot head and tough to control sometimes.

"Of course not. They deny it. Fuck 'em," Danny replied. "This thing coming up in Maine will be an off-the-record answer to that little job."

They drove in silence for about ten more miles until Danny told them to pull over to the side just outside of Foxboro on a quiet stretch of the road. Danny picked up his cane, took the tip off the end and pointed it at Marky's head.

"Don't you ever shoot up a pool hall, bar, speakeasy or any fucking thing ever again without asking me first," Danny said in an eerie, calm tone. "If you do, I'll personally put this .410 shotgun shell into your brain and splatter it across the windshield."

"I'm sorry, Danny. I was drunk."

"One pass. This is it. Just one."

"I'll never do it again, Danny."

"You're fucking right you won't. Because if you do, you'll just disappear."

Patrick sat quietly in the back seat. He knew Danny was furious about the pool hall. He had already smoothed things over with the Attleboro police chief. This murder would go "unsolved" thanks to a hefty payoff.

The three drove in silence for the rest of the ride back to the office. There was planning to do and business to conduct.

———

CHAPTER 10

HOME LIFE

No one got rich on a federal agent's salary, but Marge Connelly made it work for her family. Her husband's special off-duty side jobs often paid more than his regular week's wages which went a long way toward helping them live a bit above the other South Shore families on their block in the town of Hull. The slim, tall 33-year-old was on her second marriage and loved to enjoy some of the finer things in life. Ted cautioned her not to be overly extravagant and never to discuss the family finances with any of the other agent's wives or other ladies in the neighborhood.

He usually arrived home between 5 and 6 p.m. when working normal day hours. Marge didn't care for the overnight travel that came with the job or some of the odd hours that went along with investigative work. As a homemaker, she had plenty of time to herself during the day and enjoyed the Hull ladies bridge club. Special Agent Eric Thompson's wife, Jennifer, also attended the same club. Both ladies were members of that other exclusive, unofficial club: wives of law enforcement.

The weather was chilly, but early March in New England could swing both ways. Most people were itchy for the spring weather to kick in knowing it led to the summer they all enjoyed.

"We're going to the Cape this weekend," Jennifer said as she made herself a coffee between hands. "Eric wants to look at some property near Falmouth for future reference. I don't know what the hell that means, but it's a nice ride down there."

Marge took a sip of her coffee and looked at her cards. "We love it down there," she said to Jennifer and the other two ladies at their table.

"Do you still have that little place near Bourne?" Jennifer asked.

"We sold it last year and bought a small cottage closer to Hyannis Port."

The three women sitting with Marge looked up. That seemed to get their attention.

"What?" she asked as the women looked at her.

"Hyannis? La di da...." laughed Susan who was a regular partner.

The ladies knew what the others could afford, and this news was a surprise to them. A little place in Bourne was one thing, but Hyannis was quite a step up.

"I thought I told you. It's tiny, and we sold the Bourne property to get it. Plus, Ted works like a dog doing extra duty make it work. Sometimes I wonder if it's even worth it with good weather only a few months a year. We were thinking of renting it for the winter," she explained. Deep inside, she could hear her husband telling her to keep her mouth shut about their private purchases. The fact that he paid cash for the place would never be acknowledged to these ladies. Gossip was a favorite sport among the wives of law enforcement officers and state officials.

"It's heated?" Susan asked, now probing for more information on the place. These ladies wouldn't ask what they paid for it, but a good description of the property and its location was all they would need to get a ball-park value.

"It is. We can use it in the winter, but there's no one around during the off months. I'm not sure we could rent it even if we wanted to."

The bridge game continued. Marge was keen on changing the subject. The other ladies were not.

"How many bedrooms?" Jennifer asked as she took a good look at her cards. In some ways, she and the others were playing another card game with their friend Marge.

"Three, but it's a mess and needs some serious work. That's how we were able to afford it," Marge answered continuing to play it down.

"Well, we love looking at places on the Cape for something in the future," Jennifer continued. "We should all meet up there over the summer for a weekend barbeque or something."

Susan looked up and loved that idea. "That would be fun."

The other ladies nodded their approval of this potential plan which, as Jennifer knew, would be nothing but a fishing expedition to see what the place was like and, more importantly, worth.

"How's Eric like the travel with the job?" Marge asked trying desperately to change the subject.

"He likes it. I hate it," chuckled Jennifer as the other tablemates nodded their heads in agreement.

The game continued for another hour and a half before the ladies packed up and headed to their respective homes. Marge was able to steer the conversation away from the new summer home purchase to politics and prohibition, which never got old.

———

Young Kevin Hines was back at the Madden household as Owney "The Killer" and his two bodyguards spent a week driving U.S. Highway 1 south to the Washington, DC area on business. He was checking out the distribution operation shared between the Big Seven and a small group they called "Pols," run by four U.S. Senators. The "Pols" were nothing official in the bootlegging business, but the Big Seven recognized them as "players" due to their political capital and the fact they made a lot of money working together. The bottom line was that these four senators got kickbacks and had egos big enough to warrant some sort of label.

"One more time," Sally said to her young friend. Their time together was sporadic, and Kevin always had some phony reason to stop by. Today it was "fixing the radio plug." He had moved up a bit in the organization and was now spending some of his time as a crewmember in the Trimotor flights from Canada to Danny's farm and two other landing sites in the Northeast. Kevin loved to travel and really enjoyed the thrill of flying. Only one crewmember could fit and was needed to help load and unload the aircraft. The crewmembers always had to be on the inside given the sensitivity of their cargo. He also assisted Owney at their office with his organization skills.

"I'll try," Kevin said. He'd spent the night, and the couple had gotten little sleep.

"God, you're gorgeous," she said as he got out of bed to use the restroom.

"So are you," he felt he had to answer knowing she wanted to hear it, but they were just words to him. The attraction for him was the fact that she was the wife of one of the big bosses, and she talked favorably about his abilities not to mention the "C" note he got after every visit.

He returned, slipping his young naked body under the silk covers. Sally always got her money's worth, and this time would be no different.

She genuinely enjoyed his company. The two would have breakfast together before he would leave the house hoping no one noticed.

"How do you like flying?" she asked over an English muffin.

"Is that what you call it?" he joked.

She laughed at his innuendo. "I know how you like that, silly boy."

"Now we have a name for that move!" Kevin replied with a wink.

Sally enjoyed experimenting to see just how many different ways the two could have sex.

"Seriously," she pressed. She wanted to fly in the biggest way and was waiting for the chance. Her gangster husband, Owney, always drove or took the train. He was not a big fan of flight.

"I love it. I want to learn how to do it," he answered.

"Oh, you already know how to do it!" She couldn't resist the pun.

The two continued their small breakfast, and then Kevin finished dressing. It was the last thing he said to her that turned her stomach inside out.

"I would do it even without the 'C' note," he said while putting on his coat. She got his scarf and wrapped it around his neck. She had only a shirt on.

"Am I the only guy you have on the side?"

She stopped. That question caught her by surprise.

"Of course."

He hesitated. Then before opening the door to go out into the chilly New York morning, gave her a kiss on the cheek. "I saw you at the coffee shop with some other guy and was just wondering. I mean, I don't give a shit. But still, if I saw you, who knows who else did."

She thought fast. "He's our insurance broker."

"Oh," he smiled, paused, and then continued. "Looked like a 'G' to me 'cause I saw him get out of his car and walk in. The car screamed Fed."

"Get out of here, fly boy," she said dismissing him. "Everyone looks like a G-man these days. It's hard to tell who the bastards are," she countered. Sally then gave him a final kiss, and he was off into the morning rush.

———

CHAPTER 11
DEALS

It was not lost on most Rhode Islanders that their state was one of only two that hadn't voted to ratify the Volstead Act. Connecticut was the other, and, as pointed out in many articles in *The Providence Journal*, the people were definitely against the federal government on this issue. Over and over the state's Attorney General would try to challenge the 18th Amendment.

Woonsocket, Rhode Island was just to the north of Providence near the Massachusetts border. The city was one of the leading markets for booze as prohibition continued, and enforcement was selective at best. It was such a booming booze city that a number of smaller operators took turns at producing product with large hidden or cleverly disguised distilleries. One operation housed in the Glenbrook Worsted Company textile factory on Mason Street became big enough to include vats which could hold up to 6,000 gallons of spirits. Operated by former state representative John Kelly and two other former prohibition agents, it became one of the more well-known "secret" distilleries in the northern part of the state. The Big Seven took notice.

March was a big month for the "speak's." It included St. Patrick's Day along with a number of festival weekends. Business was good, and everyone was making money. The Big Seven estimated that the Glenbrook operation took in around 20 to 25 thousand dollars a week. While the kickbacks to the Big Seven were getting smaller and smaller, profits for Glenbrook grew larger and larger. Suddenly, they were raided by the Feds. The prohibition agents shut down the entire distillery and arrested the three men who ran it including the former state representative.

A few blocks away from the site of the raided distillery, politics played out as usual a few days later. "Today we cut the ribbon in honor of our veterans of the Great War," Governor Peter Baker said to the crowd gathered in the center of town where a statue had been erected on River Street along the bank of the Blackstone River. A number of local dignitaries and citizens were attending the unveiling followed by a short reception where they mingled making small talk as others conducted business. The weather was chilly and breezy for early March as the governor made his rounds taking pictures and seeing the people whom his executive assistant had let him know he should pay extra attention.

Jesse Young lingered toward the back of the crowd and waited for the governor to finish his hand shaking and picture taking before trying to get a few minutes with him. Both the governor and his executive assistant, Andy Parquette, spotted the reporter as soon as he joined the crowd at the ceremony. They both knew it would be hard to avoid him. The other reporters and photographers were not a problem, but Jesse was not a favorite of the Baker administration.

"Governor, do you have a minute?" Jesse asked elbowing his way toward him as the crowd around the chief executive of the state thinned. Both the governor and Andy ignored him at first, but then he became hard to avoid. "Governor?"

"Jesse, absolutely. Great to see you again," Governor Baker said in a tone that to some would seem welcoming, but to trained ears, like those of his executive assistant, was almost sarcastic.

"Governor, just a few blocks away three men, including former State Representative Kelly, were arrested for operating a distillery. Do you have any comment on that?" Jesse asked. He had his suspicions that the Big

Seven had pulled strings to have it raided in order to quell the competition, but he couldn't prove it yet.

"The Attorney General is doing his job, apparently," the governor answered with a bit of levity in his tone. "Our state continues to work with federal prohibition agents to enforce the law of the land."

Jesse wrote that quote down in his reporter's notebook and fired back another question. "What do you say to people who accuse your administration and the Feds of selective enforcement of the Volstead Act?"

"Our state, along with our federal partners, enforces all the laws of the land equally," answered the governor.

"Why was the name of your former assistant and chief of staff, Thomas Pike, found in the cash payout ledger of a murdered member of the Bristol Gang who ran booze for the Big Seven?"

At this point, Andy interrupted the interview. "Governor, we have to go or we'll be late for our next stop."

"Governor, why was your former assistants name in a payoff ledger of criminals?" Jesse pressed.

This story had not come out in the papers. Jesse was sitting on a bunch of leads, continuing to connect the dots. The ledger in question had been found by the police at a crime scene and put into evidence. Because the illegal movement of outlawed liquor was involved, the State Police allowed the Bureau of Prohibition to have access to evidence found. Jesse had a contact in the Bureau who had allowed him to see and photograph it. The names of a few low-level local officials and a couple of politicians were expected when he first flipped through it. It wasn't until he developed the pictures and dove deeper into the pages that he recognized the name of the governor's personal assistant and chief of staff. Thomas Pike was not the governor, but he was about as close as someone could get. Jesse had no direct evidence that the money was actually meant for the governor, but the reporter continued to dig around. He wanted to land a big fish, and linking the governor of the state of Rhode Island to the Big Seven would be like landing a great white shark, not to mention the accolades that would come from a story like that.

Thomas Pike had left the service of the governor abruptly not long after a Bristol Gang member was found dead in a snow bank. Jesse wasn't sure the two incidents were related or just a coincidence in timing. The official reason Pike left the governor's office was that he wanted to spend more time with his family. That was a throw away statement most reporters translated to mean "it's none of the public's damn business." Jesse tried a couple of times to contact Pike including showing up at his home to land an interview but had no luck. Pike moved just a few days before he left the service of the governor and, ironically given the statement the State House put out, had no wife or kids. There was a rumor that Pike had moved to Washington in order to work for a Florida senator, but follow up calls to both senators from the Sunshine State gave the reporter no evidence that was the case. Landing an interview with Thomas Pike could very well bring down a sitting governor, and Jesse continued to work his sources.

The governor was quickly escorted away from Jesse back to the safety of his car and hustled on to the next event.

"Did you know about this ledger?" Governor Baker asked his assistant.

"Not at all, sir. I can sniff around with the Feds or our people if you want," Andy answered.

"Well, sniff around, but quietly. We can't have it coming out that Pike was paid money from criminals. That would be a disaster for me, not to mention the next election. Keep this quiet," the governor ordered.

"Will do," Andy said while mulling over what all this meant. He had wondered why Pike had quit so abruptly and left the administration. He had some questions of his own he wanted to get answered.

———

This game was for people of means and by invitation only. Where it took place every month was on a need-to-know basis. The Bristol Gang took their gambling seriously and ran racket numbers throughout southern New England. There was a difference, however, between keeping book for regular everyday people and operating this exclusive VIP game for only a select few. Patrick ran the gambling side of the business for the Bristol Gang, mostly as a collateral duty given his dayside responsibilities moving liquor. Todd Ellis and Rudy House were his chosen gambling lieutenants. Of course, they all answered to Danny.

"Every horse won," Todd said to Rudy as the two set up the table for the evening's big stakes card game. "How the fuck does he do it?"

Rudy was unpacking the chips as the two awaited the players who were due within the hour. "No fucking clue," he answered. "He's got to have a system."

"We don't get a lot from him, but when he does put his money down, he scores every single time. And it's not just Aqueduct. He does okay at Saratoga and Belmont. But at Aqueduct, he hits every race. I don't know what the good father's system is, but I want to find out," said Todd.

Rudy was stacking chips into the rack. He would be tonight's dealer, and these "clients" expected perfection. Rudy thoroughly enjoyed dealing. He had grown up a Jersey kid just outside Atlantic City and had dealt cards since he could hold them. In high school, he was one of the youngest dealers on the shore actually working for money. "He seems to only bet on those three parks. I doubled down on a couple of his and walked away with a few 'C' notes."

Todd opened an unmarked case and starting pulling out bottles of liquor. Then he opened a second box with glasses and a few mixers. He would be the evening's banker and bartender. With his Colt .38 caliber pistol under his shirt and a sawed-off 12 gauge behind the makeshift bar, he was also the evening's security. The gentlemen at this game would not pose a threat, but he trusted no one, and there was plenty of cash in the room should someone stumble upon the game.

"Patrick asked about him too. Luck? Skill? Someone on the inside? Who knows," Todd pondered out loud.

The room they were using for tonight's game was familiar to everyone who was due around nine o'clock. They would play all night until dawn before closing down the game. The five players were invited and enjoyed each other's company. Todd and Rudy made sure the players invited to each "big" game of the week were compatible with no business or any competition between them. Occasionally a few would get hot under the collar, especially after a few drinks, if they were losing. The sound of footsteps could be heard coming up the stairs from the back entrance. It was a chilly March night and always dark near that back door. There were only two rooms on the second floor, and the men used one for the card game and the other to stage food and drink.

"Gentlemen, welcome," Rudy said as he sat at the table combining decks of cards. He was in his zone as the first two men walked through the door. Within a few minutes, all five players were shaking off the cold, getting drinks and sitting down at the table. "Max bid is going to be a thousand as we kick things off tonight, gentlemen," Rudy said as he dealt the first hand. These men were dressed to the nines and ready to play. Their wives and families were safe at home in bed.

The building was located out in the country in a small village called Chepachet around thirty miles from the capital city of Providence. Upstairs on the backside of the building, the men played cards and drank liquor until the sun came up. Downstairs there was only one man, and he would also be there until 7 a.m. He was the overnight watch trooper for this barracks of the Rhode Island State Police.

———

Even though it was March, there was still snow on the ground in Poland Spring, Maine. Some cars had a hard time on the secondary roads unless they had chains on the tires. It was a cold 38 degrees, and the snow pack was continuing to melt. Locals were hoping this would be the last snow of the winter, but in this part of the world, April was still in play for frigid weather.

When the sun disappeared beyond the horizon, lights were beginning to come on. For the speakeasy, the lights were powered by a hook-up to the grid serving the inn just up the hill. The local electrical line supervisor was a frequent customer.

The same Canadians who ran the booze down from the border also operated the place. Thanks to the inside information from the Feds, Patrick knew when the highest number of their people would be on hand. Saturday nights were typically the busiest.

"Remember, no talking," Patrick said to Marky and Joey. "Masks." he ordered as the three men donned the full-face ski masks usually reserved for people hitting the nearby slopes. They stepped out of the car into the cold night where the only sounds were coming from the speakeasy about a hundred yards down the road on the right. "No civilians," Patrick said. "You hear me, Marky? No fucking civilians."

The three men walked single file along the dark tree line toward the small building. As they closed in, Patrick stopped for a final check.

"I'm in the front door, you two in the back. Check weapons." The three men readied their Tommys as hearts starting racing thanks to the adrenaline pumping through their blood. "Let's go." Patrick walked to the front door as the other two men went around back. They knew the building and the layout. Again, this was thanks to the intel provided by the Feds.

Patrick waited about thirty seconds before taking aim at the lock on the door, knowing the doorman sitting inside was about to get the shock of his life. This was his way of knocking to get inside as he put his finger on the trigger and squeezed off a three-round burst.

Instantly the door popped open as the smoke from the rounds was sucked inside while the bleeding bouncer ran for his life toward the back of the building. Patrick entered the building, now quiet except for the sound of a record playing on the Victrola in the corner.

"Everyone freeze. This is a raid," Patrick said. He was the only one who would talk. Some tried to escape out the back door, but Marky and Joey made sure that was not possible as they entered from the rear.

"Fucking Feds," one of the bartenders said.

"Feds don't wear masks," the manager said in a serious and quiet tone while standing toward the end of the bar.

"No, they don't," Patrick said as he pointed his Tommy at the manager and pulled the trigger. The manager's body was struck three times and fell backwards crashing into the glass bar shelves filled with bottles. The smell of the liquor from the smashed bottles and the odor of gunpower quickly filled the small room. Marky turned his gun to the bouncer and shot him twice. Joey did the same with the third Canadian who had emerged from the bathroom just in time for his life to end. Patrick had a piece of paper with five names and five pictures. The first three were easy. He wanted to be in and out in a matter of minutes but could not find the other two among the patrons. There was a coatroom in the back corner of the building. Patrick went that way as Marky and Joey kept their guns drawn on the customers who hoped only to get out of there with their lives.

The door was locked, and Patrick blew off the lock. Inside was a man trying to get an operator on the phone to place a call. "Drop the phone," Patrick ordered.

The man did as he was ordered. He was a young guy around 25 or 26. Patrick looked at the photos on the paper and matched the forth Canadian bootlegger to this man sitting in front of him at the desk. "Where's Javier?" Patrick asked in a calm voice.

"Montréal. He didn't come on this trip," said the terrified young man.

"Lucky for him," Patrick said before putting his finger back on the trigger and squeezing off three rounds into the chest forcing the body to go crashing backward in the chair into a filing cabinet next to the small desk with the phone.

Patrick emerged from the small office and took another look at the people in front of him then back to the picture. No Javier. He looked at his two partners and gestured with his hand that it was time to leave. Marky and Joey went to the front door and waited for Patrick who walked over to the body of the manager. He pulled out a playing card from his coat pocket and stuck it in the mouth of the dead man as the customers watched in horror.

"Let's go," Patrick ordered while walking to the front door then outside with Marky and Joey in tow as the smells of gunpowder and spilled whisky settled across the small speakeasy. It would be a long time before drinks would be served at this place again.

———

CHAPTER 12

BOUNDARIES

Pittsfield Massachusetts sits near the border of New York State in the far western part of the state. To locals, it was about as far from the state capital as you could get, and they enjoyed the fact that life was different in this part of the state. Their thirst for alcohol and gambling was as much as anyone's, but being so far from the major cities, supply was sometimes hard to come by. The irony of the Canadian border being just to their north was not lost on many individuals who tried to bring in their own stash. Primary distribution for much of upstate New York and this part of western Massachusetts had been in question and contested a number of times over the years since the Volstead Act was passed. Chicago had clearly given New York City to the Big Seven along with southern New England and the east coast. Upstate New York along with western Massachusetts and Vermont, though, were up for interpretation of the current agreements between the families.

This was a business trip for Owney, but Sally wanted to go along and maybe do some relaxing in the upstate. Big Bill Dwyer asked Owney to run up to Albany and check on business in that part of the Empire State. After Albany, Owney was to go to Pittsfield and personally supervise an air delivery. Chicago had been operating in the area, and Owney wanted to personally see what was what. Sally also knew that Kevin would be on the aircraft making the delivery.

It was a chilly afternoon for April as Owney, his driver Pat and Sally stood near an empty hangar at the small Pittsfield Airport. The sky was a mix of scattered clouds, and a stiff northerly breeze made the 44-degree temperatures feel even cooler. The hangar was at the other end of the runway from the main building set off by itself. Originally used for military air training, it was closed and had been given to the county when the Army consolidated their newly formed Air Corps in Kentucky. The county subleased it to a dummy landscape service owned by the Big Seven.

The plane approached about twenty minutes late, circled the field and landed. It was another of the Ford Trimotors with only a pilot and Kevin aboard along with a cargo of booze destined for local establishments.

They taxied in for just a few minutes, and the pilot parked next to the hangar door then shut down the three big engines. Moments later, the door in the back of the aircraft opened up and Kevin went about his business of deploying the small stairs. Owney and his party approached the door as Kevin and the pilot came out clearly surprised to be visited by the boss.

"How was the flight?" Owney asked the pilot.

"Perfect. No issues. Some ice before we left Mercier, but we knocked it off, and she flew like a bird. Good to see you again, Mr. Madden," said Corbin, the pilot, extending his hand to shake. He and Kevin had done this trip three times. They knew the drill. Kevin would go over to the hangar, unlock the big door and open it up. Inside was a one-year-old Ford AA panel truck with "Pete's Ice Cream" painted on the side. Kevin jumped into the truck and backed it out toward the aircraft. The next thirty minutes were spent moving the cases of liquor from the plane to the back of the truck.

"We make five stops," Kevin said to Owney. "Then we come back, secure the truck and hangar, fly home. Simple stuff."

"Today I'm going with you. Corbin can stay with the plane this time. Sally is taking the car to do some sightseeing and meeting us back here in a few hours. Let's go," Owney ordered.

"Suit yourself," Kevin said still curious about the visit from the boss.

Kevin got into the driver's seat with Pat in the middle and Owney on the end. It took only fifteen minutes to drive to the first stop of the day. It was a pharmacy at the edge of town about to close for the day. Kevin pulled the truck to the back of the big gray building, then got out and knocked on the door. A few seconds later, the door cracked and, after the owner recognized him, opened wide. The pharmacy owner knew who Owney was but not by sight.

"No Corbin this time?" Jerry, who was actually half owner of the speakeasy, asked.

"Not today. Today you get to meet the big boss. Owney Madden, this is Jerry," Kevin said with a bit of awkwardness and nervous tension in his voice.

"Great pleasure," Jerry said shaking the hand of his biggest supplier.

"We've got six cases for you," Kevin said as Owney stayed silent for the moment.

"Let's get them in," Jerry said as he, Pat and Kevin went into the back of the truck. The three men made quick work of unloading six cases of Canadian whisky. Kevin had only been in the back room of the pharmacy and never into the speakeasy itself. That was for members only.

"I'd like to see your joint," Owney said with a tone that Jerry recognized as more of a demand rather a request. "Heard great things."

"Well, we're not open until seven," Jerry answered reluctantly.

"You don't have to be open. I'd just like to see your set-up," Owney pressed.

After some hesitation, Jerry finally came around. "Sure, Owney, sure thing. Come on down."

Jerry headed to what looked like a walk-in icebox with a lock. He pulled out his keys and took off the lock. When he opened the door, instead of an icebox there was a staircase leading to the basement which served as the local speakeasy that many would frequent, especially on the weekends. The three men made their way down the stairs as Jerry took the lead and turned on the lights. Owney could see it was a nice-looking place of about the standard size. There was a bar on each side of the room with tables in the middle. He recognized the smell. There was a specific smell and feel to places like this.

Owney went to the bar to his right and instantly could see that it was not just his product for sale.

"I recognize this bottle," Owney said to his customer Jerry. "It's not from us."

Jerry was silent trying to look for the right words. As a pharmacist he could make a good living. Running a speakeasy on the side, he could make a small fortune.

"This is Chicago," continued Owney. "So is this." Owney picked up one of the bottles he was pointing to. "This too," he said with a darker tone. Then he took the bottle and threw it at the concrete wall where it smashed into pieces, spraying whisky everywhere.

Jerry was clearly shaken. "I've got to buy from them. Just like I've got to buy from you," Jerry said with an apologetic tone.

"Is this not Massachusetts? Kevin, is this Massachusetts? Pat, is this Massachusetts?" he asked rhetorically.

"This is Massachusetts," Pat answered.

"Jerry, this is Massachusetts. Big Seven territory. You buy from us and us alone!" Owney exclaimed. "From now on, when my people deliver, they get access down here, and if there's one drop of Chicago booze in this speak', the bottle won't be the only thing broken."

Without another word, Owney walked back up the stairs and left the building. Pat and Kevin quickly followed. Jerry stayed back downstairs to clean up the mess. The three men got back into the truck and continued to the other four stops. Chicago booze was found at two more of the speakeasys the men serviced. It was clear to Owney that they had to make a stand in this part of the country.

It took about three hours for them to get back to the airport where Sally was waiting with Corbin. Owney was agitated and glad he had come on this fact-finding trip. They drove up to the hangar, and all three men got out of the truck. Kevin backed it into the hangar and secured the door.

"I want to fly over to Rochester and check out a couple of speak's up there that we supply. Corbin, can you fly me there, then back to Teterboro before heading back north?" Owney asked, knowing what the answer would be.

"Sure thing, boss. I'll need to fuel in Rochester and maybe again down at Teterboro, but easy deal. I only have two seats, though," Corbin said. "We may run out of daylight as well."

"We can spend the night in Rochester and start out tomorrow if needed. Honey, Pat will take you and Kevin back to the city in the car, and I'll get someone to pick me up at Teterboro when we get there tomorrow afternoon," Owney said.

"That's fine," Sally said just before giving him a kiss goodbye. Her eyes also caught Kevin's knowing the two would have some quality time together when they returned to New York.

"Okay. Let's go," Owney ordered as he and Corbin climbed back into the aircraft. It took only a few minutes to start up and taxi out.

As Pat, Sally and Kevin pulled out of the airport, the Trimotor started its take-off run and quickly faded from sight.

Hours later, darkness had long set in when Pat pulled the car up to the Madden's New York City brownstone. It was the end of a long day for all of them.

"Do you want me to walk you in?" Pat asked knowing he would pay dearly should anything happen to Sally on his watch.

"No, you're a darling. Thanks Pat. I'm good," she answered.

"Okay, Mrs. Madden."

Kevin got out with her and turned back to Pat. "I'm going to walk from here to the train. You go ahead and call it a night," he said wondering if Pat would be suspicious.

"You sure?"

"Absolutely. Get some rest. I'll probably see you over the next couple of days," Kevin replied.

"Okay. Good night." With that, Pat drove off leaving Kevin and Sally to themselves once again.

The two quickly went up the stairs and into the house. It was chilly inside, and the heat needed to be turned up.

"I'll make us a drink," Kevin said. "You can turn up the heat."

Sally couldn't let that line just sit out there. "Oh no, my boy. You can turn up the heat!" The two laughed.

In a matter of minutes, the two were sitting on the couch sipping some of their finest product.

"Who are you, Sally Madden?" Kevin asked while taking a sip of his high-end Canadian whisky.

"You know who I am," she answered in a tone so low that it could be categorized a whisper.

The two didn't wait to get upstairs to the bedroom. His shirt was off first, then hers, then everything else. They made passionate love for the next thirty minutes.

"Oh my God," he said after their first encounter of the night. "How old are you?"

She sat up, took a sip of her whisky and answered. "Old enough to know what is good and what is bad. This is better than good. I would say incredible."

They sat quietly sipping their drinks for a few minutes before Sally took out her cigarettes and lit up.

"Want one?" she asked offering Kevin the pack.

"I'm fine with the whisky."

"I'm fine with you," she chuckled between puffs.

"You going to stay with him?" Kevin asked pointedly.

"Why wouldn't I?"

"Just wondering."

"What brought on that question?" she probed.

"You don't seem happy with him or living here or anything," he said.

She was silent for a couple of minutes, surprised by how intuitive this young man was. She tried not to show on the outside that things were a bit empty on the inside.

"I'm happy," she replied.

He just sat there and gave her a look then took another sip of the whisky.

"Really?"

She thought for a few seconds. "I'm comfortable. Owney makes me comfortable."

"There's more to life than comfortable," Kevin offered. Then in the low light of the living room, he could see the tears in her eyes. "I'm sorry."

She took a napkin and wiped her eyes. "It's not you. I'm the one who should be sorry."

He poured her another drink to freshen up her glass.

Sally continued. "I wanted out a long time ago. I'm trapped. He'd kill me if I even asked. He'd kill you if he knew what we were doing right now."

"He can't kill us if he's dead," Kevin said coldly.

She was clearly shocked by that statement. He could tell by the look in her eyes. She took a drink.

"He's more than just one person. He's an empire. And you're a loyal soldier," she said.

"He's just a man," Kevin countered. "Loyalty goes both ways. I'm loyal to a point. That point is whether it's good for me to be loyal or not."

"The other bosses would also kill both of us for being disloyal," she said.

"Not if we get away. Escape to the Keys or Canada."

Her mind was racing a mile a minute, and part of it couldn't believe they were having this conversation.

"I've been thinking of an exit strategy," she finally admitted to her young confidant.

"Feds?" Kevin asked.

Sally could hold a pretty good poker face, but this was too insightful of him. Did he know something? Was he working with the Feds too? Has she been compromised? A jumble of thoughts ran through her tired mind as she slowly became more intoxicated.

"What did you say?" she asked stone faced.

"I'm just thinking out loud. I saw you in the diner with that guy. I know who you hang with, and he's not one of them. I know a 'G' when I see one," he explained.

"They could arrest me right now for being part of Owney's little empire. They want Owney, not me." She took another puff and sip of her drink. "They threatened to throw me in jail. What the fuck am I supposed to do? I'm just a guy's dame, but the guy happens to be a bootlegger and a gangster."

He sat quietly for what seemed a lot longer than a minute or two. Then he spoke. "How much do they have on you?"

"How the hell do I know? Enough to make the threats. They want some of the books and me to testify against him. For that, I get a walk."

Kevin was mature well beyond his age. He thought about this for a few more minutes. He knew she had access to money and transportation.

"Just play along for now with Owney and the Feds. Don't give them anything useful, and string them along. That might come in handy. You don't have to kill someone to make him go away," he said.

The two finished the whisky while just sitting and talking on the couch. They talked about each other's lives, passions, interests and more. When the whisky bottle was empty, they went upstairs. Soon the night had turned into day, and Kevin was giving her a kiss goodbye before heading out into the chilly New York morning. Little did he know when he was leaving on this trip a few days ago to drive to Canada to meet the plane on a routine delivery run that it would end up being a life changer.

The horses ate well, and local veterinarians looked after them meticulously because they were, in fact, athletes of a sort. The vets had full access to the track, stables and pretty much anywhere they wanted to go at most parks including Saratoga and Aqueduct in New York. Saratoga was about an hour north of Albany on U.S. 9 while Aqueduct was in Queens, New York. Either was just a half-day or so drive from Seekonk, Massachusetts.

"How's the good doctor doing?" asked Father Ralph Connelly as he approached the "B" stables at Aqueduct. He was dressed in khaki pants and a snappy, well pressed buttoned-down shirt, appearing to be any other horse owner or enthusiast. His traditional black slacks, shirt and Roman collar had been left in the trunk of the car after changing about half way along the drive to Queens.

"Ralph!" the vet said looking up from under a horse he was tending.

"Sorry I didn't come last week but couldn't get anyone to fill in for my masses."

"No worry, my friend," Doc Mason said. "Just hang out a few minutes and I'll be done in a jiffy." Dr. Paul Mason was giving a quick check-up to one of the older racehorses in the barn. Being a vet was his passion, but being rich was his goal. On the walls of his office just a few miles away from the track were degrees from the State University of New York School of Veterinary Medicine and Boston College where he finished undergraduate school and had become friends with Ralph Connelly many years before.

The short and stocky Dr. Mason finished with his horse and joined his friend from New England for a short walk back to the cars.

"Coffee?" asked Father Ralph.

"Read my mind. You can drive."

The two got into Father Ralph's Ford Model A and motored over to the local diner just a few miles away. Doc Mason was a regular, and Rose the waitress told them to sit anywhere they would like. It was a classic coffee joint that looked a little like a travel trailer on the outside but was warm and friendly on the inside.

"How was the drive?" Doc Mason asked as he took off his jacket and sat in the booth across from his college buddy. The smell of hot coffee and Danish filled the air.

"Beautiful. I think I like coming here better than Saratoga. More things to do in the city if I stay the night," Father Ralph answered.

"We've had a fine month," Doc Mason said knowing that his friend would agree. It was also code for something else.

"We did," Father Ralph replied as he pulled two envelopes out of the case he was carrying. He put the envelopes on the table and slid them across to the vet. "We did indeed."

"Doc Mason picked up both envelopes and put them in the pocket of the jacket he had just taken off that was lying next to him in the booth.

Rose the waitress approached. "Coffee for you boys?"

"You bet," Doc Mason said answering for both.

She quickly disappeared.

"What kind of numbers?" Doc asked not wanting to count what was in the envelopes in public.

"On the order of 30K," Ralph answered.

"Respectable."

"I would say so."

Rose returned. "Milk is on the side, sugar right there in the dispenser."

"You're the best, Rose," Doc said with a twinkle in his eyes. He had a wife and another girl on the side, but he always enjoyed eyeing her at the diner.

"I see you looking at her," Father Ralph said as she walked away.

"What a dame. I'm sure you want a piece of that ass. Oh, that's right, you can't," he joked with a chuckle.

"How are we looking next month?" Father Ralph asked, changing the subject back to business.

"Good. Back to Saratoga. The lineup cards should be out next week. Will your connections be good to go?" asked Doc.

"Absolutely. I've got some connected guys, and their bosses are enjoying the ride, too."

The pair had been friends for years but in business for only two of those years. Dr. Paul Mason had been taking care of horses in the racing industry for quite some time. Large animal vets were sometimes hard to come by, and both parks enjoyed having Paul around, welcoming him as one of their primary vets. Owners also had to sign off, but that was easy knowing that their horses would be in good hands. Their scam was genius and simple. Before each week of racing, the lineup cards would be published with the horses that would run each race. Dr. Mason would simply check on each horse before the races, injecting all but one with a very light sedative. He calculated the exact amount to the weight of each horse to lower the performance by a very small percentage. All but one horse would get the drug. Literally, he could rig the race for any horse to win, place and show. Sometimes, but not every time, he would have the long shot win the race. The payoff would be huge. Thanks to Western Union, he would wire Father Ralph the week's lineup card with a code indicating which ones to bet on. The code simply looked like prayer requests from out of state sick family members of parishioners. Ralph would then make bets with his guys, Rudy and Todd of the Big Seven's Bristol Gang, while sharing with them the winning races to look at.

"How's Bridget been feeling?" Father Ralph asked with a bit of priestly tone in his voice. Doc Mason's wife had been down with a bad flu the month before.

"Good, thanks. She's back to her usual self."

"Fantastic. See, prayers work."

Doc grabbed one of his envelopes from the coat lying on the seat and lifted it just enough so that his pal sitting across the table could see it. "They sure do!" he said sarcastically wagging the envelope full of money.

The two finished their coffee and catching up. Father Ralph left Queens bound for Manhattan and a night on the town before he would return to Seekonk and the parish the next day.

———

CHAPTER 13

POLICING

The Boston traffic had been stop and go all morning, and most people from the office were late. Special Agent in Charge James Warren would publicly humiliate anyone late to the morning briefing no matter the reason. He thought it was an effective way to drive discipline and keep his folks in line. To the agents and staff, it was just another line on a long list of nasty habits he brought to the office every day.

"Do you plan for traffic?" Warren asked one of the two staff secretaries.

"Yes sir, I do, but you know this town," she answered as everyone slowly made their way into the conference room which was larger than most and also used for press briefings.

"I know this town; that's why I plan for it," he replied tersely. "Okay people, we start on time, and it's now zero nine zero."

Ted Connelly and Eric Thompson purposely stood near the back of the room knowing one of their cases could be the subject of at least part of the briefing.

"We're starting with the mess up in Maine. Bottom line, once again the Big Seven hit it before we could. I'm sure our friends in the back of the room would like to brief on this debacle," Warren said.

Ted and Eric moved toward the front of the room as a few more stragglers joined the group. Ted took a good sip of his coffee and started. "Yes
sir, it seems that, at least from crime scene evidence, the Big Seven hit
the speak' we've been monitoring in Poland Spring, Maine killing two
Canadians and a U.S. citizen believed to be from Chicago. That last part
we are still trying to confirm. There may be a connection to one of the
Chicago families, but again, we're still early in the investigation. The
Canadians were from Montréal."

Eric picked up from there. "This speak' was supplied directly from
Canada and was a thorn in the side of the Seven. Apparently, they acted
before we could move in and bust them."

The room was silent for a few seconds. Then James Warren spoke.
"Apparently," he said sarcastically. "My question, gentlemen, is how the
fuck did they know we were going to bust the place? Or did they know?
Maybe their timing was just lucky. I'm hoping for option three but not
going to bet the farm on it."

Except for the sound of the coffee percolating near the wall, the room
was silent for a few moments, then Ted continued. "The usual card was
found on one of the bodies. It was definitely Big Seven work. That's not
out in the papers at the moment. We really don't want it out there anyway," Ted explained.

James took a sip of his coffee, then spoke again. "I told DC that we
were going to land some Canadians in Maine which would have given us
incredible intel not to mention a few extra feathers in our caps, but not
now. Not with them rotting in the Augusta morgue."

Most of the people in the room knew the extra feathers would have
been in his cap alone, but that was beside the point.

"When will we find out if one of the stiffs was from Chicago?" James
quizzed his staffers.

"Within a couple of days, boss. The Chicago field office is running it
down. No ID on the body, but a couple of the witnesses interviewed by
Maine State Police say he often talked about being from Chicago and connected there," Eric explained.

"Okay. Keep me advised on this," James said. "New subject. Airplanes. Seems our friends are now moving up in the world and taking to the skies. Our contacts in both Rhode Island and Connecticut confirm someone was seen moving a bunch of booze by Trimotor at the small county airport just outside Hartford. These planes can't hold as much as a boat or ship, but they can get in and out quickly. Bottom line, it extends the reach of both Chicago and the Big Seven. I want to bust one of these deliveries and seize the plane."

Everyone in the room was silent once again. They all knew it would be a huge get if they busted an aerial delivery of liquor in the act.

"That's like picking a needle out of a haystack with all the little airports in New England and New York," Jeff Howard said breaking the silence. "We will to work the CI's and see what we can find."

"Exactly," James said agreeing with his colleague. "We have one CI on the inside of the Big Seven, and the Chicago field office has a couple out their way. Our CI with The Seven is not that high up but will be a help nonetheless."

"How much are they moving by air?" asked Ted.

"Hard to tell. Really hard to tell. Looks more like strategic type deliveries for out of the way places. It may not be huge, but it extends their reach quite a bit," James explained.

He took out a map and put it up on the chalkboard with tape. On the map were four locations with red stars showing where intel had high confidence or knew an actual air delivery had been made.

"These are four deliveries we know of. No real pattern to discern. Another problem is that they're not on the ground long and take a very short amount of time. They're in and then they're out. What we need is good intel on when and where. We can be waiting on the ground and pinch everyone involved, which will send a clear message," he said. "I wanted to send a message to the Canadians by busting the speakeasy they supplied in Maine, but obviously that didn't work out," James lectured.

After the operations briefing, James went into some housekeeping business before the meeting ended and the group went about their business.

Eric and Ted walked back to their desks in the other room chatting quietly. "It's been a tough couple of months behind the power curve," Eric said to his partner. "Busting an air drop would be just the thing to break up our little losing streak."

"That it would, my friend," Ted said. "That it would."

———

99 miles to the south in the old seaport of Mystic, Connecticut, the *Black Duck* was pier side getting a boiler replaced. It was a rare sunny day in this part of Connecticut during April, and the trees were starting to show some signs of coming back to life. Captain Rick St. Pierre was very familiar with this port and town. He had friends there and could trust the workers to keep their mouths shut about what clients were in and out. They would also get some extra money in their checks in exchange for that silence courtesy of their owners, Atlantic Maritime.

"One more day and you're out of here," Eddie the foreman said to Rick. The job was a big one, and with the amount of work these ships had been doing over the last four years, he was surprised the boilers had lasted as long as they did.

"Thanks, Eddie," Rick said as he looked past the foreman, spotting his boss walking down the pier. Eddie quickly took his leave to continue supervising the boiler swap.

"How we doing?" Danny asked his senior captain.

"Should be wrapped up tomorrow," Rick answered while extending his hand to shake.

"Good news," Danny replied. "Let's get a coffee."

"Sure. Pearl Street Cafe, right over there," he said pointing to a small joint just a few hundred yards away.

The two men entered the cafe and found a table in the corner away from the other patrons having lunch and trading sea stories likely embellished to impress.

"Coffee?" asked the man who was both the cook and waiter. *Probably the owner as well*, Rick thought giving the guy the once over.

"Two," Danny answered. Then it was on to the business at hand. Danny was not much of a small talk guy. He liked to get right to the point and move on. "Can we add two more runs in May and June?"

Rick was not shocked to hear this but wasn't sure he and his team could pull it off. It was about a five-day sail south, then the same back north plus delivery time. Already they were pushing the limit. He often wondered how people could actually drink that much booze.

"We can try. Crew time gets to be a problem sometimes, Danny. They're never home with their families as it is," Rick said.

"They'll be compensated."

The waiter returned with the coffee, noted where the cream and sugar were located then took his leave.

"Oh, they're grateful for the money. Don't get me wrong," Rick replied. "It's time away that's the issue."

"There's a lot of talk about getting rid of Volstead, and that would shut us down. The time to make money is now, so we're all burning the candle at both ends," Danny countered.

"What about the rum flights? That's got to help supply," Rick said.

"It does, but they're limited in weight. You guys do the heavy work."

Rick took a sip of his coffee and looked out the window to see two men getting out of a 'G' ride Ford. "This could be trouble," he said to Danny.

Danny looked out the window to see what he was talking about. He saw the two men and instantly knew there might be some problems. Occasionally the government would harass them, but Danny didn't recognize the pair now heading down the docks toward their boat. "Anything on there?" Danny asked.

"Clean. Not a drop," Rick answered.

"Let's go over there and head this off."

The two men paid for their coffee and quickly got up to leave. A few minutes later, after crossing the street, they walked down the dock toward the *Black Duck* where the G-men were standing and looking at the boat.

The tide was out and the smell of the salt marsh filled the cool air as the breeze picked up. Danny and Rick approached the men.

"Gentlemen, can I help you?" Rick asked the two.

"Are you the captain of this vessel?" the man in the black coat asked.

"I am."

"I'm Lieutenant Fred Myers and this is prohibition agent Tim Edwards. We would like to go aboard for a quick safety inspection."

Rick looked at Danny and then back at the taller man now identified as a member of the U.S. Coast Guard. "Safety inspection? We're having a boiler replaced, but sure thing. Feel free to come aboard. It's a little messy below where the guys are working."

The prohibition agent didn't say a word. Danny played along. The four men boarded the boat, and the Coast Guard officer started looking over the safety gear. The prohibition agent began checking the storage bay, berths and engine room.

"What do you do?" Danny asked the prohibition agent.

"Look for people like you who run booze," the agent replied with a terse tone.

Danny didn't need any hiccups to his operation, and losing one of the big three boats would be a real problem.

"We've got some reports of this boat operating off Stonington along the rum line," said the Lieutenant after he finished looking at the gear and ship's logs.

"Must be another boat," Rick answered. "There are a bunch that look like this one."

The lieutenant and special agent looked at the new boiler going in. "That's got to be expensive," the Coast Guard officer observed.

"It is. Now, is there anything else we can do for you two gentlemen today?" Rick asked.

"Protection is important, and I'm sure you would agree," the agent said to Danny.

Danny was silent. He was never one for saying a lot, especially to a Fed.

"Protection can be bought," the agent continued. "I'm the eyes and ears in this part of Connecticut for the bureau."

It was clear to Danny that this was a shakedown, and these two were working together. He didn't mind paying off the Feds. It was a common practice he and his crew did all the time. Bottom line, it was the cost of doing business.

"We're not doing anything illegal," Rick offered. "We're just doing maintenance and will be out of here tomorrow."

The Coast Guard officer spoke next. "We could hold this vessel here for a closer inspection which may take a few days or a week."

Rick spoke up. "This vessel is registered in Canada, and we have all of the required Canadian seaworthiness certificates."

"You're in a U.S. port. Didn't clear customs. Just showed up for some work," the Lieutenant said.

Danny couldn't have one of his three big ships out of service and decided to play along.

"I'll bet you two could help us out. We were just saying over a cup of coffee how good it would be to have a safety inspection of the vessel. I'm sure your time is valuable, and perhaps five 'C' notes each would cover any of your costs," Danny offered.

The two men looked at each other. That was more than they had expected. The agent felt greedy. "Six each," he countered.

"Done," Danny started walking up the dock toward his car parked on the street. "Come along, gentlemen," he said waving his hand.

Rick took his leave, went below and grabbed his camera hoping like hell there was some film inside. It was a 1928 Rolleiflex TLR they kept aboard to document some of the trips and any funny business that may go down. He quickly returned to the dock then quietly took a detour jumping off the dock to the sand below. He moved to the opposite side of the fish house building that was adjacent to the dock making sure the three men on the street near the car would not see him. He made his way to the corner of the building to get a clear view of the transaction that was about to take place.

Danny always kept plenty of cash available for times like these. In the big scheme of things, this was a rather small payoff. He opened the trunk of the car and inside there were two locked steel boxes. He used a small key to open the one on the right and counted out twelve one hundred-dollar bills. He also pulled out two bottles of fine Canadian whisky from the case that was toward the back of the trunk.

"Gentlemen," Danny said to the men who were at the front of the car and couldn't see what he was doing in the trunk. "I've got something for you," he said and then slammed the trunk down. The men walked to the back of the car. "This is local ginger ale from New London. I thought you should each have a bottle." With that he handed each a bottle and then reached into his pocket and counted out six hundred-dollar bills each. "I'm sure this will cover the extra inspection you can do for us."

"Your ship just passed inspection, Danny," the Lieutenant said with a smile on his face.

"I'm glad it did, Lieutenant. And just to be sure, we always document our inspections," Danny said looking off to the corner of the fish house building where Rick was photographing the transaction. Rick even gave them a little wave.

The men were speechless.

"I'm glad we were able to meet up for this inspection, and I'm sure that this should be the last one for quite a while. If it's not, I can always mail over the photos to the Coast Guard commander and head of the Bureau to prove it was completed."

After an awkward goodbye, the men took their leave, and Danny returned to the dock where Rick was waiting.

"Good job, Rick. Get those developed and file them in case we need the pictures. I highly doubt we will, but I like insurance. Safe voyages," Danny said shaking Rick's hand and returning to the car for the drive back up to his farm in Charlestown.

Rick smiled as he walked up the brow onto the *Black Duck*.

———

New York was full of characters who all loved to cheat the government and each other. Big Bill Dwyer was one of those at the top of the heap when it came to the rackets and big city underworld. Like the other members of the Big Seven, Big Bill had his side deals and kept his people in line by paying them a little extra or burying them in the Jersey landfills. Loyalty was the most important character trait he wanted and expected from those whom he employed.

Judge Louis Franklin had been on the Superior Court bench for five years and dreamed of becoming a Supreme Court Justice in the years to come. He was an appointed judge indicating that he was rather connected when it came to politics. Because of his position, he couldn't be seen in public with the likes of his pal Big Bill Dwyer; that was why they would meet for lunch at out of the way places where no one in the joint would dare say who came and went. The judge was a big man and looked young for his 57 years. He would always arrive after Big Bill.

At exactly one o'clock in the afternoon, after the lunch rush was over and most people had gone back to work, His Honor left his chambers and walked over to the dry cleaners a few blocks from the state courthouse. He walked in, picking up the distinctive smells of a laundry, to get his two white shirts. The young lady at the counter pulled his shirts forward from the rack as he pulled out two quarters.

"Thirty cents, sir," she said knowing who he was and being respectful.

He put the coins on the counter. "The change is all yours, doll," Judge Franklin said.

With that, he took the two shirts and instead of walking back to the front door, made his way around the side of the counter and into the back room of the laundry. In the corner, Big Bill Dwyer was sitting at a table that was set up with lunch for two. It was a nice meeting place, and the only down side was the occasional whiff of bleach from the washing machines on the other side of the building.

"Big Bill," the judge said greeting the man he'd known since high school.

"Louie!" Bill said giving his pal a big bear hug. "Pastrami from the Philly Pollak down on Seventh Avenue."

"No one does it better. How the fuck are you?" The judge asked.

"Super, thanks."

Not wasting any time, the two jumped right into their sandwiches. Then it was time for some business talk.

"FDR wants to put you out of business," Franklin said. "My people in Washington said the states are coming together to repeal."

Big Bill took another bite of his sandwich and a sip of his milk. He always drank milk with his meals even if there was alcohol at the table. Then he spoke. "That would kill us."

"Better start planning for the future, my friend. It's getting traction, and people like Representative Jimmy Brown of Pennsylvania are raising their voices for it. I saw him a few weeks ago in Atlantic City, and he told me it was going to happen."

The two continued their lunch. Both knew the repeal of the 18th Amendment was in the future, but how much into the future was always the question. Insiders like this helped Big Bill and the Big Seven in many ways, and this was one of them.

"By the way, there's a cop captain in the Bronx named Hanna. Know him?" Big Bill asked.

"I've heard of him. Don't know him personally. Why? Trouble?"

"Putting the squeeze on some of our Bronx speakeasys. I know he's got to do his job and all, but that's the Feds' jurisdiction, and we take care of them for just that reason," Bill explained.

"Technically, local law enforcement can also enforce Volstead. Really any law enforcement can," the judge said with a bit of a professorial tone in his voice.

"What can you do?" Bill asked.

"I know the borough commander and will chat with him. Anything else?"

"Nope. Always appreciate it, my friend."

The two finished their lunch and got up to leave. They gave each other another hug, then Big Bill left through the front door with his shirts, and the judge took the back exit returning to his chambers for the rest of the afternoon.

CHAPTER 14

TRACKS

It was 10:30 at night when the doorbell rang. Patrick was in the shower, and Jeannie walked down the stairs to see who could it be out there at this hour. She thought maybe it was their crazy neighbor. After unlocking the three dead bolts, she opened the door to see Marky standing there wet in the rain.

"Marky!"

"Hey Jeannie. Where's Patrick?"

"In the shower. Come in, dry off," she said.

Marky stepped into the house but stood near the door dripping on the wood floor. The rain had been relentless over the last couple of days and wasn't showing any sign of letting up. She noticed a deep red, almost black stain on the bottom of his pants but didn't say anything.

Both heard the shower turn off upstairs.

"Patrick, Marky is here," Jeannie yelled, hoping not to wake up their two kids.

Patrick got out of the shower, wrapped a towel around himself then went to the top of the stairs.

"What the fuck Marky? It's after ten."

"I need to talk to you."

Patrick walked down the stairs to the front door. Then he turned to Jeannie. "Go check on the kids, doll. They might have woken up."

Jeannie went back up the stairs to see if Mary and Patrick, Jr. were okay. She was used to the unusual hours and work schedules her husband kept.

"What?" Patrick said in a very annoyed tone.

"We've got a little problem down at the mill," Marky said.

"What?"

"We've got to go over there so I can show you."

Patrick took a deep breath and had a feeling he knew where this was going. He went back upstairs, got dressed and told Jeannie they were going out to take care of some business problem.

The two drove in Marky's car back to the mill where the second floor operated long after the first-floor employees ended their workday. When they walked into the entrance, the front desk girl just looked at Marky and was quiet.

"How many guests are left upstairs?" he asked the girl at the desk.

"Two," she answered.

With that Marky led Patrick up the stairs to the second floor and room six which was down the hall on the right. Marky reached into his pocket, pulled out the key and unlocked the door. He looked around to make sure no one was going to walk by, but with only two customers left a few rooms down the hall, things were quiet. Marky opened the door and walked in. Patrick followed. Marky then closed and locked the door behind them.

"Holy shit," Patrick said. "Holy shit. What the fuck?"

Marky just stood there and didn't have much to say.

"Who is this?" Patrick asked his subordinate. "Who *was* this?" he corrected himself tersely.

There was a half empty glass of Scotch on the table next to the bed. Marky went over and picked it up. He drank the remaining Scotch in a single gulp and put the glass back on the table.

"Lili," Marky said. "At least that's what she said her name was."

"Are you kidding me?"

Lili's lifeless, naked body was half on and half off the left side of the bed. Her hands were tied to the headboard. Blood was everywhere, and her clothes were all over the floor. Patrick didn't want to step another foot into the room.

"Marky, you're cleaning this mess up. "You're digging the fucking hole. I'm done with you," Patrick barked. "If Danny finds out about this, it's both our asses."

"He won't. I'll clean it up, but I need your help getting her out of here. Once they're done down the hall, the place will be empty, and we can take care of it," he said confidently.

"Jesus, Mary and Joseph, Marky. What's up with you? We're in business, and this place is part of the business, not your sick personal playland." Patrick was steaming mad and wanted to put a bullet in Marky's head, but he also knew that wasn't the solution. At the moment, he had to make sure this mess was straightened out and that the place was ready for business the next night. He also had to keep this from Danny, who actually would put a bullet in Marky's head.

The two went to work cleaning up the room, stripping the bed, washing the floor and rolling the body up in the rug that was just big enough to fit the young lady who would now turn up missing. The wood on the floor and part of the headboard was cleaned, but there was a slight stain left from the soaked in blood, and the ammonia and Borax they were using took away some of the finish. The smell was very noticeable all the way down the hall. Marky opened the few windows on the second floor. The last two "guests" had already left along with the front desk clerk at midnight.

"Get her head," Patrick ordered as he picked up the end of the rug where Lili's lifeless feet were tucked just inside. "Let's go."

The two moved the body down the stairs and waited to make sure things were clear before they went out the door to the trunk of Marky's car. All they would need was for a cop to come along and ask what they were doing. Ironically, the police chief had a piece of this very business, but they didn't want any hassles.

They drove up U.S. 1 to a wooded area outside of South Attleboro where some farms were located. They turned off the main highway onto a small dirt road that ran for a couple of miles leading to another even smaller dirt road.

"Take a right," Patrick ordered. The sun was about an hour from rising. The Chrysler Imperial's L-80 headlights were working overtime and fading. At the end of this second dirt road was a small but deep pond. They stopped the car and took out the chains and cement blocks collected back at the mill originally used to weigh down some of the textile machines on the first floor.

Thirty minutes later they tossed the package into the deep end of the pond hoping no one would ever find it. The drive back to Patrick's house was silent. He didn't know what to say to his muscle man and enforcer. *Maybe it's a mental problem*, he thought. *Maybe he was just drunk*. Marky pulled up to the house and Patrick got out.

"Sorry, man," Marky said sheepishly just before Patrick closed the door.

"Be in at noon, and get rid of those clothes you're wearing," Patrick replied coldly.

Marky pulled out as Patrick went in the front door of his house, still unlocked from their late-night departure.

"You're just coming home?" Jeannie asked her husband as she gave the kids breakfast.

"No, I was up and down and helped Marky with his car. I wanted to come back to have breakfast with my two favorite kids in the world. How about some coffee, doll?"

Jeannie fetched Patrick some coffee, and the family ate breakfast before the kids headed off for another day of school.

"So, you've got yourself a beach house down at the Cape," Sergeant Jeff Howard remarked as he made small talk while the two agents were sitting in a small truck on the other side of Norwood Field. "I love the Cape."

Ted Connelly had tried to keep that on the down low, but his wife loved to open her mouth and brag. "Just a little one. We had another one before but sold it and decided to get something we could also rent in the winter. It's definitely a fix'er up type of place."

The two agents were on their fourth airport surveillance shift of the month. Ted's usual partner, Eric, was on vacation, so Jeff was pinch-hitting.

"I would love that. Too rich for my blood, though, with two kids going to private school," Jeff explained.

One of the CI's (confidential informants) the office had working in the local speakeasys had given up some interesting information about the flow of booze from Canada by aircraft and a few of the airfields they were said to be using. Norwood Field was just about twenty miles south of Boston and on that list. Covering all of these fields 24/7 was impossible, but keeping an eye on a couple of key fields was within reason.

The truck they were sitting in was a 1925 Ford panel van with "Earl's Plumbing" painted on the side. Ted looked forward to the days after his retirement when hours of mind-numbing boredom would be replaced with hours on the golf course in Florida during the winter and on the Cape during the summer.

The two men were about to call it a day when a plane matching the description of the one the CI had given them flew over, circled the field then landed. Both men in the truck sat up and took notice. They could see the other end of the field with no glasses, but binoculars gave them a much better look.

"He's not getting off the runway," Ted said. "Looks like he's just sitting there. Maybe it's some sort of training flight."

"Give it a few minutes," Jeff said. Over the years, Jeff Howard had become a great special agent and was a patient man. "I'll bet that's a runner."

The two men watched the aircraft sitting at the far end of the runway still running. Finally, the plane revved up and taxied just off the end of the runway onto the paved taxiway. At that precise moment, a truck similar to the one they were occupying could be seen driving between hangar buildings and heading toward the plane.

"Bingo," Ted said.

"Yup."

They continued to watch as two men unloaded the airplane. Ted tried to take a couple of pictures, but their position was much too far away to get any good shots.

"3:35," Jeff said noting the time.

Thirty minutes later, the truck was full of booze, and the Ford Trimotor was powered up once again set to take the active runway. These smaller fields had no control towers allowing planes to come and go on their own.

"Now we can call it a day, Mr. Connelly," Sergeant Howard said. "I'm logging this now, and we'll see if there is a pattern. I'll bet a month's pay they're back same time next week."

Ted cranked up the truck, and the two G-men headed back to Boston knowing they would be back to Norwood in short order.

———

Miami Beach was the new playground of the rich and famous. The Big Seven met annually in the spring to share updates on their various businesses and operations. *This two-day train trip was worth every minute,* Danny thought as he put his feet into the turquoise blue tropical water. The Flamingo Hotel had become the winter meeting venue the Big Seven used as their excuse for a tropical getaway. There were always plenty of fine-looking women, great weather and good food. Because of the times, the beverages were served in dark glasses and always tagged as "soft drinks" or "sweet tea." Locals like developer Carl Fisher were on the inside track with local officials and law enforcement. They used to joke that prohibition ended on the mainland and didn't extend to the new town of Miami Beach, which had been incorporated just thirteen years before.

Formerly Alton Beach, the new Miami Beach quickly billed itself as the place where summer spends the winter with billboards in places like Times Square, Boston and Chicago promoting the exotic new destination to the rest of the country. Wives were not invited to this annual meeting but became familiar with the playground on other visits during different times of the year.

"The best cigars are made right here or over in Havana," Big Bill Dwyer said to his associate as they sipped some of the Canadian whisky their outfit supplied this popular hotel. "You're missing out."

Danny was not a big smoker but did enjoy the product that made them all rich men. "I can tell by how many you smoke," he said. "Owney is on his way out here. Probably a late night." Both men chuckled. It was just shy of ten a.m., and already the drinks were flowing.

These men were some of the original members of the Big Seven, and on this trip some of their business associates, who by now were starting to work more closely with them, were here to relax and talk business. Arnold Rothstein and Charles "Lucky" Luciano made their way downstairs to the pool as well.

"Thanks, doll," Lucky said to the waitress who had rushed over to meet him holding a tray with a plain donut and what looked like a cup of coffee. In the cup, however, was Russian-made vodka brought down by way of Canada.

Owney arrived to meet the others as they sat in the shade of palm trees next to the pool. He had a coffee in his hand. Inside the cup was actual coffee.

Lucky and Rothstein didn't meld too much into the operational side of the Big Seven, but as close as they were to the primary members and the business each brought, they were given all due respect and briefings on what was happening. This meeting was to address a certain territory infringement that had been festering for a few years now.

"We can't let Chicago get away with taking money out of our pockets in what is clearly our territory," Danny said turning the conversation from pleasure to business. "Just not going to do it." With that he took a sip of his drink. This was a thorn in his side more so than the rest. His percentage of the business from that part of their territory was the highest. He had already dealt with the competition in Chicago on a number of different occasions hoping to send a message each time. It was apparent to him that some of these incidents had not changed the problem.

"You might just have to suck it up," Lucky said with his trademark, matter of fact tone.

"I've seen it first hand," Owney said entering the conversation. "It's not everywhere, but it's evident."

"I agree it's been a problem," Big Bill chimed in.

"What about a sit down?" Lucky asked.

"Maybe we negotiate something in person," Rothstein suggested. "Carve out a little taste for them we can all be happy with."

This didn't sit well with Danny. "A little taste?" he asked, clearly agitated. "Then I want 'a little taste' of the Cleveland business."

"They control Cleveland, Danny. You know that was ironed out years ago," Lucky lectured.

Danny knew how much the Cleveland territory meant for the Chicago families including Capone. The Big Seven had pulled out of that territory after a nasty spat years ago that left two of Owney's lieutenants buried in the ice of Lake Erie only to be found during the thaw that occurred months after their demise.

"Fuck Chicago," Danny said in a defiant tone. "We earned all six New England states and part of upstate New York. I'm not giving back an inch of that territory."

The other men sat back and enjoyed their early morning tropical drinks, whisky or coffee. The bottom line was that everyone was making money. No one wanted to disrupt this kind of cash flow with a war over a small piece of western New England. For now, they would let Danny blow off some steam and then power on with business as usual.

"Who's first?" asked the young lady who had just walked over dressed in white and ready to massage her first client of the day.

"I say we let Danny go first. Maybe get rid of that hard on he's got for Chicago," Lucky said with a chuckle as the other men roared with laughter. No one ever accused Danny of not having a sense of humor as he, too, laughed it off.

———

CHAPTER 15

FEELINGS

Fred Rockwell enjoyed the power he commanded as an executive editor of the state's largest newspaper. The *Providence Journal* was the paper of record and respected around the nation as a strong journalistic shining light. It had broken numerous stories ranging from crazy government spending to local corruption and more. Fred enjoyed a fine home life with his wife of almost 15 years, two kids and a dog. They made their home in the Providence suburb of Cranston where his wife, Linda, was a schoolteacher.

At lunch, Fred would head over to Federal Hill and his favorite small Italian restaurant. Sometimes he would come with a client, colleague or like today, by himself with a copy of his newspaper in hand. The irony of reading the paper at lunch was that he was directly responsible for much of its content and knew everything that would be in print. He would, however, read over the stories and note any typos or misspellings, rare as they were. He also liked to look at the ad layout.

The weather had finally broken, and spring was starting to bring out the flowers and the pollen that was blowing in the air. He sat in a back booth already knowing what he would have to eat even before the waitress approached.

"Tea?" asked the young lady approaching his table with pad in hand.

"Sure, and a small meatball grinder," answered Fred. "Grinder" was a Rhode Island term for sub sandwich.

"Yes, sir," she said then disappeared to the back.

Fred opened his paper and started with the sports section to see how his teams were doing.

"How are you, Fred?" the strange voice asked from the booth behind him.

Fred was startled but turned around to see a man he did not recognize also reading a *Providence Journal*. The man did not look at Fred. He just sat there reading his paper.

"Good." He paused and tried to think of who this might be. Then he continued hesitantly. "Can I help you?"

"I'm here to help you," the stranger said again into his paper and not directly to Fred.

Fred got a sick feeling in his stomach not knowing what this encounter was about.

"With what?" Fred asked.

"Keeping your job and family."

"Who are you?" Fred asked now with a serious tone to his voice.

"That doesn't matter. It's who you are that does. You're in a powerful position, Mr. Rockwell. You've got Linda and the kids to take care of," the stranger continued.

At that point, the waitress returned, and both men went silent. She left the tea and returned to the kitchen.

"What do you want?" Fred asked.

"It's what we don't want, Mr. Rockwell. We don't want the governor embarrassed. He's an important man and does important business around the country with some of our associates. This Jesse Young has been asking a lot of questions lately. Too many questions."

Fred took a sip of his tea before responding. "I don't control what my reporters ask or report on."

"They work for you, Mr. Rockwell. That's all we know." The man turned the page of the paper he appeared to be reading. Then he spoke again. "We also know the girl you've been sleeping with on and off now for almost a year. She works for us. We've also got pictures of the two of you. Now, I'm sure this is all just a misunderstanding, and those encounters can go unreported."

Fred was breathless and had nothing to say at this point in the weird conversation with the stranger in the next booth.

The man closed his paper and put money on the table to pay for his coffee and cannoli. He got up out of the booth and dropped an envelope on Fred's table. "Try the cannoli," he said coldly before walking away. Fred opened the envelope and looked inside. Without pulling them out, he could see the black and white pictures that could end his career and marriage. Suddenly his appetite was gone, and he paid his tab without eating a bite of the meatball grinder that had just been delivered to his table. It may have been springtime, but a cold chill came over Fred as he left his uneaten food and walked out of the diner.

—————

The bingo had been doing well at Saint Mary's, and the parishioners enjoyed the Thursday night games so much that Father Ralph had recently added a once a month Saturday edition. Sister Judy Ann made her rounds to the regulars who were clearly having a really good time.

"I'm at mass every week, and I still can't win," said one of the faithful.

"The Lord works in mysterious ways, Timothy," Sister Judy Ann answered with a chuckle in her tone. "We're here for family, fun and community. Winning is just a bonus to our fellowship."

The man took a sip of his coffee as he watched the ten cards he was playing while Father Ralph called out the numbers. "I'd love to experience the bonus," he laughed.

The mix of cigar and cigarette smoke hung above the crowd like a cloud toward the end of the evening. Women had begun smoking a new brand of cigarettes called Lucky Strike because of their catchy ads promoting thinness and well-being. Even Sister Judy Ann would sneak an occasional cigarette when a parishioner would offer one or two for later on.

"Almost done for the night," she said to Father Ralph who had finished his last call and was starting to pack things up.

"Good night for the church," he replied.

After the parishioners left the hall, the two continued to clean up as the clock approached midnight. Their goal was to finish the last cards at eleven o'clock giving a good hour for the crowd to disperse and cleaning to take place. The toughest part always came with the noisy folding and stacking of the chairs. Father Ralph and a couple of the male parishioners would handle that task. "Thanks, gentlemen," the priest said to the two men as they finished the stacking and headed out into the night.

Ten minutes later Sister Judy Ann was ready to call it a night.

"I'm starved," Father Ralph said as he put the last of the tablecloths in the closet.

"Same here," Sister said. There was never a lot of time for the two to eat between setup and the bingo from 7 to 11. "Everything is closed."

"I've got some amazing chicken salad over in the rectory. Come on and have some with me," he offered. He lived by himself in the church rectory. The place had three bedrooms for three priests, but at the moment, he was the only one living there since the Bishop of Fall River had reassigned his assistant pastor. Currently he was waiting for a new priest to be assigned.

She hesitated for a few seconds and then agreed to come across the street for a bite to eat.

Sister Judy Ann could count on one hand the number of times she had been inside the rectory. Usually it was to help one of the priests inside with boxes or something that needed to be brought over. Once she and another of the sisters had used the kitchen when the stove in the church hall failed just before soup kitchen night. Dining there would be a first.

"Make yourself at home," Father Ralph said as he went into the icebox to bring out the chicken salad. "It's a little warm in here, but that's always been the case. Not a lot of ventilation."

She put her coat down on the chair in the dining room and started to look around. "Beautiful paintings," she said noting the art displayed around the house.

"Thanks," Father Ralph yelled from the kitchen. "I'm a bit of a collector."

Sister Judy Ann knew her art as well and enjoyed visiting museums and galleries during her time off. She took note of a particular painting above the fireplace in the living room. "This print looks very French, like a Matisse," she said loudly so he could hear her in the kitchen.

A couple of minutes later, Father Ralph joined her in the living room. "Good eye," he said. "It is."

"I thought so," she said. Then she looked closer at the painting. Then she stopped and was silent for what seemed a long minute. "That is a Matisse! An original?"

Father Ralph laughed. "Like I said, you have a good eye for art."

She gave him a curious look as he handed her a drink.

"I'm a collector. A guy my brother Ted knows in Boston was able to bring one in, and I got it cheap," explained the good father.

She took a sip of the drink and almost spit it out. "This is whisky," she exclaimed.

"Ted also hooks me up with a few extra benefits from time to time. He's a Bureau of Prohibition agent and gets his hands on some of the goods sometimes. Thought you would enjoy a sip."

Sister Judy Ann smiled. She did like the occasional sip of whisky, illegal as it was. It was truly a rare treat. She also knew Father Ralph's brother was in law enforcement but now it was clear what agency. The two sat down at the dining room table and after saying grace, enjoyed some chicken salad and sweet rolls Father Ralph prepared. The two had a lot in common always enjoying each other's company.

After dinner they both retired to the living room for another drink and to talk about art. Sister Judy Ann found herself relaxed and in awe of Father Ralph's impressive collection.

Their eyes met a couple of times in the natural progression of a man and woman being attracted to each other. It was the forbidden fruit each knew they could not eat.

"How long have you been collecting?" Sister asked trying to change the focus a bit.

"Four or five years, I guess. Kind of hobby," he answered then took a small sip of his drink.

"Is the painting of the horse races oil?"

"Sure is. Once again, good eye, Sister."

"You like horses, I see," she continued and pointed to one of the small sculptures on the end table.

"You could say that," he chuckled.

She looked back at him and for a split second felt something inside herself that she hadn't felt in years. He looked back at her. That second felt like an eternity.

"Well now," she snapped with a bit of breathlessness in her voice. "I should be heading back to the convent. It's really late."

"You sure you don't want to stay for one more?" he asked.

"Oh no. I have to get up early anyway to do some cleaning before mass."

Father Ralph thought for a minute then spoke. "Okay, good. We should have a professional service come into the convent every couple of weeks. You shouldn't be burdened with spending what little time you have cleaning. I will put in a call to our housekeeper and have her do the convent, too."

Sister gave that some thought and very much appreciated that offer from her pastor. She wondered why he seemed to always have money for this and that as he helped her put her coat on. Once again, their eyes met as she started buttoning. Once again, an awkward pause. Then she spoke. "Well, thanks again for supper, Father."

"Any time, Sister. Be careful walking home," he answered while opening the door. The convent was just down the street from the rectory and housed only two RSMs or Religious Sisters of Mercy. The convent had four bedrooms, but at the moment it was just those two sisters living there.

He shut the door behind her and made a mental note to call the housekeeper on Monday morning; he paid her personally and not out of church funds. Then he picked up his newspaper and looked at the race results from around the northeast.

———

The road trip to Albany took about four hours from where Danny started in the central Massachusetts town of Framingham. The Big Seven had full control of all the establishments in that part of Massachusetts he was visiting on business, but he wanted to make an unscheduled run to the capital of New York. He drove his personal Chrysler Imperial L-80. The trunk was full of his product, and he had plenty of cash for payoffs should he be stopped by a G-man or local cop.

The sun was starting to cast longer shadows on the beautiful day as he crossed the state line headed for the capital. The Chicago Drucci gang, which had given Danny headaches in the past, secretly ran one of the larger speakeasys in Albany. He suspected the Drucci gang was also responsible for pushing their product into his territory. Today he was going to send another subtle message.

"Yeah?" barked the guy who opened the small window in the door after Danny rang the bell.

"Empire traveler," Danny responded with the correct code to gain entrance to the speakeasy.

Three seconds later the door opened and Danny walked in. He was pointed to the stairs leading to the club in the basement of the old warehouse. The smell of the old mill was quickly replaced by those of cigar smoke and fried foods as he descended into the large club which was starting to get busy during the early evening in upstate New York.

The manager was named Johnny, and Danny knew him from a few years back in Providence. Johnny had actually worked for Danny and the

Big Seven for a while back in the mid 20s. Johnny was a big man of six feet, five inches and a commanding presence towering over both the bar and the young bar maids. He didn't see Danny until he sat at the bar toward the far end. A knot in his stomach turned as Johnny tried to put on smile and welcome his old boss.

"Danny Walsh, what brings you into our neck of the woods?" Johnny asked. "What are you drinking?"

"You know why I'm here. That's Chicago booze up there," Danny said getting right to the point and gesturing at the bottles lined up on the shelves behind the bar.

Johnny was clearly surprised by the visit and didn't really have a good answer. "We serve your product, too, Danny."

"Give me three fingers of something we sell you."

Johnny knew he was in a spot. "We don't have any in stock, but I'm sure you guys can hook us up."

Danny looked around the speakeasy. He estimated there were about ten customers. "I've got some in the trunk. Why don't you and I go get it and bring it down here?"

Johnny didn't want to make waves with the Big Seven. "Sure thing, Danny."

The two went upstairs, and in a couple of trips they moved six cases of various whisky and Scotch product from his car and trunk.

Johnny opened one of the cases and put the bottles on the bar. Then he pulled out two glasses and poured a drink for each of them.

"Neat?" Johnny asked, still a bit nervous.

Danny nodded his head.

"Salute. To good business friends," Johnny said with a chuckle as he raised his glass.

"To business," Danny said lifting the glass and in one long gulp, emptied it. Then he reached into his coat pocket and pulled out his .32 caliber Colt Savage and fired six 71 grain bullets into the whiskey bottles lined up behind the bar smashing them to bits and spraying their contents all over the floor. The sound of the gun was amplified across the basement speakeasy and felt like a cannon to the untrained ears. Patrons screamed and some hit the floor while others hid under tables. Johnny was shocked.

Danny pulled out another clip and calmly reloaded. Then he took aim at whatever was left on the bar. The smoke from the gunfire filled the air.

One of the patrons was an unarmed local cop, but he didn't make a move to stop Danny. Within three minutes, the entire Chicago inventory of liquor was destroyed and the speakeasy fell silent with only the smell of gunpowder and sound of heavy breathing filling the air.

"Now you have no choice but to serve our product," Danny said to Johnny in a low, nonchalant voice. Johnny was literally shaking. He knew these folks didn't play games and had a reputation of protecting their business. "If I or any of the other Big Seven bosses come back and see Chicago product on that bar, we won't be shooting at the bottles next time."

Danny poured another shot from the bottle that was sitting on the bar. That bottle was one he had supplied. Picking up the glass, he drank the shot then slammed it down on the bar when finished. "Have a nice night," he said while at the same time putting his gun away. Danny turned around, went back up the stairs, got in his car and headed south to Providence.

———

CHAPTER 16

THIN BLUE LINE

The meeting spot was one of three that the men felt comfortable using. Taunton was a small town about thirty miles south of Boston and not too far from the South Shore where Special Agent Ted Connelly lived. They didn't meet in person often and usually had a location drop for payoff money. This meeting had been arranged by Ted who wanted to kill two birds with one stone.

Timing was important, and they liked to meet after the morning rush but before lunch at the small diner just off the town square. It was the slowest time of the day, so usually there were only a few people around. Ted arrived first and sat in a booth toward the back of the diner facing the entrance. Patrick McDuffy entered the diner with Joey Cardin in tow for security.

"Why don't you sit at the counter and have a coffee," Patrick said to Joey. "I want to talk to Ted alone."

"You got it, boss," Joey answered.

Patrick went over and sat in the booth with Ted. The two shook hands. Patrick pulled out an envelope from his jacket, put it on the table and pushed it toward Ted.

"Thanks," Ted said putting his hand on the envelope and placing it in the inside pocket of his jacket.

"What do you have for us?" Patrick asked coldly, getting right down to business. He didn't like Feds and didn't want to be seen with one.

"They know about your little airplane flights," Ted said. "We've been watching some of the airports and have established a pattern of delivery."

This was news that Patrick absolutely didn't expect, and he tried to keep a poker face when hearing that the Feds were onto their air operation.

"How?"

"How what? How do we know?" Ted asked.

"Yeah. Who's the snitch in our organization?"

"Don't know. Someone dropped us the airplane information, and our guys are looking into it. I was at Norwood myself when the Trimotor came in with a shipment."

Patrick let this sink in for a few minutes. He needed to get this information back to Danny and the Big Seven bosses before one of the flights got busted.

"Find out how you got that information," Patrick ordered.

"I'll do my best, but nothing guaranteed."

"Fuck you. You work for us, and we keep you very comfortable with that little beach house on the Cape," Patrick said. "Remember, that type of money is easy come and easy go."

Ted looked Patrick in the eyes. "Are you threatening me?"

"Just find out who leaked our air operation," Patrick replied with a nicer tone.

"I'll do my best, but you people need to watch your asses," Ted said looking around and lowering his voice to a whisper. Ted took a sip of his coffee and a bite of the powered donut he had ordered before Patrick arrived.

"Is that it?" Patrick asked.

"That's enough," Ted answered with a chuckle in his voice.

Patrick got up from the booth without another word and walked out of the restaurant. Joey quickly took a last sip of his coffee and followed his boss out the door.

Ted finished his breakfast, paid his tab and also left the restaurant. He walked two blocks to where he had parked his government-issued Ford, ready to drive back to the office in Boston.

After Ted left the diner, another man paid his tab and left. He was also headed for Boston and the same building where Ted worked, but on a different floor.

———

"Do it again," Sally said to her young lover who had stopped over for "lunch" while Owney was once again out of town on business. "Tie me up this time," she begged. "Tie me up."

Kevin was not into that sort of thing for the most part, but he played along just for her sake. He tied her arms to the bedpost and proceeded with what she called her prescription for loneliness. That was their secret code. She would call down to Owney's New York office, ask for Kevin and tell him she needed him to get her "prescription." Sally would be crushed on those occasions when the people on the other end of the phone told her Kevin was traveling with or for Owney.

For years New Yorkers took elevated trains until the IRT opened the first underground system in 1904. It made for an easy and quick run up to Owney and Sally's 5th Avenue home. Their time together had begun to feel more than recreational for Kevin. He walked as quickly as he could to the house from the new subway station just five blocks away. For a while he had pushed it off, ignoring the feelings. Now they were clearly lovers and wanted to spend as much time as they could together without getting caught. Getting caught, as they both knew, would end badly for both. Kevin continued to run scenarios in his mind of how the two could escape Owney's hold on them and live a life far away someplace warm like

Florida. Then there was the FBI problem as well. So many complications to work through.

"Oh my God, Kevin," she tried to say but was as breathless as an Olympic athlete after a run. "Jesus."

"You're incredible," he said back to her as he rolled to the opposite side of the bed and sat up before reaching for his pants sitting on a nearby chair.

She sat up in bed pulling the sheets up to her neck to cover her naked body.

"What? Now you're shy?" he joked.

"Now I'm lonely."

He gave her a mock disgusted look, and then they both laughed out loud.

After ten minutes of cooling down and dressing, they met downstairs in the kitchen for a coffee.

"Any thoughts on what we need to be doing?" Sally asked trying to address the big elephant in the room.

"I'm working on it. Keep feeding that 'G' bullshit or something so he stays interested. I'm still looking into what we can give them on Owney that would send him away forever. I've got an idea of what they would take. You mentioned the ledgers, and I also had an idea. I've got movement records of the shipments from Canada on the *Black Duck, Goose and Gander*. Plus, I'm pretty involved in the flights now. Bottom line, your next visit with Agent Davis is important. You need to ask exactly what will buy us a way out. After that, we may be free to escape to Florida," he said in a bit of a monotone.

"*If*," she said. "*If* they just let us walk away," she countered.

"One step at a time, Mrs. Madden," he said with a reassuring tone. Sally felt secure around him. She felt he was strong and smart.

"I never reach out to Agent Davis. He usually contacts me with notes in the flowerpots out front," she explained. "It's been a while. Or he'll just show up someplace like the diner."

Kevin thought about the flowerpot notes and how simple but brilliant it was. Owney would never take a second look at one of those. Kevin also knew they would have to be very careful with both the FBI and the Big Seven. Getting out from under the arms of both would require timing and skill, two things they both understood.

———

The farm in Charlestown was large and private. Danny liked it that way. The drive in from the main road was almost a mile and a welcome sight after he had been working or traveling. Some nights he would elect to stay at one of his two places in Providence; others he came back to the farm. He was passionate about horses and horse racing. Most of the horses Danny owned were there on the farm. Unlike some of the other heads of the Big Seven who enjoyed seeing their names in the newspapers, Danny tried to keep a much lower profile. Having a racehorse, however, meant the owner needed to be a public figure or at least have some sort of public persona. Danny used an alias as the owner of three racehorses he had up at Aqueduct. When someone would call for Roger Thompson, he knew it was in reference to the horses. His rider and trainer were one in the same, a practice that was not too common in horse racing. Usually the race horses had separate trainers, but with only three of them housed at the same track, Danny was comfortable with John Cowen, known around the paddocks as JC, doing both jobs. JC was a young and wiry 23-year-old who had grown up racing horses on Long Island. Danny hired him after their first meeting because he was so impressed with the young man who had been born in Ireland before his family immigrated to New York when he was just five years old. JC didn't know that Roger Thompson was actually Danny Walsh of the Big Seven and one of the biggest bootleggers and gangsters on the east coast. If he had known that, he may or may not have had second thoughts about working for him.

"Roger, it's JC at Aqueduct, and I'm calling with some bad, sad news," JC started when Danny answered the phone. The connection was sketchy being long distance.

"Hi JC. Is there a problem with the horses?" Danny asked (as Roger).

"I'm afraid there is. Revolution was found dead in her stall this morning when I made the feeding rounds. I immediately called Doc Mason to come right over, and he said there was nothing he could do. It was too late. He thinks she might have had a heart attack or something in her sleep," JC explained to his boss.

Danny was silent for a few seconds which felt to JC like an eternity. Then he spoke. "How are the other two horses?"

"They're fine. I checked on both and found no problems. I'm so sorry to have to tell you this. I loved that horse," JC said with a sad tone.

"Heart attack?" Danny asked with some skepticism in his voice. "That horse was four years old. Just ran last evening, didn't she?" Danny questioned.

"I know. Yes, and you can be proud, she won in the third. There was one other horse that didn't look good last night as I was making my rounds, but he's okay today," JC noted.

"So, what happens to her now?" Danny asked.

"Doc says he will have someone take her away and handle the remains. It's not free, and I'm sure they'll bill us, but I have no idea how much. I will ask, though."

Danny thought about this for a few minutes. "Okay, don't worry about the cost. Just have them bill you and put it on my tab," Danny said. "I heard another horse died last month up there. Is that true, JC?"

"Yeah, it is. Harmony died last month, also of a heart attack at night."

There was something not right about this Danny thought as he gazed out his kitchen window at his farm and other horses nearby. "Okay, JC. Keep me advised on all this, and have Doc give me a call when he can,"

"Will do, boss. Again, I'm so sorry about this." With that, JC ended the conversation he had been dreading.

Danny was not the sentimental type, especially given the business he had chosen, but horses had a special place in his heart, as did any animal. Something just didn't sit right with this, and he made a mental note to check up on it.

CHAPTER 17

INK WELL

It didn't take long for the waiter to come over and take Jesse's drink order. The resort was well known to the wealthiest Floridians and cold weather transplants. Having just opened months before, the Don Cesar had become known as the Pink Palace on the Gulf of Mexico just outside St. Petersburg. The already iconic Mediterranean revival design and bright pink colors attracted visitors from around the country and the world. Jesse was taking vacation time from the paper, but this was hardly a social call.

"Sweet tea," the waiter with the sharp bowtie said as he handed the drink over to the guest from Rhode Island who would have preferred a liquor drink. "Will someone be joining you?" he asked.

"Yes, thanks," Jesse answered in a tone that was all business and recognized by the waiter as the sign of a person who wanted to be left alone.

Jesse waited another thirty minutes or so until his guest finally arrived. Thomas Pike was dressed in a typical South Florida linen shirt, lightweight and pastel yellow. Most people would look at him and guess he was a native because he was so good at playing the role. His hat was floppy and kept the sun off his pale New England skin. The weather had started to turn hot and tropical with afternoon rain showers just about every day.

"Is this seat taken?" Mr. Pike asked the reporter sitting at the round poolside table.

"No, not at all," Jesse answered. Both men were suspicious of each other. Thomas Pike had never once talked to a reporter off the record. All his dealings had been done in a public setting and mostly through a spokesperson. This clandestine meeting showed Jesse that the former assistant to Rhode Island's governor and chief of staff was scared about something.

"I don't have a lot to say," Thomas started. Jesse knew that statement usually meant quite the opposite. "I'm not sure why I decided to take this meeting."

"Because I found out where you were, who you were pretending to be and that for some reason the Big Seven wanted you gone from Rhode Island and especially the governor's office. Should I go on?" Jesse explained.

Thomas sunk into his chair a bit as the realities of what was going on sunk into his brain. A waiter approached again.

"Drink?" the waiter asked.

"Water with lemon," Thomas said. Then the waiter disappeared.

"Your name was in the ledger of a murdered Bristol Gang member, and then you disappeared from the state. Something weird is going on here, Thomas," Jesse explained. "The people in the governor's office sure are spooked by this."

Thomas sat quiet for a couple of minutes. The waiter returned with his water and quickly left the two at the table. Finally, Thomas spoke. "That office has a lot of people. Most of them know I know a lot. Being chief of staff was the only job I ever really wanted. It was my dream job. I didn't want to be the king, just the king maker. I wanted to be the guy who had the power behind the power. It is who I am..." he paused and began to get choked up. "Or was."

Jesse just sat and listened. He always felt during these types of interviews that he was part therapist, part parent and part detective. Thomas continued. "I'm afraid for my life," he said coldly. "If what I know gets out, the governor and a number of other high-ranking officials in the state are done, including some judges."

That definitely got Jesse's attention. He felt like he had a hundred-pound tuna on the line and had to slowly reel him in before the line snapped and the story got away. "Have you talked to the Feds about this? About some protection?" Jesse asked gently.

"They're all in bed. I was told to disappear and start a new life. Told to keep my mouth shut or they would shut it for me permanently. I was given money and a window of time to fall off the face of the planet."

Over the years and many hundreds of interviews, Jesse had learned to be patient and keep his poker face no matter what the subject was saying. This was a test for sure. "Who told you that?" he asked.

"Can't say."

Jesse probed a little deeper. "How much money?"

"Can't say."

"That's not giving anyone up, Thomas. How much to keep you in exile down here in Florida?" Jesse asked. "I'm just curious what the going rate is these days to disappear."

"Not that it matters, but in the neighborhood of 100 K," Thomas answered.

Jesse sat back and let that sink in. That was a lot of money and would more than take care of Thomas Pike for the rest of his life. Thomas' official salary had been around ten to twelve thousand per year as listed publicly with the State of Rhode Island.

"Do they know where you are?" Jesse probed a little deeper. "I assume they know your alias in case they need to communicate."

"Not exactly. They know I'm in Florida but not where and under what name," Thomas explained. "That was the deal. I'm out."

"Suppose I use you only on background and as an anonymous source. No name or alias or anything," Jesse offered.

Thomas sat quietly for a minute or two. Then he spoke. "Liquor is going to be legal again. It's just a matter of time. Our D.C. delegation has been pitching this legislation for a couple of years now. Finally, people are coming around to the idea. When it's legal again, the gravy train stops for a lot of folks."

Jesse knew that the Volstead Act's lifetime was coming to an end and also figured it would be in the next couple of years. The fact that the elected officials charged to enforce it were profiting from illegal liquor sales was his biggest story yet. He had gathered some decent evidence from insiders here and there over the last couple of years, but this was the first confirmation that it went all the way to the governor's office.

"Thomas, once your name was found in that ledger, they dropped you like a hot potato. Out of sight, out of mind, and out of the way. You gave your entire professional career to the party and the governor. They paid you back by dropping you off the face of the planet."

"With 100 thousand thank you notes," Thomas inserted.

"Your name is going to come out someday. Same with the others like the judges. The fact that your name was in the ledger is a giant story. The fact that I asked the governor about it in a public setting means other reporters are now going to be looking into it. Your name and reputation are going to be washed down the sewer. You might be rich living in Florida, but you won't ever work in politics again," Jesse said.

"I did nothing wrong," Jesse insisted. "My name was in that ledger because I was the delivery boy. I didn't solicit bribes. They gave me envelopes, and I handed them over. That's it," Thomas explained.

"Is that what they were? Bribes?"

"What the hell do you think? You're the reporter."

"I just needed to hear it from the source."

"Well, you just did. Big Seven people would give me the envelopes at lunch or someplace, and I would give them to the governor. End of story."

Jesse sat silent for a few seconds. Then he spoke. "Technically that's not the end of the story. That's illegal, Thomas. You were the one to receive the bribe. You were the official on the receiving end. You were…"

"Fuck you," Thomas interrupted. "I just handed it over. Nothing more."

"That's naïve, chief. You know the law," Jesse said. "If the AG…"

"The AG?" Thomas interrupted. "You're the one who's naïve, mister big ass reporter. The AG?" Thomas laughed out loud. "The AG is not going to prosecute me. He got part of the money. Don't you see? Everyone was paid off! And the Big Seven wasn't the only contributor to these people. There were others."

Jesse, along with most reporters and, in fact, the public at large knew other organizations paid off officials to keep the raids and arrests down, but the governor and Attorney General were way up in the food chain. "If your name comes out, they'll blame you, and that will be the end of the story. You're their fall guy. You'll be the one going to prison."

That was exactly what Thomas knew and didn't want. Deep down inside, he didn't want his reputation as a public servant and political guru tarnished. He knew they would step all over his reputation, and his family would be the ones who would be embarrassed. He had seen this play out many times with others.

"If you do a story that I was not the recipient of this money but just the go between, do you think there would be a better outcome for my reputation?" Thomas asked.

Jesse thought about that for a minute before speaking.

"It's the only way to save your reputation. You were just following orders. Technically speaking, you have no idea what was in those envelopes. You worked for the governor, and those were his orders," Jesse answered. "Put it this way. You can stay tucked away down here under another name while, at the same time, save your legacy and allow the people of the state to see who was giving the orders and getting all the pie."

Thomas sat back in his chair. He knew he would never be in a position to go back into politics even if the story came out that he was only the middle man. It just didn't happen. All he could hope for was to save whatever scraps of his reputation were left and carry on. After it all settled down, he wanted to go back to using his own name.

"What would I need to do?" Thomas finally asked feeling a queasy twist in his stomach when he did.

"We would just talk. I ask questions. You answer them. I don't say where you are or what you're doing now. Pretty simple."

Thomas sat silent again for what seemed like an hour to Jesse. Then he spoke. "When would it run?"

"Not sure. Depends on how much more reporting I have to do. Probably sometime over the next couple of months. Meanwhile, you stay tucked away down here in paradise," Jesse explained knowing his fish was now firmly on the hook.

The waiter returned to ask if the men would like to see a menu. Thomas had no appetite. Jesse was starved, but food would have to wait with so much to ask and so little time.

Thomas Pike took a long sip of his sweet tea. "Where should I start?"

———

CHAPTER 18

SLY FOX

Paperwork was the least favorite thing Ted had to do as a prohibition agent. The Bureau surveillance reports were a pain and, in Ted's mind, a waste of time. The morning meeting was scheduled early, and the scuttlebutt around the office was that something big was afoot.

Special Agent in Charge Warren called the meeting together as the glassy eyed agents made their way into the dark and musty conference room in their Scollay Square office. Two men were smoking so Special Agent Eric Thompson opened the only window in the room to get some fresh air.

"Close that," James ordered with a bit of anger in his tone. Eric looked back at his boss and then closed the window. "This meeting is secret."

"You think the birds are going to tell someone what we're doing?" Eric asked breaking the tension in the room as everyone laughed. James did not laugh.

"You never know who may be in earshot, Agent Thompson. Proper operational security is what I follow, and I hope you do, too," James replied tersely.

The men began to quiet down as James waited for the stragglers to arrive. "Glad you made it, Sergeant Howard," he said not able to resist the urge to be an asshole.

That earned James a dirty look from his second in command. Sergeant Jeff Howard had found out about the early arrival time just an hour before as everyone else had.

"Okay everyone, listen up. I'm waiting for one more person." At that moment, the door opened, and an agent no one recognized joined the group. "This is Special Agent Kyle Foster of the New York Field Office who will be helping us out over the next couple of weeks. With his help and some pretty good intel that you guys have come up with, we are going to make a significant bust today."

Ted along with the others looked at each other not knowing what this was all about. What bust? None of the men seemed to know what Warren was talking about. Each agent knew there were some raids scheduled over the next couple of weeks, but nothing this day or even this week.

James continued the briefing. "Today at fifteen hundred local, we are going to intercept a booze running aircraft at Norwood Airport and put a dent into the Big Seven's little liquor airline. Then later tonight, our brothers in the Coast Guard will intercept a ship known as the *Black Duck* off the coast of Rhode Island, and that, my friends, will be the icing on a giant cake."

Each agent in the room was genuinely surprised. Ted spoke up making a joke but knowing each agent was thinking the same thing. "Why the New York agent? You don't trust us, boss?" All the agents in the room laughed, but each thought the same thing. Ted, however, knew this was bad on a number of different levels and felt a sick feeling in his gut.

"I trust each and every one of you, but we can't be too careful these days. Special Agent Foster has been working this op for a few weeks using our intel along with their own. New York is handling the *Black Duck* intercept with the Coasties as a joint operation, and they were good enough to do some preplanning for our little piece of the pie. I'll let Agent Foster brief today's op which is code named 'Sly Fox.' Agent Foster."

Kyle Foster was of medium build, a no-nonsense federal prohibition agent who didn't suffer fools well. He started, "An aircraft is scheduled to land at Norwood Airport around 1530 this afternoon. We will be standing by disguised as a fuel crew. Their SOP is to land, unload and refuel quickly for the trip back to New York State. The truck and uniforms are standing by at a location we picked out just a couple of miles from the airport. Nothing is going to be risked as far as the security and secrecy of this operation are concerned. We think some of the airport people are being paid off by the Big Seven. There are not many of them, but we can't be too careful on this one. Questions?"

Ted spoke first. "Will we have local help from Norwood PD?"

"No. Next question?"

Ted followed up. "We usually get help from local law enforcement as a back-up. Why not now?"

"I don't trust them at all, and it's only a small crew on the plane. I'm sure we can handle it," Agent Foster answered curtly.

All of the agents in the room knew what Agent Foster meant. Local police were not a lot of help, and there were plenty of leaks.

"We saddle up in fifteen minutes. No one leaves this floor until we all do at once," Foster said.

James had a big smile on his face and was glad for the help from New York. He didn't care whether his own agents resented it. "Okay everyone. Let's get geared up. Standard raid gear," he barked.

The feeling in the room among the Boston agents was that this had been well planned and they were not being trusted by their own higher ups. Ted knew he couldn't reach out to his contact with the Big Seven. He also knew that he would have to answer for this should both raids succeed.

"Come left to one seven five," Captain Rick St. Pierre ordered as the *Black Duck* motored around Cape Cod headed south southeast making way toward the coast of Rhode Island. "Steady as she goes. Maintain twelve knots." Their first port call was Block Island, a frequent fuel stop before heading six miles northeast to sit on the rum line just off Narragansett Bay. Danny's organization ran the liquor distribution on Block Island and paid off the dock workers who fueled the *Black Duck*. Captain St. Pierre wanted a full fuel tank after the trip from Canada before his offload just in case the Coast Guard or Feds showed up and they had to make a run for it. The sea state was choppy, and the old oil tanker turned rum runner rolled up and down on the turbulent Atlantic. The sound of the twin engines hummed as seagulls hovered nearby hoping the boat was a fishing vessel. Business was good, and this was an easy run for the crew. Each would profit handsomely after they delivered and returned to Canada. Connecticut had been their drop point for a number of months until the Feds started to notice. Now Rhode Island offered perfectly situated quiet inlets to offload the smaller boats that ran in from the *Black Duck*. Depending on the sea state, Rick would sometimes push past the rum line and into the bay itself under the cover of darkness.

"We might go in further this time," Rick said to his first officer Jim Studley. Darkness was seven hours away, and they hadn't refueled on Block Island yet. Both men were experienced operating all of the Big Seven's rum running ships. The *Black Duck* was their favorite, though. This trip required *Black Duck* because of its larger size and cargo capacity. Another crew had sailed the *Goose* down the coast just a few days earlier delivering a perfect offload for Danny's crew.

"Your call," Jim said. Both men knew the risks were much higher going into the bay versus offloading to the smaller boats out along the rum line beyond the jurisdiction of the Coast Guard and Feds.

Three hours later they were tied up at the pier in New Shoreham, Block Island. The requisite payoff was made to the dock workers and harbormaster along with a couple of bottles of fine Canadian whisky. Law enforcement was mostly non-existent before the tourist season kicked in later that month.

About an hour before darkness set in, Captain St. Pierre ordered the release of all lines as the *Black Duck* slid slowly out of the harbor back into choppy Long Island Sound. As he closed to within a mile of the rum line, the sun dropped beyond the horizon. "Let's take it in," he ordered. "Too choppy out here. Signal the boats we will sit just off Prudence."

"Aye, sir," Jim answered. They maintained radio silence for most of the trip, but when a change to the rendezvous point was made, they had no choice. The small boats Danny operated would now go to near Prudence Island in Narragansett Bay and wait for the *Black Duck*.

At that moment, the U.S. Coast Guard patrol boat *Vigilant* slipped out of the small waterfront village of Galilee heading to a point about a mile south of Point Judith as darkness took over.

———

Hours earlier, the Norwood Airport was having a quiet afternoon. A few miles away, Special Agent in Charge Warren and New York's Special Agent Foster parked their vehicles next to an old barn on the farm of a local, retired Army officer. The officer was thrilled to help in this operation by allowing the Feds to stage from his property. A decoy fuel truck had been delivered to the property just 24 hours earlier.

"Agents Connelly and Thompson will drive the fuel truck. The rest of us will pile into the delivery truck scheduled to arrive at any minute," James said to the group.

"They thought of everything," Ted whispered to his partner.

"Everything except us," Eric replied.

Right on schedule, the men heard the roar of a truck's gas engine and saw what appeared to be a delivery truck approaching. Sure enough, the truck pulled into the farm and up to the barn. The men didn't recognize the driver.

"This is Special Agent Greenburg from the New York Field Office," James said making a quick introduction. "Okay, let's go."

The men jumped into the back of the delivery truck with their guns as Ted cranked up the engine on the fuel truck. "Follow me," James said from the passenger seat of the delivery truck to Ted just a few feet away.

"Yes, sir," Ted answered with a slight sarcastic tone trying not to sound bitter that neither he nor any of others had been aware of this operation.

The men drove the trucks just up the road and down the hill to a turn which led to the back gate of the airport. The gate was opened, and they continued down a winding dirt road ending at the building which served as a hangar on the far end of the airfield. The Boston agents were already familiar with this after their surveillance of the area weeks before.

"Position the fuel truck over there," Special Agent Foster ordered pointing to a place where the fuel truck had typically been when the Trimotor had landed in the past. "The delivery truck can stay next to the building."

Ted parked the fuel truck where Agent Foster ordered and got out of the cab. He walked over to Agent Foster. "Any other orders?" he asked with another touch of sarcasm in his voice.

"Listen up," Agent Foster said loudly. "When they land they'll taxi back here and open the rear door of the aircraft. We wait until the aircraft is completely shut down and all three men are off. They will think we're fuelers. The rest of you will wait in the hangar. When I announce we are federal agents, you two come out of the hangar," he said pointing to Ted and Eric.

"What about us?" asked Jeff.

"I want the rest of you in the tree line just over there in case they make a run for it."

"Run for it? There's only three of them and eight of us," Jeff noted.

Special Agent Foster walked over to Jeff and in a condescending tone said, "I'm cautious, Sarge."

Jeff and his crew headed for the tree line about one hundred yards away. Foster turned to the others. "Fifteen minutes out. Let's get in place."

Ted and Eric went to the hangar and stepped inside through the side door. The smell of spilled liquor was familiar to both, but no booze could be seen. They would have to crack the door open a bit in order to get a view of the ramp and aircraft when it arrived.

Twenty minutes later everything was silent. Ted looked at Eric. "Maybe Mr. Wonderful from New York got his intel wrong."

A minute later that would be proven false as they heard the telltale sound of a Ford Trimotor aircraft flying over the field. Just as they had witnessed during their own surveillance, the plane circled twice looking for anything suspicious.

"Wait until I give the signal," James yelled to all as the aircraft made its final approach to Norwood Airport.

The aircraft touched down and turned off the runway onto the dirt taxiway then made another turn to head to the end of the field to where the agents waited as dust from the props filled the air behind it. The plane pulled up to the same spot where they had seen it a number of times before when under surveillance. Three Wright R-975-1 300 horsepower air-cooled radial engines shut down all at once replacing the deafening roar with a calm and almost eerie silence. About a minute later, the latch to the rear door turned and in one move it opened downward. One man stepped off the aircraft and quickly put chocks against the left main landing gear. James was waiting for a signal to approach the aircraft with the fuel truck. Ted and Eric had the side door cracked just enough to see the aircraft about fifty yards away. The men in the woods could see pretty clearly and sat tight for the moment.

Right then, the pilot and co-pilot emerged from the aircraft onto the sand taxiway. Ted recognized the co-pilot. He was a member of the the Big Seven. Ted also thought he recognized the other crew member as a possible part of the Bristol Gang or the North End Gang. He then looked over to the fuel truck and saw James and Kyle waiting for a hand signal to approach. At that moment, Ted took his Tommy gun and pushed on the door they were standing behind so that it would open a little wider. He stepped out enough to be at least partially seen by pretending to trip and fall against the door making a noise.

"Who's that?" The co-pilot asked the other crewmember still standing near the wheels. The air crew was about to wave in the fuel truck and then head to the old hangar near the prepositioned cargo truck sitting inside just a few feet away from Ted and Eric.

"Feds!!!" the co-pilot yelled. "Let's start up and get the hell out of here."

As the crew member pulled the chocks off the wheel, the co-pilot jumped back into the aircraft and headed to the cockpit. The pilot was right behind him.

"Go! Go! Go! Go!" James yelled as he started the truck and moved toward the aircraft which was still shut down. Ted and Eric came running out of the old hangar toward the aircraft with weapons in hand. The crewmember pulled out his pistol and fired at Ted and Eric missing both. Eric trained his Tommy on the crew member and fired a burst of automatic rounds. The crew member was dead before he hit the dirt.

"Screw you," the co-pilot yelled out the open window as he tried to strap in and start the engines. At that moment, Sergeant Jeff Howard was approaching from his side of the aircraft charging in from the woods. He aimed his Tommy and fired a burst into the cockpit killing the co-pilot.

"Take the pilot alive," James ordered still pulling the fuel truck closer to the plane in order to block it. Ted raced to be first to the aircraft then jumped inside noting the steep grade of the cargo bay full of whisky cases. Sweat was pouring down his back as he worked his way forward and up toward the cockpit. The pilot turned from his seat and put his hands up. He saw Ted approaching between the cases of whisky. "I know you," the pilot yelled recognizing Ted instantly.

James and Kyle parked the fuel truck in front of the aircraft to stop it should they get the engines started. They then jumped out of the truck and headed toward the cargo door.

Ted looked at the pilot and also recognized him. He had been a member of the Big Seven for years and worked directly for Owney. Now he was flying as one of the air coordinators. The pilot put his hands out showing he had no weapon. Ted looked back and couldn't see James or Kyle. Eric was still standing outside the aircraft. Ted had a split-second decision to make as the two men's eyes met. At that moment, Ted aimed his Tommy, putting his finger on the trigger and squeezed off a burst of bullets directly into the chest of the pilot killing him instantly while spraying blood across the cockpit windows and instruments.

Eric climbed into the aircraft his with weapon drawn seconds later followed by James and Kyle. With all the cases of booze, there was only enough room for one or two people.

"We're clear," Ted yelled. "We're clear."

Eric couldn't fit into the cargo bay very well as he was a tall man and with the amount of whisky cases stacked from floor to ceiling. He crouched at the back of the cabin as Ted started to back out. James and Kyle along with Jeff and the others arrived at the cabin door out of breath from running.

"Hop out," Ted said to Eric who was just inside the door blocking the way. "We're clear. Both men are dead. I thought the pilot was going to fire back," Ted said as he slowly climbed out of the cabin.

James walked up to him and was not pleased. "I said alive," he barked. "Did you not hear me? Did they have weapons?"

"The aircraft was a weapon. If they started this thing up, they could have driven right into your ass sitting in a fully loaded fuel truck just feet off the nose. So, you're welcome!" Ted said in a defensive tone.

"Mission accomplished," Kyle offered to all. "They're bad guys. We get bad guys. Good day all around."

James just looked at Ted and shook his head. The two had no love lost for each other.

"I want photos. I also want the press to get them. This is a big dent into the Big Seven's operation. They won't be flying around dropping booze all over New England without thinking twice," James announced proudly.

Ted knew this would be a tough bust for the Big Seven. He also knew Patrick or someone would come to one person to ask about it. That person was himself. There was much to explain.

———

Prudence Island is the third largest island in Narragansett Bay and almost in the dead center of this large body of water. It sits just off Bristol and

Portsmouth, home to only a few people. It was a favorite place to off-load the small boats running in from the rum line. Danny's boys were in place as the *Black Duck* sailed to about one thousand yards east of the island to drop anchor. Captain St. Pierre came out to the deck as his crew secured the anchor and made contact with the small boats using their code words. Three of the smaller boats tied up alongside the *Black Duck*. Each had large barrels that would receive the whisky direct from the *Black Duck's* tanks using a hose and pumping system made originally for transferring oil. At the same time, other crew members would start a chain of men passing cases of bottled liquor from the cargo hold up to the deck and onto the smaller boats. It was done mostly in darkness or with as little light as possible in order to stay hidden. The weather was cool for early summer, and the men worked quickly in order to allow the *Black Duck* to sail before daybreak.

Just to their south, the Coast Guard vessel *Vigilant* was closing on their position. Apparently the *Vigliant's* captain had misjudged the rendezvous point having patrolled for a few hours just off Point Judith at the mouth of the bay looking for the active rum line. It wasn't until the *Black Duck* was completely unloaded that they decided to search inside the bay.

"Weigh anchor," Capt. St. Pierre ordered. "Let's get out of here. Make ready revolutions for ten knots."

"Small boats away," Jim yelled as the tenders with their eighty and ninety proof cargo made the last short trip over to Prudence Island and Bristol where trucks were waiting.

"One six zero and ten knots," Capt. St. Pierre ordered. Except for being caught, his biggest fear was running into another ship while operating mostly silent and dark in the predawn hours. He had a mate on the ship's forecastle with a lantern who would relay a signal back to the bridge should anything be spotted. Rick was familiar with Narragansett Bay having made many trips over the last few years. He would rather have stayed out on the rum line, but the sea state and download timing had given him good reason to take the risk.

As they sailed south toward the mouth of the bay just off Newport, the man on the forecastle yelled, "Ship ahead. Ship ahead."

"All stop," Rick ordered. "One blast."

Jim pulled the handle at the top of the wheelhouse to release one blast of sound from the ship's air horn.

"One o'clock," the lookout yelled.

"Left to one six zero," Rick ordered.

"One six zero," the helmsman repeated.

Two hundred yards off their starboard bow, the Coast Guard ship also came to a stop. Technically, the *Black Duck* was legal. Not a drop of liquor was aboard. The Coast Guard could, however, check their oil tanks and would know immediately that oil had not filled them in years. They could order the ship seized for further inspection now that it was in American waters. For Captain Rick St. Pierre, that was not an option. He had a job to get the *Black Duck* safely and quickly back to Canada in one piece and ready to make another run.

"Signal the other vessel that we are a passing and will keep him on our port side," he told Jim.

"They want to board us," Jim said after receiving the light signal.

"Prepare the special package," Rick ordered.

Jim quickly left the wheelhouse and headed below. Rick and the helmsman remained on the dark and chilly bridge of the ship. They were stopped but drifting slowly. "Ahead one knot," he ordered in order to stay in the channel and in the right direction. He wanted nothing more than to get out of there and back into international waters. He took the signal light and told the Coast Guard ship they would stay on course making way at one knot and to send their skipper over in a small boat.

Jim returned to the wheelhouse a few minutes later with a package in his hand.

"Here they come," the forward lookout yelled. "Go to starboard," he said to the small boat with the lantern on the bow helping the men to see their way through the darkness.

The small Coast Guard tender tied up alongside the *Black Duck* as the ranking officer climbed a small rope ladder to the deck. Rick came down from the wheelhouse and was waiting for the officer.

"U.S. Coast Guard with a warrant to inspect this vessel," the captain said to Rick.

"You don't need a warrant, captain. It's yours to search. We're just an oiler headed back to sea," he explained. The Coast Guard didn't need a warrant at all to inspect a vessel. The fact they had one told Rick they knew what the *Black Duck* was doing and wanted nothing to come back to bite them in court should they find the liquor they suspected was aboard.

Three other men climbed off the Coast Guard tender, up the rope ladder and onto the deck.

"Search the vessel," the young captain ordered to his men.

"Can I offer you a coffee, captain, or something to eat?" Rick asked politely. He was always nice to the American officials.

"No thanks."

"Here's some pastry to take back with you Captain. It's made of fine dough."

This was the moment Rick knew could go either very badly or very well. It was always a great big gamble. Should this captain be a by-the-book guy, he could order the entire ship's company arrested for attempting to bribe a federal officer. The fact that Danny and his crew were friendly with most of the local Coast Guard officers could pay off on this chilly night in Narragansett Bay.

"Thank you, captain. That's mighty thoughtful," the Coast Guard captain said in return with a bit of a southern accent while taking a peek into the brown bag Jim had brought from down below.

"Our pleasure," both Rick and Jim replied.

The Coast Guard captain was silent for a few seconds while looking around. Rick and Jim held their collective breaths. Then he spoke. "Let's go," the captain yelled to his men who were inspecting pallets tied to the ships deck. "These men need to get underway and are free to go."

Just as fast as they came aboard, the Coast Guard men departed on their tender returning to their ship trailing a couple of hundred yards behind.

"Make revolutions for twelve knots. Same heading. Let's get the hell out of here," Rick said as black smoke rose from the midship stack into the early light of a new day dawning. A half hour later, the *Black Duck* crossed into international waters just as the sun crossed the horizon.

———

CHAPTER 19

COMPLICATIONS

When the milk box out on the front steps of the Madden's brownstone had a note from the milkman saying he was going to be back later in the week, Sally would destroy it. The next day she would make her way over to Mel's diner a few blocks from the house at precisely two o'clock in the afternoon. Owney was once again out of town, so it was no coincidence the note showed up this week. She actually wanted a meeting as well.

"You're so punctual," Special Agent Kent Davis said to her as she sat down in the booth toward the back of the diner. A waitress quickly came over. The sound of Glenn Miller's orchestra could be heard in the background from a radio that was near the lunch counter.

"Coffee?"

"Sure, with milk and sugar," Sally answered. Dressed in a light coat, hat and sunglasses, she didn't want anyone to recognize her sitting with the 'G' man. Even if someone did, she would just shrug it off as the Feds trying to squeeze her for information to which she told them to fuck off.

"I have that document you asked for," Agent Davis started. He pulled out a manila envelope and slid it across the table to his informant.

"It took a while," she said.

"Lots of hoops."

She opened the envelope with her name on it and pulled out the document from the U.S. Attorney's office guaranteeing her immunity from prosecution in exchange for her conveying records belonging to Owney and others in the Big Seven.

"He would kill me and probably you if he found out we were doing this deal," she said while looking over the paperwork.

"I have a lot of people who would like to kill me. It's against the law to harm a federal officer," he countered.

She just laughed out loud. "Law?" She laughed again. "Apparently you don't know these people very well. And isn't it against the law to harm anyone?"

He took a sip of his coffee choosing to ignore her sarcasm. "So, what do you have for me?"

She went into her purse and pulled out a small book. Kevin had been helpful in finding a taste of what she could provide. "Here's a little sample," she said while handing it across the table to him.

Agent Davis opened the book. Inside were delivery schedules for the New York metro area speakeasys. He wanted more substantial records like payouts, but this was a start.

"We know about a lot of these. We watch the movement of the product pretty carefully, doll. What I need are more records that have numbers and specifics on who is getting paid," he explained. "Names and figures."

"I know," she said. "It's coming." She paused, then continued. "There's one other little thing."

"What's that?"

"Kevin."

"Your love interest?"

"Now you're being an asshole, and assholes get left out in the cold," she said. With Owney as her husband, Sally Madden could hold her own after a lifetime around gangsters and bootleggers.

"What about him?"

"Same as me. Full immunity."

"I can't do that. He's got dirt on his hands, and he's broken who knows how many laws moving booze."

She sat back and took a sip of the coffee again. This was a negotiation.

"Well, enjoy your little book there. Kevin can get you the big stuff. We're a package deal."

Agent Davis took a deep breath. "I'll see what I can do. We have to move along on this."

"I understand. Next time, if you get Kevin under the umbrella, we'll come together and bring enough good things to get you promoted, Agent Davis. Now, you have a great day," Sally said with a bit of a smart tone. Then she got up out of the booth and left the restaurant.

Agent Davis put the book she had given him into his briefcase, a quarter on the table and headed out of the diner headed for One Scollay Square where he would have to write up her request.

———

"Excuse me?" Owney said into the phone with a very surprised tone. It was a very bad connection to Danny who was standing in the small office of one of their Providence speakeasys. Danny was there checking on the cash flow of the southeastern Massachusetts and Rhode Island speak's.

"Patrick and Marky just came and told me. All three are dead and the shipment seized," Danny explained. "They were waiting at the airport when the plane landed."

There was silence on the phone for a few seconds as Owney collected his thoughts and tried to keep his cool. Danny was an equal partner, after all, even though Owney still thought of him as a subordinate at times. Finally, he spoke in a low, calm tone which, as Danny well knew, was a sign that he was very angry. "Danny, what are you going to do about this? This is your territory. Your crew. Our organization," he said in almost a low whisper.

"I'm looking into it, Owney. We have some moles on the inside, and I want to know why we didn't get a typical heads up. I'm as pissed as you are," Danny replied.

"This flying thing has been a sweet deal for us. It gets us around the Coast Guard on the water and prohibition agents on the ground. We can't move as much in bulk, but we can add more flights and look into a few more planes. I don't, repeat, *don't* want this fucked up," Owney said sternly caring more about the operation than the three men they had lost in Norwood.

"Same with me, and I've got more stake in New England than you do. I'm on it, O," Danny said. "Let's talk later tomorrow, and I'll update you."

"Fine." With that, Owney put the receiver on the hook ending the call.

Danny turned to Patrick. "I want a sit down with Ted the Fed."

"Why don't you let me do it. That keeps you more insulated," Patrick suggested.

"Not this time. We lost three people. Set it up."

"Will do, boss," Patrick said knowing he would have to make contact with Ted and put together a meeting. That meeting wouldn't be a good experience for Ted, Patrick thought as he finished off an early, stress-induced rum and Coke.

———

"They're not going to like this down in Providence," Kitty said to her current squeeze. "They're not going to like this at all."

Angelo ignored her and continued to pack up a few things into an overnight bag. As head of the North End Gang, he had no love lost for the Big Seven and Danny's operation in New England. They had an agreement to stay out of each other's business, but every once in a while, the two families would bump up against each other.

"Did I mention they won't like this one bit down in Providence?" Kitty continued.

"Fuck you."

"No thanks. Goodbye. I'm going to Evelyn's house until you get back," she said in a brush off tone.

"Keep your mouth shut about our business," Angelo said knowing he really didn't have to. She knew what the outcome would be if she started to tell people his business.

"What do you take me for? I'm an educated dame."

"No denying you're a dame, I'll give you that," he said giving himself a bit of a chuckle. He finished packing the small, black overnight bag by putting his trusty Colt .45 in last.

"I'm off for Concord. Go see Evelyn. I'll be back from New Hampshire later tomorrow," he said as he put his hand on her behind giving her a push out the door. Angelo didn't want to be late because the people he was meeting with from Chicago didn't tolerate lateness.

———

Safe deposit boxes were in the second vault at the Old Stone Bank on Washington Street in Providence. Jesse had rented one ever since he had a scare in the early 1920's when someone threatened his life after a series of stories on tax fraud. His wife had the second key and instructions to access it if anything should happen to him. It was his own personal life insurance policy in case someone thought they could intimidate him or worse.

"Thanks," he said to the guard who kept watch over both vaults. The guard had no idea who he was or what he did for a living. To the guard, Jesse was just another bank customer, probably hiding things from his wife.

Twenty minutes later, he was back in the newsroom pouring a cup of coffee, his second of the day.

"You got a minute?" Fred Rockwell asked as he also poured himself a cup of hot Joe.

"Sure thing, boss," Jesse said as he took the sugar and sweetened up his cup.

The two finished fixing their morning caffeine and headed to Fred's office.

"How's the building code story coming?" Fred started.

"Slow, but getting some good background now. They are changing the codes as the builders build, and it's driving them all nuts. Should have a draft in about a week," Jesse said before taking a sip of his coffee.

"Jenny said you were vacationing in Florida all by yourself," Fred said in a measured, nonchalant way. "How was it?"

"Good. Only a few people knew I went down there. I'm working a source in the Big Seven corruption story. Very juicy. I'll let you know when I'm ready to go to print on this one."

"You're pretty hush-hush about it," Fred continued to probe without seeming to probe.

"On this one, I have to be."

"How big a deal?"

"Can't say. Depends on this source in Florida. But it has potential to end some careers," Jesse said without going into any more details.

Fred tried not to seem too interested in knowing who his reporter's source was but wanted as much information on this story as he could get. The two were more than just boss and employee. They were longtime friends in the newspaper business.

"Keep me posted. This could shake a few people up the chain of command," Fred explained.

Jesse knew Fred had to answer to the publisher who was friends with the governor and other politicians. What he didn't know was that Fred's own life was at stake with the dirt the Big Seven had on him.

"Got to get to work. I'll keep you posted," Jesse said.

"You bet."

Fred took a sip of his coffee as Jesse left the office. That sick feeling returned to his stomach, and he wasn't sure how to proceed on this one.

———

CHAPTER 20

MOLE HUNT

"We have to talk," Agent X said to Special Agent in Charge James Warren. "Later," James barked as he walked out of his office on the way upstairs to start hammering out next year's budget. He was afraid the Bureau of Prohibition would go away once the repeal actually happened. The only unknown was when it would happen. That part was political. He feared he would be mixed in with other supervisors and get demoted or moved to another agency. It was all about self-preservation.

Agent X was not known to most people in the building. He had an office upstairs, and most thought he was a civilian who worked in the accounting department. That's where his office was. He even used another name. James called him Agent X because, being a supervisor, he was on the need to know list.

The irony of the moment was that James was headed for the very office Agent X had come downstairs from. Agent X walked with James as he headed out of his office area and toward the stairs.

"We need to step outside for a few moments," Agent X insisted. James knew it had to be important if this guy came down into his office looking to chat.

"A few minutes is all I have. This way," James answered pointing to the steps that would take them down rather than up.

They quickly descended two flights and walked through the lobby and out the door into the bright sunshine of Scollay Square.

"What is it?" James asked in a tone saying that this was a waste of his time and that he didn't want to be there.

"There's a problem in your squad. We think there's a mole," Agent X started.

"Not a chance. Not on my watch," he said pausing for a few seconds. "What else?"

"What else?" Did you hear what I just said?"

"I keep a very close eye on all my agents and what they do in and out of the office. We have no problems in my squad," James explained.

"A close eye? So, tell me why Special Agent Connelly is meeting with members of the Big Seven? How does he afford a new, larger beach house on the Cape? Why did he shoot that pilot on the plane during the raid in spite of being told to take the guy alive? Some of your other agents who were there swear the pilot had his hands up."

James was silent for a few seconds. Then he spoke. "Connelly?"

"Yeah. He met with one of the higher lieutenants of the Big Seven recently. We've been watching him for some time now," Agent X said with a matter of fact tone.

"Maybe it's one of his CI's," James countered. Most agents had a number of confidential informants in their back pockets to keep them up with what was going on in the streets.

"We thought that at first, but the pattern is wrong for a CI. This guy he met and others he has spoken to are well inside," Agent X said trying to talk over the noise of the busy city but still remain confidential.

James let that sink in for a few minutes. A bad agent in the Bureau was a direct reflection on him. "What do you want me to do?"

"Nothing for now, but just remember that he may be leaking important intel to the bad guys. Think about your failed raids over the last year or more. This may be the reason. Connelly was part of every single one."

"That would explain a lot," James said knowing that on the flip side, Connelly being exposed would show to the upper managers that James was not at fault for those failures.

"We might set up something to see if we can get him in a mouse trap. I will be back in touch. Until then, business as usual, and don't contact me directly. I will find you outside the office."

James took a deep breath and nodded his head in agreement. Agent X left and walked across the street for a coffee while James headed back into the building with more on his mind than the upcoming budget.

———

Mary McDuffy finished the dishes while Patrick was getting ready to head out on a bright and warm Rhode Island morning. There was much to do with upcoming deliveries and staying ahead of the voracious demand for spirits. Marky usually picked him up exactly at 8 a.m.

"You coming home on time tonight?" she asked her husband.

"Don't know," he said not paying too much attention to her.

"Let me know if you can. I can get supper done with the kids, and we can have a drink later. Maybe more," she hinted.

"Okay."

Mary was getting aggravated with Patrick for not paying attention to what she was saying. "Okay? Just okay?"

He looked over to her and walked a few steps to give her a kiss on the mouth. "I'm sorry. Just a lot to keep up with. Sure. Later works. *Mystery House* is on the radio tonight too."

Patrick was clearly a different man at home with his wife and kids. When he left their house, he moved back into a world where money ruled as did the firepower they would all sometimes have to use.

The sound of Marky's '27 Ford could be heard pulling up. Patrick grabbed his briefcase, kissed his wife and both kids, then went out the front door to the waiting car. He noted two people in the car. The one in the passenger seat quickly got out and held the door for him.

"Thanks, Tony," Patrick said. He didn't mind having Tony along and sometimes welcomed the extra body on cash pickups. Tony shut the door for Patrick then quickly got into the back seat. He worked for Marky, who worked for Patrick, who worked for Danny.

"Stop for a minute at the corner. I want a paper," Patrick ordered.

Marky dutifully did as told and stopped the car just before the corner of Atwells Avenue where a newspaper stand stood. "Get the boss a paper," Marky ordered Tony.

Tony got out of the car and walked over to the guy selling newspapers.

"He's been a big help," Marky said to Patrick.

"Good."

"I was a little worried at first, but it seems to be working out. He's becoming an earner."

"Good," Patrick said again.

"You okay, boss?"

"Yeah, sorry. Just tired. Yeah, he's an okay kid," Patrick said. "That shit he wears is the only thing I don't like. Weird flowery smell."

Marky nodded his head in agreement. They watched through the windshield as Tony paid the paper guy and started walking back to the car.

"I would expect a smell like that from a wop, not an Irishman," Patrick said.

"Want me to say something about his aftershave?" Marky offered.

"No, no. No big thing. Let's get going."

Tony got back into the car, and the three raced off to meet Danny for their morning meeting. Patrick had good news for his boss who would relay that information to the other members of the Big Seven. Business was good. They were all making money. Booze was like gold, and running gambling numbers was the gravy.

———

Two hundred or so miles south, Mrs. Owney Madden and Mrs. William "Big Bill" Dwyer finished their weekly coffee and went their separate ways.

The Big Seven wives were all close. It was a club they and they alone could understand and once a member, nobody could leave. At least that's the way it had been for years. Sally's next move would be a step in breaking that tradition.

She walked six blocks up town and turned down Chambers Street. She was a long way from their townhouse but liked a coffee shop not too far from South Street Seaport. Once reaching the corner of Chambers and Broadway, there was a different coffee shop she went into. The place was busy with business people and the sound of clanking dishes as well as the smell and haze of cigarette smoke filled the air. Toward the back of the shop she saw who she was meeting with. Keeping her sunglasses on, she made her way toward the booth where agent Kent Davis was sitting.

"Good morning," Kent said. "Almost afternoon."

"Almost. What do you have for me?" Sally replied getting right down to business. The less time she spent with him the better she felt. She also felt the less time with him was safer given that her husband wouldn't take to their meetings very kindly.

"Hello to you, too," he joked.

A waitress walked over.

"Coffee for me," Sally said then dismissed the waitress like a personal servant.

"Same deal for Kevin if…."

"If?" she interrupted.

"*If* he can deliver the ledgers from the last three years. We know he has access to them, Sally. We also know what he's done and continues to do. He's dirty, and we could bust him tomorrow. This is a gift from God. It had to go all the way to the top," Special Agent Davis whispered in a down low tone.

The waitress returned with the coffee. Sally took out a cigarette. "Got a light?" she asked the waitress.

"Sure," the waitress said taking out a match book and lighting the guest's Lucky Strike.

Once again, the waitress walked off.

"Tentative yes," she answered.

Kent took a sip of his coffee. He was hoping for a yes. This would be a good catch for him and feather in his cap.

"Tentative?" he questioned.

"He has access, but he would have to get the ledgers and get out. I'll work with him on an exit strategy and get back to you shortly," she said.

"Understood."

"Once those are missing, Owney will go ape shit. They'll turn the place upside down and look at everyone. Kevin will have to make an excuse to move them or do something before handing them over to you," she explained to Kent who knew everything she was saying was true.

"Fine. But time is ticking by. We want to break this up before Volstead gets repealed," he admitted. Everyone could tell that a repeal of the Volstead Act was in the future, but they all wanted to make as much money or, in this case, brownie points before the laws changed. He also knew many in this gang were guilty of murder, assault, book making and breaking about a dozen other laws. These ledgers, though, were hard evidence that would shut their booze and gambling businesses down.

"Being a 'G,' you would know more about that than me," she said. "I'll be back with you soon."

Before he could reply, she got up and left the booth headed for the door leaving him with the tab.

With midday approaching and a newspaper in front of him, Agent Kent Davis decided to treat himself to lunch with the knowledge that he could be on the edge of a big get.

———

CHAPTER 21

COST OF DOING BUSINESS

The men met in Connecticut instead of New York City for their quarterly get together. The speakeasy was a company-run establishment, and the manager had been working overtime for the last couple of days to make sure it was ready for their arrival. He had only been given a three-day notice that the big bosses planned on using his place just outside New Haven for their meeting. Everything had to be just right. He had prepared a separate room with a round table and some extra chairs along the wall in the back.

Except for the loss of the three men in Norwood and a few smaller busts, the Big Seven bosses were pleased with how things were going. Business was good, but they each knew that sometime in the future, their product of choice would become legal once again. That was a reality that looked them all in the face and clearly was the near future.

"Did we ever figure out what happened in Norwood?" Big Bill Dwyer asked as he sipped his Canadian whisky.

Danny had an answer ready for that question because he knew it was coming.

"Yeah, we figured it out, and we're going to take care of it," he said confidently. "Our guy in the Bureau let us down. End of story. We had no idea they were going to be on the ground with a team of 'G's. I'm on it."

"It's your territory, Danny. Your men. Your problem. Your fix," Owney added.

"I'm on it," Danny repeated to the group in an authoritative and confident manner. These men respected each other and each other's territory. At this table, they were equals.

It had been a tough couple of weeks for Danny's crew, and the others understood the complexities in the northeast and New England. It was one of the hardest places to operate because of the number of Feds, population and amount of geography covered. New York was relatively contained to one area along with the mid-Atlantic and Florida.

"Kevin, give us a quick rundown on the air operation," Owney ordered. Kevin had become one of his most loyal, top lieutenants.

"We're up to three flights a week in New England and three to Philly which covers Atlantic City, the Shore and down to Delaware. We're looking at doing the same for Florida. The only thing about Florida is the distance and stopping for fuel at secure locations," he explained. "With the loss of the plane in Norwood, we're down to two."

"Can we get another one or two planes?" Big Bill asked.

"We're working on just that," Kevin answered respectfully. "They're expensive to buy and run but worth it when it comes to speed and reach."

"Tell them what the take is on one flight," Owney ordered.

Kevin pulled out one of his ledgers and opened the book to a marked page. These were the latest numbers he would have. "Given the number of cases and units sold from each case on individual mixed drinks, close to sixty thousand after expenses," he said.

The men liked that answer and knew it was in addition to their shipping operation using the boats.

Another round of whisky was served as Kevin returned to the back of the room and sat down.

"One third of our business will be gone when they get around to re-pealing," Big Bill said addressing the elephant in the room.

"We'll still have gambling, cigarettes and protection," Owney countered.

"That's not enough to fill a hole this big," Danny said speaking up and having an idea of what he wanted to do after liquor became legal.

"What would you suggest?" Big Bill asked with a tense tone.

"We get licenses and sell it legally. We open stores across our territories. Yes, we'll pay taxes and have to hand some back to the government, but we still control the supply. All of the headaches caused by liquor being illegal will be over. We can also think about increasing the gambling side of the house and look ahead to the next big thing which is narcotics."

The men reflected on that point for a few minutes while sipping their drinks.

"Chicago is not happy with your little stunt in Albany," Big Bill Dwyer said breaking the momentary lull in conversation. "That was not a good move, Danny," he said then took another sip of his Canadian whisky on the rocks.

"Fuck 'em. They don't control me or my territory. That was---"

"Not your territory. That's the issue," Big Bill countered.

"I opened that speak' along with a few others east of Albany. Chicago also came into Vermont and tried to put product into one of my places near Burlington until I finally found out about it."

Owney weighed in on this conversation. "Well, it's our consensus that we need to keep the peace with Chicago, and you stoking the fire is not helping. Especially if we move into narcotics after Volstead."

Danny took a long sip of his drink then spoke. "I hear you all, and I'll back off. But they have to show some respect for our operations in the northeast and New England."

"Let's move on," Big Bill said and signaled for the waitress to refresh their drinks. Each member briefed the group on their ongoing business and shared some stories of the road. They were business partners but also enjoyed each other's company. Like any family, there was always some infighting.

———

Aqueduct was more crowded than usual for a Saturday as race fans filled the stands on a muggy summer evening. The distinctive, mixed smell of hay and occasional manure would sweep over the track from the barns as the sun began to set across New York. Father Ralph had driven down the night before after Friday evening mass knowing he didn't have to be back to St. Mary's until Sunday morning. His priestly black outfit and white collar would stay back in the rectory when he made these trips to see the action, place bets in person and see his pal, Doctor Mason. The two met up in the stands well away from anyone in range of their voices.

"You have money for me?" Doc Mason asked.

"Nice to see you, too," Father Ralph said sarcastically.

"Sorry, it's been a long month. We also need to take a break. Drugs are one thing, but when we have two overdoses in a single month, it raises eyebrows," he explained.

"Who's asking questions?" Father Ralph asked.

"Everyone. The trainers, the owners and even the guy calling the race upstairs."

Father Ralph let this sink in for a few minutes. Then he spoke. "I understand. We can take a little break."

Doc Mason nodded his head.

Father Ralph continued while reaching into his pocket for a thick manila envelope. "Let me know when you'll be comfortable resuming."

Doc Mason put the envelope into his back pocket. "How's that little sister? What's her name? She's a little---"

"Fine, and end of story," interrupted Father Ralph trying to change the subject.

"Alright then. But she is fine little dame," Doc Mason said.

"Any other people suspicious of our little operation?" Father Ralph asked finally moving the conversation in a different direction.

"The cops asked a few questions as well as the owners of both horses."

"What did you tell them?"

"They had heart attacks, plain and simple."

"Did they believe it?"

"Of course, they did. Because the horses actually *did* have heart attacks. No worry."

Father Ralph took a sip of the now cold coffee he had in his hand. "Good, let's keep it that way."

The drive from St. Mary's all the way to Aqueduct took around six or seven hours in his Model A, but the effort was worth it to Father Ralph knowing that his retirement would be a comfortable one. He also lived for the adrenaline of the races. Fixing them with his old college buddy, Doc Mason, was another thrill he couldn't share with anyone.

Making the rounds in Boston was always a pleasure for Danny. Patrick and his crew usually handled cash pick-ups in this part of Massachusetts, but Danny had decided to make this week's circuit personally. He wanted to show his people that he was watching everything and that he could show up at any time.

His last stop was a discreet little club just off Beacon Street not far from the capitol. Most of the state's legislators could be found on any given night here or at one of the other three speakeasys in the Back Bay neighborhood.

Coming out of the back door of the building this speakeasy was using for covert customer access, Danny could smell the Charles River flowing past only blocks away. It was dark, and the only light shining into the small parking lot was coming from the building next door. For a big city, Boston was rather still on this summer night. Danny walked across the lot toward his car. On this night, he had no driver and no bodyguard. He had enjoyed a nice dinner with a lady friend before making his rounds and hadn't wanted any extra company. Just himself.

As he approached his car, he stopped and turned around. Nothing. The night was eerie and quiet. For an unknown reason, he thought someone might be following him. Shaking that off, he continued toward his car parked about fifty feet away. The wind shifted from the Charles River to the general direction of the back of the building. In that instant, the smell of the river was replaced by something familiar, but he just couldn't quite place it. The smell intensified as he got closer to his car and the wind blew from his back. Two seconds later he heard a pop and immediately knew what it was when he felt a fire run up his back and down his leg. He heard another pop and again felt the same agony of a second bullet entering his back forcing him to collapse face down on the ground. He could hear the steps of someone running away, then a car door, then the car pulling out. As his eyes closed, that smell returned. He knew the odor but couldn't place it. Confused semi-darkness followed. His last memory before completely losing consciousness was of indescribable pain and that awful smell.

———

CHAPTER 22

THREE FLOWERS
BRILLIANTINE

The house was quiet as Jeannie and the kids slept peacefully in their beds. The sound of crickets could be heard outside the opened upstairs window on this mild summer's night. Patrick had turned in early not knowing just how busy his next day would be. At 3:30 in the morning, the phone next to his head on the bedside table rang. He woke from a deep sleep wondering if this was some sort of dream. The phone continued to ring, bringing him to the reality that something was going on for him to be called this late. He reached for the heavy black telephone, lifted the receiver off the hook and brought it to his ear as he spoke into the phone.

"Yeah," he said quietly trying not to wake his wife.

"Patrick, it's Marky. Danny's been shot!"

It was almost like an electric shock being pulsed through his body; Patrick immediately sat up, now completely awake, listening to the news from his associate.

"Come again?" Patrick asked looking for some confirmation that this was not a bad dream.

"Danny was shot in Boston, and he's in pretty bad shape at Mass General," he explained. "You need to pick me up, and we have to get up there."

"Jesus, Mary and Joseph!" Patrick exclaimed. "Who the fuck---"

"Did this? Or who would do this?" Marky interrupted finishing his question. "We'll find out. Only a few people knew he was headed to Boston for pick-up."

"What's his condition?" Patrick asked.

"Critical."

"I'm on my way. Get your guys ready to go. We'll meet at your place in an hour," Patrick ordered taking command and hanging up the phone.

"What is it, dear?" Jeannie asked as she also sat up in bed, now wide awake.

"Danny's been shot in Boston," he said with an all business tone while climbing out of bed and getting dressed.

"Oh, God," she said.

"I'm heading up there with Marky and some of the boys. Not sure when we'll be back," he said. After getting dressed, he reached into the top drawer of his dresser and pulled out his Colt pistol and a box of ammo.

"Please be careful," she begged. "Promise me you'll be careful."

He stopped for a minute, looked at his wife and bent down to kiss her. "Always," he said before walking out of the bedroom, down the stairs and then out to his car.

Fifteen minutes later, he was sitting in front of Marky's most recent apartment. Marky had a way of getting kicked out of apartments.

The windows of the car were open letting the muggy summer night air in. Marky came running out of the dark building and got into the waiting car.

"Where are the boys?" Patrick asked.

"Heading that way, I wanted separate cars in case you need to get back here."

"Good thinking."

The two men were quiet as they headed up U.S. 1 to Boston's Massachusetts General Hospital.

About halfway there Marky broke the silence. "Oh, by the way, cops said it was not a robbery."

Patrick looked over at Marky's face mostly hidden by the darkness of the early morning.

"What?"

"No robbery. He had about five grand in cash on him which seems about right given where he was and the hour. It was his last stop of the night," Marky said.

"Then it's a hit. Fucking Chicago!" Patrick vented. "I bet a hundred K it was Chicago."

The rest of the ride was silent. When they arrived at the emergency entrance, they were met by Todd and Joey. The new guy, Tony, had also shown up but was in his own car.

All five men took the stairs to the third floor waiting area. Danny had been moved out of the emergency department to the critical floor. Shortly after his arrival, an emergency surgeon had removed two .32 caliber bullets from his back. Patrick told the nurse on duty that they would like to talk to the doctor treating Danny.

Twenty long minutes later Dr. Matthew Fulton walked in. "Good..." Dr. Fulton paused to look at his watch. "Morning, gentlemen. It's been a long night. Here's an update on your friend. He was shot twice in the back by a .32 caliber gun, and by God's grace, both bullets landed in almost the same place next to the right kidney. There was some damage to the kidney which we repaired and should heal over time. He could actually lose that kidney and live a normal life. I don't think that's going to happen, though. His right leg may have some nerve damage as well, but it's way too hard to tell how much at this point. Right now, he's still groggy from the anesthesia, but in a few hours, Mr. Walsh should be awake and able to see you. I can't have a crowd in there; only two at a time, please."

All five men nodded in agreement, and Patrick spoke for the group. "Thanks, doc. We appreciate it, and I know Danny will show his appreciation as well once he's up and back to work."

"That's going to be a while. At least a week or two here, then a couple weeks at home," Doctor Fulton said with a "doctor's orders" tone. "Does his work put stress on his body? Manual labor and such?"

Patrick handled that question. "He has lots of stress, but not from that. No, he's in management."

"Okay, that will help things along. I'll be leaving the floor in a couple of hours, but Dr. Knowles will take over, and I'll be back tomorrow night," he said while reaching for Patrick's hand. The two men shook, and the doctor quickly left the waiting room headed back to check on his other patients. Dr. Fulton would soon be headed to his home in Quincy and bed.

The crew waited for the doctor to walk down the hall, then Patrick shut the door to the waiting room. Joey spoke first. "BPD told me he was shot from behind, and they gave me this envelope of cash he had on him. No robbery. They suspect it was a hit, too. They know who we are and who he is. The only problem is that we don't know who to blame for the hit."

"I know who the fuck to blame," Patrick said.

Todd interjected, "We can't jump to conclusions. It could have been---"

"Chicago. We know it was Chicago, Todd. Who else?" Patrick asked.

"Maybe it was just a local kid or something."

"And a kid didn't walk away with all this cash?"

"True enough," Todd conceded.

The men were silent and each wanted a drink.

"I want security 24/7 now," Patrick ordered. "Marky, you set it up."

Marky nodded his head. He had figured that was coming. Thankfully he had a few new men to help with the added task of protecting the boss. Patrick waited a few hours for the sun to come up and morning to take hold before calling and informing the other members of the Big Seven. Just as a precaution, he suggested each of them have increased protection until tensions diminished between their operation and Chicago. Coffee instead of whisky would have to do as he waited for the boss to wake up and get a take on just what happened and why.

———————

Special Agent Ted Connelly heard about the hit on Danny Walsh and wanted to learn more. He had a good contact in the Boston Police Department and decided to seek him out. Leaving his office in Scollay Square, he walked a couple of blocks and took a taxi the rest of the way to BPD Headquarters.

"Hey, Teddy," Captain Ray O'Rourke said, pleased to see his old pal from downtown. "How the hell are you?"

"Good, my friend," Ted answered.

"How's Marge?"

"She's good. Everybody is hanging in there. I'm still chasing bootleggers."

"Stinks for you, my friend. No one gives a shit about booze anymore. They're going to legalize it again anyway," O'Rourke told his buddy.

"Let's go outside for a minute," Ted said signaling that he wanted to talk in private. They both knew the walls had ears.

Both men made a cup of coffee and walked outside into the Boston late spring sunshine.

"What do you know about the Danny Walsh hit?" Ted started.

"Who said it was a hit?" Ray asked.

"Come on! You're talking to me," Ted said knowing his pal would spill the beans if he had any. There were both, after all, brothers in law enforcement.

"Word is that it was a contract hit. We have no clue who the trigger man was. Clean get-away, no prints, no robbery, nothing."

"Fuck. I figured as much. Danny is a big deal. He's one of the Big Seven," Ted said.

"Big Seven?" Ray asked.

"Yeah, the Big Seven. Some people call it 'The Combine.' They run the booze up and down the east coast. New England is Danny's territory. The others handle New York, Mid Atlantic, Southeast and so on. Big dollars. Lots of political pull."

Ray took a sip of his coffee and let that sink in. He handled mostly Boston and local crimes. He had heard of the syndicates but was not very familiar with their names.

"What else?" Ted probed.

".32 cal, probably a Colt. No gun recovered. Clean job."

"That's it?"

"Yeah, cold. Not much else. Definitely a professional job, but that's about it," Ray said.

Ted was thankful for his friend and any info he could share. "I appreciate it, Ray."

"Any time. How's that little place on the Cape?"

"Good. We upgraded to a bigger house out there. Super, though."

"Oh, I'm glad you're enjoying the big federal bucks," Ray joked.

Ted laughed it off as the two walked back toward the station.

"Thanks, Ray. I owe you lunch," Ted said reaching to shake his friend's hand.

"Any time, Ted. Best to Marge. And your brother the priest."

"We'll talk soon. Thanks again," Ted said then turned to walk a few blocks to the "T" station near Park Street.

———

A little more than an hour later, a phone call was made.

"He left the building, got into a taxi, ended up at BPD, went into the building, then came out with Captain Ray O'Rourke. The two walked toward the Common then came back. After that, he took the 'T' from Park Street to Scollay Square, but he didn't go directly back into the building. He went to a coffee shop across the street. Why would a guy who just had a coffee, want another one?" special Agent Robbie Boone, better known to the people on the top floor as Agent X, asked in a matter of fact tone. Boone was part of the Internal Affairs Division of the FBI which also had oversight of all Bureau of Prohibition special agents.

"Good question," James Warren said on the other end of the phone. "See what you can get out of the workers at the coffee shop."

"I know how to do my job. Technically I don't report to you, and I'm telling you this as a courtesy so that you can be measured in what you say to Connelly. Remember all this when handing out assignments, too," Boone said reminding James of the hierarchy.

"And I appreciate it, Mr. Boone. I truly do. Thanks again for the intel, and we'll be in close touch," James said ending the phone call. He had never been a big fan of Ted Connelly and displayed a rare smile on his face as he got up from his desk to use the restroom.

———

The hospital room was private, and a set of armed guards stood outside in the hall 24/7 on eight-hour shifts. The new guy, Tony, had the duty at the moment as Patrick approached from the elevator. He was returning after running back to the office to take care of some work before returning to Boston to check on the boss. He knocked on the door then entered.

"You're awake, boss!" Patrick said with a happy tone in his voice. It was the first time he would be able to speak to Danny since the shooting and surgery earlier that morning. Now it was just after sunset. Danny was groggy but awake enough to talk to his number two.

"Awake and alive." Danny said with a slight hint of humor in his tone.

"Indeed," Patrick answered. "Good thing."

Danny was weak but struggling to sit up. His voice was soft, and he was clearly in pain. He finally spoke. "This was a hit."

Patrick looked into his eyes. "Yup. It was, boss."

Danny took a few minutes and a sip of the water sitting to his right on a table. Pain shot up his back, but he knew that was okay given the alternative.

"Who? Chicago? North End?" Danny asked.

"My guess is the Drucci Gang. Got some feelers out. Getting as much intel as we can. I even sent Marky to Chicago to poke around," Patrick explained.

"They'll see right through that," Danny said with a wave of his hand. "Drucci or even North End up here is my guess."

"We'll see. For now, you need to get better and stronger. Too much shit going on to have you down for the count," Patrick said.

"I may be down, but not out. That doc said I should be back up and going in a few weeks. Luck of the Irish with this one, my friend," Danny said appreciating his top guy and their closeness. There were only a couple of people he could trust completely, and Patrick was one of them.

"I'm heading back to wrap up this shitty day. I want you to get some rest. Let's talk again tomorrow," Patrick said.

"You do what you have to do. Run the business. Don't be sitting up here worrying about me," Danny ordered. "It'll take some time, but I'll be fine."

"You got it, boss. And there's someone 24/7 just outside your room keeping watch," Patrick told him. "Tony, come in here," Patrick yelled toward the door hoping he would be heard. A few seconds later, Tony stuck his head into the room.

"Yeah, boss?" Tony asked.

"Look who's up," Patrick said pointing to Danny in bed.

"Hey, Danny! Looking better," Tony said looking down and not making direct eye contact with the boss.

Right at that moment Danny's stomach turned. He motioned for Patrick to come close so he could whisper.

"What's that smell?" Danny asked quietly.

"What are you talking about?" Patrick asked Danny.

"That fucking smell. What is it?" Danny asked again now louder with an angry tone.

Patrick looked at Tony. "What is that Tony?"

"Oh, Three Flowers Brilliantine. It's in my hair," Tony explained to the two men.

"Smells like you used the whole bottle," Patrick joked then took Tony's arm headed for the door. "I'm out of here, boss. See you late tomorrow."

Before Danny could answer or talk to Patrick, he was gone. Tony was again stationed outside the door. The smell inside the room lingered. Danny reached for the telephone and told the operator he wanted Perry 24469. A few moments later, Marky picked up on the other end.

———

CHAPTER 23

CASH MONEY

The payoff money always came in cash and always in a brown envelope. The meeting place was just down from the State House near Union Station. The man sitting on the bench facing the Providence River worked for the governor. The man handing him the envelope was one of Patrick's people. About once a month, Danny or Patrick would typically give one of their crew the envelope which would then be taken to Providence. Ever since the ledger had been found on the body of one of their members, they stopped making notes of the payments. It didn't matter anyway. Cash was cash, and the Big Seven had plenty of it. Today, Patrick took care of this business as Danny continued to recover in Boston. He gave the envelope to Tony who met the man on the bench. The total transaction time was about thirty seconds, and then both men were on their way. About one hundred yards away, Jesse took notes and snapped a couple of pictures pretending to aim at the riverfront looking like an artist or tourist. Most days the riverbank had plenty of both. Things were starting to add up. Jesse walked away thinking that he had a hell of a story to write.

The woman joked that she could drink like a sailor and proved that to be the case. The vodka was on the rocks as she took another sip then wanted to go back to bed for more. Marky had rented the room for six bits a night. It was not in the best part of Chicago, but that was on purpose. He wanted to keep a low profile and knew some of the women the Drucci Gang had in their stable.

"Again?" she begged. He thought of himself as a ladies man and could hold his own, but four times in one night may have been his limit.

"Come on, doll…" he said walking back from the little bathroom.

"Come on what?"

"I've got to sleep," he said.

"Fuck sleep," she insisted.

"Let me ask you again. You actually know this guy Tony?" he said for the third time.

"Yeah, but his name is not Tony. It's Manny," she said. "I don't know his last name, but yeah. He works with Gino and some of the others."

Marky had brought along the only picture he had of Tony with him from Providence. It was a group shot taken recently at Aqueduct when Danny had treated a few of the guys for a weekend of racing down there.

"Has Manny been working with the Druccis lately?" Marky continued.

"Not for a while. The other guys have been, but he's not around," she replied. "Gino said Manny was on assignment in New England."

Marky knew this information would be worth the long overnight train ride to Chicago. By asking women who worked the streets for the Drucci Gang, he figured someone may recognize the picture. The Big Seven kept good background information on the gang's operation, interaction with Capone and some of their independent work like prostitution. This was when good intel paid off.

"One more time? Pretty please?" she begged.

He went over to the bed and picked up one of the pillows.

"Kinky stuff? Sure!! Tie me up, baby!" she said, almost too loud for his liking.

Marky took the pillow over to the chair where his pants were. He reached into the pocket and pulled out a .38 caliber pistol. She didn't know what to make of that. He walked toward the bed and asked her to lie down.

"What's that for?" she asked.

"I'll show you. Close your eyes."

She complied.

He took the pillow and put it over her face with one hand and pointed the pistol into the middle of it with the other. Then he pulled the trigger. Her legs jumped off the bed as the bullet entered her face. He pulled the trigger three more times. Blood filled the pillow while feathers floated around her dead body.

Quietly he put the pistol back into his pants pocket, got dressed quickly and left. Other business needed his attention back in Rhode Island.

———

The office in New York where Owney did most of his business was rather small for the size of the operation he and his partners were running. There were two secretaries, an accountant and Kevin, who had been elevated to a pseudo office manager. Owney was once again on the road in Long Island looking after some of their speakeasys. It was standing policy that nothing ever left this office unless Owney personally approved it.

Kevin was in early after a late night with some of Owney's boys playing pool and drinking to their hearts content at one of the "company" speakeasys in the Bronx. He and Sally had been spending a lot of time together and talked about getting married once they started their new life with each other. He was ready for the future but first needed to deal with the present, and that meant getting over a few major hurdles. The accountants usually showed up around 9 a.m., so Kevin timed his arrival for about an hour earlier.

"Good morning, Kevin," was the greeting he got from Dotty, one of Owney's long time secretaries. Owney Madden knew it was important to take care of the people who took care of his business. He was very good to the office folk giving them bonuses, many days off and taking care of their families. Dotty was like family. Owney trusted only a few people and demanded complete loyalty. Kevin was one of them, but oddly, the office keys and security were the responsibility of Dotty. She always opened and closed the office. Kevin ran things, but she was the glue that kept it all together.

"Good morning, Dotty. I'm going to Connecticut later for a delivery. That crew needs all the help they can get," he said while pouring himself a coffee. "Monday's pick-up also needs to be recorded."

The ledgers were always kept in the safe along with any cash on hand as well as the check books. Kevin had the combination to the safe, and it was routine for him to go into it for the books to make entries. After fixing his coffee, he waited a few minutes for Dotty to make her way back to her desk near the front of the office. She was the only other person in the office as they awaited the others.

The ledgers were always started on the first day of January and ended at the end of the year before new ones were created. The accountants were meticulous in how they kept the books. They made most of the entries except for when Kevin or Owney himself recorded a pick-up. Today was one of those days. Purposely, he had not recorded the last pick-up in order to have an excuse to go into the safe and make the entry. The crackling sound of Dotty's radio could be heard coming from the front office as Kevin bent down and dialed in the six-number combination. With a click and a snap of the handle to the left, the door of the heavy safe opened slowly. As he had done many times before, he extracted the current ledger and put it on the top of the five-foot tall safe. Then he reached back inside and pulled out three more ledger books which were tied together with red string. He looked around to make sure no one was watching and then untied the string to separate the ledgers. After he separated them, he placed them on the top of the safe momentarily. At that moment, he reached into his trench coat where he had made three temporary pockets, two on one side, and one on the other. He carefully pulled out three identical ledgers he had made in the days before. Quickly, he put the fake ledgers on the top of the safe. After another look around to see if he was still alone, Kevin put each of the real ledgers into the trench coat pockets. In his hand was the red string which he then proceeded to wrap around the fake ledgers, tying them together before returning the books to the inside of the safe. He stood up, reached for the ledger where he was going to record the pick-up and opened it to the appropriate page. Reaching into his pants pocket, Kevin pulled out the notes he had made during the pick-up. Just as he started to turn around, he felt a tap on his shoulder which almost stopped his heart.

"Hey Kev... need any help?" asked Glen, one of the accountants who had just arrived. Kevin had almost jumped out of his skin but tried his best to act normal.

"Hi Glen, no... no thanks. I'm just going to put in yesterday's pick-up figures," Kevin said trying to not to sound surprised.

"I'll get it. Just tell me the numbers." Glen replied while grabbing the ledger out of his hand. "Lock it up and I'll put this back later," he said pointing to the safe then turned to walk back to his desk.

"Very good," Kevin said confidently as he shut the door of the safe and spun the combination lock. He then returned up front to Glen's desk to give him the receipts of the pick-up which needed to be recorded.

"Here you go," Kevin said to Glen as he counted out the receipts and left them on the accountant's desk.

"I saw you," Glen said as he started separating the pick-up receipts.

"Excuse me?" Kevin asked while feeling for the bulge of his Colt .38 Special under the long trench coat.

"I saw you. You think you're going to keep that a secret?" Glen asked.

Kevin's options started to spin around in his head. Accountants were not the muscle end of the business, and Kevin knew he could take this guy out if needed. He paused before answering. "Keep what a secret? Saw me where?"

"Come on, my brother! I saw you and Sally having dinner the other night!"

If that was all Glen was talking about, Kevin would be relieved more than this guy would ever know. He quietly exhaled the breath he was holding.

"Where?" Kevin asked.

"Mia's Kitchen on the West Side."

"Oh, she's lonely with Owney on the road all the time and asked if I would keep her company."

Glen chuckled and continued to count the receipts in front of him. Then he started to record them into the ledger.

"Don't worry. My lips are sealed," he said with a bit of a sarcastic tone.

"I've got work to do. So do you, Glen. Let's keep our eye on the ball," Kevin said ending the conversation as his heart rhythm returned to normal.

With that, Kevin picked up the schedule on his desk and headed for the front door. "I'll be back later on or in the morning, Dotty."

"Okay, Kevin. You be careful," Dotty replied with her usual maternal tone of caution.

He opened the front door and walked out as the cool New York air hit him in the face and wondered if he would ever see this place again.

———

Seekonk, Massachusetts was a sleepy little town where everyone seemed to know each other's business. This was even more the case within the church community. Father Ralph was having coffee at a local place called the Ritz Diner a couple of miles from St. Mary's when one of his ushers noticed him sitting alone.

"Hi, Father. How's it going?" Bruce the usher said taking the good father by surprise.

"Good, Bruce. How are you?"

"Good, thank God. Just getting a coffee. Are you alone? Do you want some company?"

Father Ralph was expecting someone and looked at his watch. "Oh, thanks Bruce, but I'm waiting for someone. Great to see you, though."

"Same here, Father," Bruce said. "See you Sunday."

"Absolutely, God Bless." Father Ralph answered then went back to his newspaper.

A few minutes later, two men entered the diner and walked over to Father Ralph's table. "Anyone sitting here?" Todd Ellis asked.

Without looking up from his paper, Father Ralph replied. "No, I'm waiting---"

"For us, yes you are, Father," interrupted Todd.

"Oh, hi, Todd. Hi, Rudy. How was your trip down from Providence?" Father asked making some small talk.

"No G-Men, no problems," Todd replied coldly. "You have something for us?"

"You have something for me first?" Father asked just as coldly.

There was a pause. Todd reached into his coat and pulled out an envelope fat with cash and quickly slid it across the table.

Father Ralph did the same. He reached into his coat and pulled out an envelope and pushed it across the table to the men. This envelope, however, didn't have cash inside. It contained something better. "I've got to tell you, only two races this month."

Rudy looked up. Of the two men sitting with Father Ralph, typically he didn't say very much, but with a tense tone he asked, "Two?"

"Only two," Father answered. "More next month, but we need to be really careful. Guys, a few horses have died. That's drawn unwelcome attention."

"Last month we had only four. If this is a trend, our people are not going to like it," Todd injected into the conversation.

Father Ralph took a sip of his coffee. "We'll be back to between five or six races soon."

The two men opened their envelope and pulled out the paper with two races noted on it. "Your cut may have to be adjusted," Todd explained.

"My cut is the same whether it's one race or ten races. I make less with only two, but the percentage remains the same," Father Ralph said in a not very priestly tone.

Todd folded the paper up and put it back into the envelope. He motioned for Rudy to get out of the booth. As he slid across the bench seat to stand up, he looked into Father Ralph's eyes. "Don't forget who you work for. See you next month."

With that, the two men quickly left as Father Ralph returned to his newspaper knowing Doc Mason was the key to this whole operation and that he could be compromised if someone started digging.

CHAPTER 24

BUSINESS

The *Black Duck* unloaded in the darkness of the overnight to the rum
runners just off the coast of Point Judith. Captain Rick St. Pierre had
planned a fuel and food stop after the booze offload. He had the option
of Block Island, but after a radio message, he had decided to head for the
small seaport of Galilee which was just a few miles away, much closer than
Block Island.

Marky, Patrick and Tony were waiting on the dock as the *Black Duck*
approached. It was a chilly morning for late spring, and the wind continued to blow from the northeast under cloudy skies. The sun had just
come up. Seas were a bit choppy for the latest offload of Canadian product. Captain Rick hated what the sailors called a northeast fetch. Those
were winds coming from the northeast pushing up the seas and causing
problems for the smaller rum runners which would have trouble tying up
to the larger, more stable *Black Duck*. Captain Rick knew the three men
waiting on the pier, but he was not sure what their purpose was now that
the offload was complete.

"Ahoy," Patrick said as the boat slowly approached.

"Lines forward and aft," yelled Captain Rick to the deck hands. In total, there were four men on the boat. Two of them handled the lines throwing them to Patrick and Marky on the dock who quickly tied them off while Captain Rick came out of the wheelhouse. Black exhaust continued to puff out of the large stack as the engine was put in idle but still running. Patrick boarded the boat and climbed to the wheelhouse to intercept Rick before he could come down to the main deck. Marky and Tony waited on the dock as the deck hands started to clean the rails after the large offload at sea. There would always be some breakage, and they didn't want a 'G' dropping by asking for their registration while finding whisky and traces of other liquor on the rails, deck and in the holds of the ship.

A few minutes later Rick and Patrick came down the steps from the second deck. "Guys a little change in plans. We've got to go out and rendezvous with one of the runners who will come out of the bay with some VSOP that needs to go back up north," Captain Rick explained. The men were tired after a long cruise and offload, but those were the orders. At least it wouldn't be too long. Just three miles off the end of Narragansett Bay. The men began to make preparations for getting underway as Marky and Tony boarded the boat.

Ten minutes later, they were headed through the channel in Galilee with the wind giving them a push toward the open sea.

Tony was on deck when Marky came back up from down below. "Tony, give us a hand down here," Marky said pointing to the hatch and stairs. Tony looked around and saw the two deck hands just standing around toward the rear of the boat having a cigarette. Then he looked toward the direction they were steaming and did not see the smaller rumrunner that *Black Duck* was headed to intercept. *Maybe it's running late*, Tony thought. When he started walking toward Marky who was standing at the top of the passage steps, he noticed Marky's boots had a bunch of white power on them. It looked a little like flour, he thought.

"What do you need?" Tony asked as he approached Marky and the steps that led below.

"We've got to move some booze down here," Marky said. At that moment, Tony remembered he hadn't seen Patrick since they left the docks. "Come on, let's go."

As Tony entered the passage that led below deck, he could smell something familiar. Marky followed him down the steps after closing the passage hatch behind them creating a large noise. Tony was startled by the sound of the hatch as he came off the last step into the forward hold where whisky cases typically were stacked to the celling. Now the hold was empty except for one barrel sitting in the corner. Patrick stood next to it. He also had the same powder all over his shoes. At that moment, Tony saw a bottle of Three Flowers Brillantine on a table to his right. Marky stood behind him.

"Is it Tony?" Patrick asked. "Or is it that even your name?"

"What are you talking about?" Tony asked now with a sick feeling in his stomach.

"Maybe it's Manny? Maybe you're not even Irish?" Marky asked now with anger in his voice.

"O'Shea, huh?" Patrick questioned in a mocking tone. "That's Irish, isn't it, Marky?"

"Yeah. But Morelli isn't," Marky replied.

Tony was silent.

"So, this stuff for your hair. That's pretty good stuff, right? I mean, you use a ton of it. Enough so that everyone can smell it for miles around. Everyone including the boss right before you shot him in the back," Patrick said.

Marky grabbed Tony and pulled his arms behind his back as Patrick picked up some rope that was sitting on the floor near the barrel. The ship rolled left and right as Captain Rick stayed on a steady course away from land. Patrick tied Tony's hands behind him tightly as Tony struggled in vain. Marky pulled him down to the floor and Patrick lashed his feet together with more rope.

"We just want to know if you're working alone or are there more from the Drucci gang in our organization? Patrick asked. "Believe me, you'll want to answer."

Tony was silent.

Marky grabbed the bottle of Three Flowers Brilliantine and walked over to Tony who was lying on the floor. "Answer the man's question," Marky ordered.

Tony was silent and now shaking.

"Here's some truth serum that may help you remember," Marky said as he took the bottle and poured it into his mouth. Tony spit up the hair liquid then choked and coughed. The smell was strong in the small below deck space.

"Any more of you pieces of shit in our organization?" Marky asked.

"No. Just me." Tony admitted.

"You're sure?" Marky asked.

"Just me. Let me go back, and I'll be your guy in Chicago."

Marky looked at Patrick and smiled. Patrick didn't say a word but shook his head with what was clearly the answer no.

"Get his feet," Marky said to Patrick.

"No, seriously, let me go be your guy in Chicago," Tony begged.

"No one takes a shot at our boss and gets away with it," Marky said as he and Patrick dragged him to the end of the hold where the barrel was. Tony could smell something else now. Then he saw the bag of cement sitting half empty in the corner.

Patrick looked down at Tony, a.k.a. Manny, lying tied up on the floor. "I have one question which may work in your favor if you answer truthfully. We have the evidence but want to know for sure. It was you who took those shots at the boss in Boston, wasn't it?"

Tony looked up at both men then spoke. "I was ordered to. I swear to God."

"Feet first," Marky said as he and Patrick hoisted Tony's squirming body up then into the barrel. Tony yelled and tried to resist by kicking his legs, but they were tied close together, so it was futile. His legs went into the barrel and into the thick, wet cement that had been mixed on the way out to sea. Tony was surprised it felt as cold as it did. He was silent knowing that his fate was sealed.

Both Patrick and Marky held Tony down into the barrel. Half of his body was in the cement while his chest, head and bound upper arms were exposed to the air. It didn't take long for the cement to harden.

"Let's get this piece of shit up on deck," Marky said as he went up the steps and opened the hatch. After he returned, Patrick picked up one end and Marky the other and they lifted Tony, now cemented into the barrel, up the stairs to the deck. The wind continued to blow, and the deck hands stood well aft, purposely looking the other way.

The *Black Duck* had a deck access door on each side of the vessel's midships. The ship's rail was wooden and stood around 3 feet up from the deck completely around the vessel. A wooden access door opened all the way back at the stern where it was flush with the deck rail for easy access to the ship.

"Let's go," Marky said loudly so that Patrick could hear him over the sound of the ocean, wind and engine. The two men dragged Tony and the barrel where he was cemented to the opening. The sea was racing by below them in the dark as the ship continued to steam east. Marky took Tony's left arm and Patrick his right. "On three..." he yelled. "One.... Two.... Three..."

Tony's final, horrifying moments on this planet consisted of falling from the ship, striking the cold Atlantic waters then instantly sinking below the surface where no one would ever find his remains.

"You can still smell that shit in his hair. It's all over my hands," Marky said closing the deck access door. "You think Chicago will strike back?"

Patrick shook his head. "Strike back for what? I didn't see anything. Tony just left as far as we're concerned," he said.

Marky laughed. "Exactly," he replied.

"Let's head in," Patrick yelled to Captain Rick who was up in the wheel house looking forward intently. He finally turned to look aft toward where the men were standing. Captain Rick acknowledged with a wave then spun the ship's wheel 180 degrees pointing the *Black Duck* back toward Point Judith where beer and dinner awaited.

———————

"Lucky" was the adjective the doctors kept using every time they examined Danny, and today wasn't any different. The only difference was that Danny was doing a follow up appointment by going to their office rather than the doctor visiting him in the hospital room.

"A little better, my friend. As I said last time, the healing will be slow, but you're making good progress," said Doctor Weisman who was one of the best orthopedic minds in the Boston area. "Just a little to the left and your luck would have run out."

Danny rolled his eyes when he heard the mention of luck again. The doctor's office was about an hour's ride from his office, and either Patrick or Marky was still having to drive him every place he went.

"Keep doing the exercises, Danny. Don't overdo it. See you in a month," instructed Dr. Weisman.

"Patrick has something for you and the crew," Danny said as he got up to leave.

"You don't have to do that, but it's always appreciated."

Every trip to see this doctor, Danny made sure he brought enough product for the entire office. Patrick left a case of Canadian whisky in the business office before helping Danny back to the car. For the most part, Danny could walk on his own but still needed the help of a cane. Because his cane happened to be a disguised .410 shotgun, Danny had elected to leave it in the car for the appointment and use Patrick's arm instead.

The ride back was mostly quiet. Patrick knew the boss was still sore and not in a great mood.

"Is Chicago looking for their man?" Danny asked.

"Haven't heard. I assume they would be seeing that there's been no contact. But then again, not sure how much contact he actually had. I figure he didn't report back very much. They may not even notice for another month or two," Patrick answered.

"Fuck 'em," Danny said coldly. "On another subject, Owney and Dwyer are thrilled with our last few months. We're moving more than anyone else in the Seven."

Patrick smiled. "That's what we do, boss."

"They're worried about repeal," Danny continued. "And, in my opinion, they should be. We're not going to make jack once it's legal."

"We'll have to find something else," suggested Patrick knowing the boss was right.

"Yeah, but what? The good news is that the numbers aren't going anywhere for now. Same with the races."

"That's true, boss. Plus, the protection money. That's not slowing down either. Same thing with the unions," Patrick said.

The business of controlling unions was good, reliable money for the Big Seven along with protecting local officials from outside threats.

Patrick had some other news for the boss that he knew would not make Danny happy. "So, our people in upstate New York found out that Chicago and some people direct from Canada are moving product near Albany again. Got a telegram from Owney's people. One of them was tipped off and decided to check for himself. Sure enough, he saw a delivery."

Danny sat silent for a few minutes. Then he spoke. "That territory is ours, but nobody seems to give a shit down in Manhattan. As long as their prize territories are protected, ours seem to be like a red headed step child. But who brings in more each month? We do! I don't get it."

Patrick continued driving south on U.S. Route 1 back to Rhode Island without another word. Danny didn't like the Chicago families, and they clearly didn't like him.

———

Fred Rockwell was running late and didn't attend the morning editorial meeting. As executive editor, he delegated most of those meetings to his city editor. Jesse saw the boss headed to the elevator and wanted to give him a quick update on his investigative piece on the Big Seven and the governor.

"Got a second?" he asked as Fred pushed the button for the elevator which was notoriously slow as the operator moved between floors waiting for anyone who needed more time.

"Depends on this new elevator operator," joked Fred. "What have you got?"

"Gold!"

"Gold? What does that mean."

"Gold, literally. Pike said the Big Seven not only paid the governor in cash, but they lavished him and his family with jewelry and other nice stuff. Best part," he paused, "He's got a record of it!"

Fred seemed taken aback by this news. He knew his pal Jesse had done his homework, but he hadn't really been sure where this story was going. Now he knew.

"No shit! A record of it? How?"

"The governor gave his wife a ruby necklace for her birthday last year. Now think back, do you remember that big late-night robbery at Tiffany's in New York two years ago?"

"Yeah, millions stolen. FBI said a couple of the Big Seven were part of the gang who were arrested. I thought they got all the loot back."

"That's what the press reports said and the line Tiffany took. Truth is, that necklace was one of a few pieces that were given to Owney Madden as tribute from the guys who did the job. They gave it to him before they were caught and arrested. Tiffany didn't want to admit that some of the goods got away before the arrests. They were embarrassed." Jesse explained.

"You're saying that the governor's wife's necklace was stolen from Tiffany by one of the Big Seven gang members?" Fred asked.

"That's exactly what I'm saying and that Owney used it as part of a down payment to buy influence. He gave it to the governor. Pike was there. He told me himself. It happened on a state business trip to New

York the governor took. I asked the NYPD for a list of the stolen goods, and there it was on the list," Jesse said trying to contain his excitement in telling the boss about his scoop.

Fred decided to pass on the elevator as Jesse briefed him on his story. So far, Fred had only caught a few bits and pieces of this investigative report. This part was huge.

"Is Pike on the record with all this?" Fred asked.

"Absolutely. He has more to give us, too. I would like to go back down to Florida and interview him again. This time on the company dime," Jesse said knowing that the paper would likely spend the money for his trip.

Fred was silent for a few moments. "Well, let's see were this goes," he said without actually looking at Jesse.

Jesse waited a few seconds before speaking in a more insistent tone. "Fred, we need to talk to Pike again."

"We will. Try calling him," Fred offered. "That's an expensive trip and would be better if we did it on the phone."

"He won't talk on the phone. You know those phone operators. A lot of them are snoopy and stay on the line sometimes. They're mostly all party lines. That's why I had to go down there myself the first time. We need to go back," insisted the reporter.

Fred pushed back. "Look, we're trending down when it comes to budget targets. See what you can do from here, and we'll look at it again in a month or so."

Jesse had not seen this side of Fred in a long time. Fred was a journalist first, company man second. Today, Jesse thought the contrary was true. "This is new for you. I'll get this story, and I'm sure you and the other bean counters will be glad to take credit," replied Jesse with a terse tone.

"I've got a meeting. We'll take another look at this later, Jess," Fred said ending the conversation and walking toward the stairs not waiting on the slow elevator.

Perplexed, Jesse walked away wondering what just happened.

———

CHAPTER 25

FEEDBACK

The car was something Ted's wife had wanted for a long time. For many people, cars were still a luxury they could simply not afford, especially during the depths of the depression. The job of a prohibition enforcement agent came with a car, so owning one didn't make financial sense for Ted, but Marge liked the idea of showing off. First it had been the larger beach house on the Cape, and now she had her sights set on a new Ford.

The dealer was one of only a few in New England where the cars were shown and sold. The good news for Ted was that he could meet Marge down at the dealership and be back after lunch.

"It's twelve hundred even," the sales person said as he showed Marge the 1930 Ford Model A Town Car sedan. "It's what everyone is talking about."

Ted spoke up. "I thought they were in the 700 range?"

"This is the Town Car edition. I can show you a Tudor at around 750," said the sales person who was already having a great year so far. Cars were quickly becoming the thing to have in everyone's driveway.

"Oh Ted, look at the craftsmanship on this," Marge said.

"Let's look at the Tudor," Ted replied.

The couple and the salesman walked the lot and landed next to a 1929 green Model A Tudor. This was the latest model, and Marge quickly opened the door and sat in the driver's seat. "Oh Ted, can you imagine taking friends in this?" she asked.

"What's the price on this one?" Ted asked still not enthused about the idea of buying a car.

"750," the salesman offered.

"Any wiggle room?"

"Maybe a little. Let me ask my boss."

"Law enforcement discount?" Ted asked.

"Stay here," the salesman said then walked to the brightly colored building a few steps away.

Marge continued to look at the car and decided to try all the seats. "Can you see the kids back here?"

Ted looked at her in the back seat and noticed the salesman returning with another man. Probably the sales manager Ted figured.

"Officer," the sales manager said extending his hand to shake.

"Agent, but no worry. Hi. Ted Connelly."

"Oh, agent. Very nice. So, Agent Connelly, how's $500 flat sound? We take care of our law enforcement here at Flannigan Ford."

Marge almost came out of her skin with joy.

"What's the catch?" Ted asked with a suspecting tone. He couldn't do anything else to cause a problem with his job.

"No catch, Agent Connelly. We discount all our cars for state and federal law enforcement officers. It's all legal, and we ask for nothing in return. Really a company 'thank you' for your service to our community," the sales manager responded with the same line he used many times before.

Ted looked at his wife. "How can we say no to that deal?" she asked him with wide eyes.

"We'll take it," Ted said closing the deal.

Marge was thrilled. Ted and the sales person walked back to the office as the manager and Marge went over the car's features.

Twenty minutes later, Ted emerged from the office and handed Marge the keys.

She almost knocked him over with a giant hug.

"You drive that home, and I'll drive my 'G-ride.' Be careful," Ted instructed.

As the two left the car lot headed home, the manager came back into the office as the salesman counted the cash. They didn't get many cash settlements on cars, but a sale was a sale he thought.

Across the street in the parking lot of the Celtic Bar, Special Agent Robbie Boone took a few pictures and then headed north for the office and to put his report of this transaction on paper.

———————

The light rain continued to fall on the barns around Aqueduct Racetrack. It was cool, and some of the horses had coats on. Doc Mason was making his rounds. He always checked all of the horses every Thursday before a big weekend of racing. Molly's Gem was a third-generation thoroughbred owned by one of the Rockefellers. They had lost two horses over the last three years to heart attacks. The fact that the horses were young and in good shape made the deaths even more odd. Doc Mason was inspecting Molly's front right shoe. He was also going to give her a vitamin shot. One of the barn hands was looking on. This particular barn hand had started six or seven months earlier, and Doc Mason was noticing that the new guy wasn't very good at some of the chores that came with the job. He was a young man named Eli with blond hair and a pale complexion. Except for Eli, all of the other barn hands were African Americans.

"Want me to hold the reigns, Doc?" Eli asked.

"Yeah, Eli. Just hold her steady. This one shoe looks loose," Doc Mason said as he put the three syringes he was holding in his hand on the ground. Molly was not a very good patient. She started making noise and backing up a bit. Both Doc Mason and Eli had to be careful.

"I'll hold her here if you want to get the saddle in the other stall," Eli suggested after seeing this technique done time after time to settle a horse. Once the saddle was put on the back of the horse, she would likely settle a bit. Doc Mason nodded in agreement, got up and went to the other stall leaving Eli alone and holding Molly. Eli looked down and picked up one of the syringes, quickly putting it in his coat pocket. Then he replaced it with an identical one. The syringe he replaced it with was a true vitamin boost.

"Let's try this," Doc Mason said upon returning with the saddle and lifting it up onto the back of the horse. Just as predicted, Molly calmed down so the doc could do his job with the shoe. A few minutes later, he finished by giving her one of the three shots and moving on to the next horse a few stalls down. She was scheduled to run in the first race later that evening. Eli stayed close to his boss in case he needed more help. Later on, Eli went for a coffee at a diner down the street where he handed the syringe he had taken to Detective Hal Robinson who joined him in the end booth.

"If this is the same as the last two, we're in business. I suspect it is," Detective Robinson of the NYPD said to his colleague who was more than ready for this undercover assignment to be over.

"I'm sure it is. That's the one that killed the horse last time and probably the time before that. This is a bad doc," Eli said. "Got to get right back. I'm tired of shoveling shit and ready for this thing to be over. Let's talk tomorrow." With that Eli got up and took his coffee to go.

———

Big Bill Dwyer wanted his crew to know that there would be consequences for going against the family and organization. What happened with Danny in Boston would not be repeated with his New York people. He took no prisoners when it came to disloyalty. He let them know, as did Owney with his crew. Kevin was with Owney when he called a meeting about loyalty. By the end of the meeting, each man knew what happened with the guy from Chicago and what the outcome would be should they decide to be a rat or worse.

"Anyone you suspect...anyone," Owney said looking at Kevin, now one of his top captains. "I want to know about it immediately. Kevin, I want fucking loyalty."

"You got it, boss," Kevin replied smartly. "We're on it."

The same message was repeated by all of the Big Seven bosses to their crews. The message was clear and out there on the streets: be disloyal and end up at the bottom of a river.

CHAPTER 26

DOUBLE DIPPING

James Warren was in early, but he didn't go directly up to his office. Instead, he went down to the basement of the Federal Building where he would find out if what he suspected was the truth. Special Agent Robbie Boone liked to meet in an old room that had once been used for interrogations. No one ever went down there unless it was to look for an old file or find some peace and quiet away from the bustle.

"Close the door," Robbie said to his equal. James led the squad upstairs, but Robbie worked directly for the regional director with no chain of command under him. That fact kept him independent from anyone else in the building.

"What have you got?" James asked. "Or should I guess?"

"Bad 'G' in the house. He's on the arm of the Big Seven, and he delivers," said Robbie in a matter of fact tone.

"Evidence?" James asked.

"He just bought a really nice car. Has a second house on the Cape, and we have pictures of him meeting with some of Danny Walsh's crew. Oh, and we have some photographs of him with a mystery woman. We're not sure who that is but suspect he has a little action on the side. Is that enough?" Robbie asked in a snarky tone.

James had never been a big fan of Ted Connelly. The two hadn't gotten along from the time Connelly had been assigned to his squad. In a way, he felt excited about busting one of his own.

"This went on right under your nose," Robbie continued with an accusatory tone. "Right under your nose."

Now James was annoyed. "Listen, you little piss ant, I have a whole squad to run. We do some great work upstairs. Connelly being an informant for the Big Seven has nothing to do with how I run my squad. He's a bad fish. That's all."

Robbie backed off a bit then asked, "How do you want to handle it?"

James didn't want to just bust him, but he really needed to catch him in the act.

"I have an idea," James said.

———————

Sister Judy Ann was walking down the path between the convent and the church when Father Ralph looked out the open window. "Good morning, Sister," Father Ralph said shouting out like a school kid. "How are you today?"

She looked up at the window and could see him behind the half opened stained glass. Laughing, she waved and said hello.

As she continued her morning walk along the path, the sun was just starting to get bright through a few clouds, and the birds were chirping on the mild early summer's day.

"Let's go to the beach!" Father Ralph said now walking out the back door of the church to catch up with her. The sound of the door slamming behind him was a familiar one. "I've got nothing pressing, and you love to look for shells."

The two had been to the beach together in the past, but only as good friends and to keep each other company. This time his tone seemed different to the young nun.

"That's temptation right there, Father," Sister replied.

"Really. Let's take a ride and get some sun," he insisted. Being the pastor meant he was in charge, and it was indeed a quiet Friday. "We've worked enough this week."

She thought about it for a few seconds. "Okay," she said with an excited tone. "Let me change."

A half hour later, Father Ralph and Sister Judy Ann were driving south down U.S. Highway 1 toward the town of Narragansett both now wearing civilian clothes.

"How about we stop and get some clam cakes?" Father Ralph suggested.

"Sounds like a plan," she answered.

An hour later the two were sitting by the ocean at Nicks Seafood splitting some of New England's finest food and sipping from a bottle of Bordeaux disguised as less than 1.28% alcohol content wine which was allowed under the Volstead Act.

The conversation was upbeat and almost festive as the two talked about music, sports and their childhoods. "Ever think of doing something different?" Father Ralph asked quietly.

"Today?" she asked, knowing that was probably not what he meant.

"You're silly," he pronounced. "Just silly. No really?"

That was not a question she had been expecting, and she had to give it some thought.

After an awkward minute of silence, she looked up at him. "Once in a great while. You?"

"Every time I look at you," he said as his words drifted into the air. They both sat silent. Then, he looked into her eyes and she did the same. The attraction was real. He touched her face and leaned in.

"No!" she said snapping out of what felt like a trance. "No, we can't, Ralph. We just can't."

He backed off disappointed. She took a sip of her wine. They were quiet as the waiter approached.

"More wine?" asked the young man who picked up the bottle and prepared to pour.

"Oh, none for me," Sister said. "Ralph?"

He was a bit aloof and finally said no to the waiter dismissing him.

"I want to marry you, Judy," he declared. "I will leave the priesthood and teach high school. You can do the same."

She sat silent for a moment or two.

"I can't leave the priesthood," she said then they both broke into loud laughter breaking the tension.

The two finished their lunch and wine, then went for a walk along the rocks high above the ocean which ran the length of the restaurant. Not another word was spoken about what he had proposed. The conversation went back to church and school business like nothing had happened.

Later that night as Sister Judy Ann returned to her lonely little room in the convent, her mind couldn't escape the words he had spoken. She decided she would pray about it, and maybe they would talk again another day about the future.

———————

"Hey we've got a problem," the editor told the governor during a meeting that had been scheduled weeks earlier. During this meeting the two men were supposed to be talking about future access for the paper and its reporters. "Pike is talking to one of my reporters. My guy is working on a story that will ruin both of us."

Always a thoughtful person, Governor Baker let this process before responding to his old friend. Rockwell had scored many kickbacks over the years on the down low. The money came from various sources, but mainly the Big Seven who looked at it as an investment to keep their guy in office.

"Who is it?"

"Jesse Young. My political reporter. You know him," Fred said then took a sip of the tea that the governor's assistant had provided before leaving the two alone in his State House office.

"Yeah. He's a pain in the ass. So, what are we going to do about it?" the governor asked.

"I'm trying to kill the story or at least keep him going in other directions. I'm also keeping him on other projects. I like Jesse. He's a friend and a good journalist," Fred answered.

"Don't you worry about the small things," lectured the governor. "I'm sure it will all work out. How far along is the story?"

"Sounds like he's still working on background. He asked to go back down to Florida and interview Pike again. That's his---"

"Pike! He's a fucking rat," the governor interrupted. "I thought he would just stay retired down in Florida."

"I squashed the Florida trip, but that doesn't mean Jesse won't go on his own dime," said Fred. "You just needed to know this should any of your people get an interview request from him. Also keep an eye on any staffers who may be talking to him. This place can leak like a rusty faucet sometimes."

Governor Baker took a sip of his tea then returned the cup made of fine china to its matching saucer. He sat silent for a few minutes. It was a bit awkward. Then he picked up the burning cigar and took a puff. "Don't you worry about it, Fred. This is small potatoes," he said with smoke coming out of his mouth at the same time. "Small potatoes."

Fred just nodded in agreement. They sat for a little longer and changed the subject before Fred took his leave. Governor Baker then picked up his phone which rang one of two secretaries.

"I have to stop by the pharmacy on the way home. Please tell Warren."

"Of course, governor," she said on the other end of the phone. Her next call was to the governor's driver for today, State Police Trooper Warren Lamb, letting him know of the slight change in his normal afternoon ride home.

———

CHAPTER 27

SOUTH SHORE

The smoke in the room was thick and acrid because almost everyone smoked. A few agents were non-smokers, but they all seemed oblivious to the haze in the conference room.

"How's it going, Ted?" asked Sergeant Jeff Howard who was walking into the room and saw his friend standing next to the wall, not yet seated at the long table.

"Good, Jeff," answered Ted. "How's Julia?"

"Super. Doing well. Heard you got Marge a new car. That's big stuff,"

"She earned it. Also got a good deal. Everyone's getting one these days," Ted explained trying to downplay the purchase.

"Too rich for my blood, but good luck with it," Jeff said to his longtime pal.

At that moment, James Warren came walking into the room as people started taking their seats.

"This won't take long, people. We have a little operation going down on the South Shore possibly later this week or next. Seems like the Big Seven is going to do a warehouse drop near Plymouth. Still getting some intel on this one, but looks like they need more room to store booze to sup-ply the speak's down there and on the Cape," he started.

"How big a warehouse?" asked Jeff.

"Big enough to hold a few truckloads, I'm sure," James answered. "Still thin now on details, but I'll let you know more as we get closer. Meanwhile, see what you can sniff out, and keep this in house for now. I don't want the local jurisdiction getting ahold of this. I want this one for us."

Each member of the squad knew that James was trying to add up his wins to show the bosses upstairs just how good a Fed he was. He hated sharing the credit for a good raid with any other agencies, especially local police.

"That's it for now," James said ending the meeting which had lasted only a few minutes. The agents filed out of the smoky conference room headed to their desks or the coffee pot. Agent Ted Connelly decided to go across the street for his coffee, a move Special Agent Robbie Boone noted from his window on the third floor.

———

The summer in New York could bring some nasty thunderstorms as was the case on this muggy afternoon. Kevin had the ledgers and a few days to play with knowing Owney's schedule and the fact that they would not be missed until the boss got back. He also wanted a guarantee from the Feds that his escape with Sally would not be a problem and that neither of them would face charges of any kind. They had been over this in the past, but he wanted to hear it once more before they made their move. Sally met him near Penn Station, and together they walked on the crowded New York streets to a deli on 33rd Street.

The sound of clinking dishes and smell of fresh doughnuts hit them in the face as they walked in the door. Special Agent Kent Davis was sitting just where he said he would be toward the back of the restaurant. They picked lunchtime because busy New Yorkers getting their food would pret-ty much ignore everything else going on.

"Right on time," Special Agent Davis said greeting the two before they sat across from him in the booth. "You want to get something to eat?"

"Kevin, get me a coffee and whatever you want," Sally said to her lover. With that, Kevin got up and went to stand in the line near the counter about half way to the entrance.

"Are we still good?" Kent asked his CI (confidential informant).

"We are," she replied. "Kevin wants to hear it from you again before we make our move."

"Okay. How's my friend, Owney?" the FBI 'G' man asked.

"He's not your friend. Believe me. He's out of town."

"Figured that from your phone call."

Kevin returned with two drinks and a big doughnut. He took a bite of the doughnut and a sip of his coffee. Then he spoke. "Talk to me," he said to the FBI guy across from him.

"We're all good. No worry. Once I get the ledgers, you two are free as birds to go wherever you want. We don't give a shit. We just want the records of Owney's business and the inner workings of the Big Seven," Agent Davis assured his freshest catch.

The noise of the crowd and workers in the deli made it so they had to speak up. Kevin didn't want to say too much. He just wanted that guarantee before they broke away to escape. His plan was to take Sally to Arizona for a couple of years under a different name and cover before finally settling in Florida once they were forgotten about. He figured Owney and the Big Seven would be weakened when Volstead was repealed. Clearly, they would still be a force to deal with in organized crime and the rackets, but Kevin was confident that their escape would be clean. Plus, he figured the distance would be too far for the Big Seven to worry about even if they found out where they were.

Sally just sat there as Kevin ate his doughnut and the 'G' man watched. "Is that all we have to talk about?" she asked her lover and future husband.

"Yeah, doll. I'm good," Kevin said. Then he looked at Agent Davis. "You can go. Instructions on where to pick up the ledgers will be forthcoming."

"Ah, no. We don't pick them up. You hand them to me, on my terms, then you're free to go. When you're ready to make the drop off and then escape, you let me know," he informed his informant.

Kevin really couldn't argue with him. Davis could have arrested them both on the spot with a list of charges that could put the two away for a long time. This deal was too sweet to mess with, and he didn't want to screw up his plans.

"Fine. Goodbye, Agent Davis. You can leave," Kevin said coldly. Sally sat silent and waved as the FBI agent got out of the booth and left the deli.

"I love you," Kevin said to Sally. "We're going to be so happy and so far away." He finished his doughnut, and the two got up and left the deli headed in different directions. Sally was going home to finish packing the essentials she would be taking. Kevin would do the same. Their plan was to drop the ledgers at the end of the week, one day before Owney was scheduled to return. It was all coming together nicely Kevin thought as he walked down busy 33rd Street thinking about the Arizona sun and warm weather that awaited the two.

———

Patrick got the call a few minutes after he woke up and barely after his first sip from the first coffee of the day. Mary was feeding breakfast to the kids. She knew it was Marky on the phone, and whenever he called during odd hours, it usually was not a good thing. The telephone operators listened in on many of the conversations they connected, so Patrick would talk generically then go to where he was told to get caught up on whatever was the real reason for the call.

"Marky is going to get you arrested, Patrick," Mary lectured as Patrick began to get his stuff together. Usually Marky would pick him up, but today he would have to drive himself. "He's a troubled kid," she continued. "Are you listening to me, Patrick?"

"Yeah, yeah. I hear you. He works for me. And if he works for me, he works for Danny. He's just a hot head and a kid who doesn't think sometimes before he acts," Patrick replied.

"I'm scared he's going to get you in trouble or bring trouble here to the house where the kids and I are," she said in a harsh tone.

Patrick took another sip of his coffee after getting his briefcase ready. Then he looked at his worried wife. "Has he ever before brought business to the house?"

"He brought liquor a few times."

"Mary, that's not trouble."

"It's not legal. The kids know it. I'm just tired, Patrick. Tired of worrying about you," she explained.

Patrick walked over to her and looked her in the eyes. "He's not going to be a problem, and we're not going to get in trouble. Not from Marky, the Feds or anyone," preached Patrick. "I've got to go. I'll be back at the usual time."

With that he went out the door, down to the car and drove a few miles to the office where Marky and Joey Cardin were waiting.

"What the fuck, guys?" Patrick asked with a tone clearly showing he was their boss.

"Two of our girls got into trouble last night with some clients," Marky started.

"How much trouble?" Patrick asked knowing he didn't want to hear the answer.

"The clients were cops, and both girls were about to get arrested," Joey said breaking his silence. "I was there."

Patrick looked over at Marky. "Were you there?"

"I came later. Joey was running the night. But that's not the whole story." Marky said.

"What else?" Patrick asked now looking at Joey who seemed scared.

"It seems one of the girls really didn't want to go to jail, so she took one of the cop's gun and shot him. Then she went next door and shot the other who was with Linda. The good news is that they were the last clients of the night."

The expression on Patrick's face couldn't hide the surprise and shock of this news. Always the company man, Patrick had to ask the toughest question. Did Danny know? The answer was probably no. Danny was smart to keep all of these businesses a few steps separated. He didn't like to hear this kind of thing.

"Marky! What the fuck man?" Patrick was now genuinely mad at both of these men. "They killed two cops? Do you know how big that is? Where are they?"

"The girls or the cops?" Joey asked.

"Both," Patrick snapped at his lieutenant.

"The girls are gone to Boston to get lost for a while. We dumped the cops in the Blackstone River," Marky said as a matter of fact with little to no emotion in his voice. A this point Joey was silent.

"Don't you two clowns think they're going to wash up someplace?" Patrick asked.

"Nope, we weighed them down good," Joey said proudly like he had done a good deed. "Used chains and some blocks. Did it around three in the morning."

Patrick looked at both men now pointing a finger at each. "I don't want Danny to know about this. He's just about back to full speed and doesn't need to hear any of this shit. I don't want you two talking about this ever again. They're going to come around asking for these guys. What do you suggest we tell them?"

Joey spoke first and had a nervous tone to his voice at the moment. "We say they were here but left after midnight. We ditched their cop car down near the falls, too."

"You've got their asses covered, but remember this: if it went down any differently than you're telling me, you'll both end up with them in the Blackstone. Read me?" Patrick said with a low but angry tone.

At that point Danny was coming in through the front door. The men had been talking in the back. They walked up toward the front where some desks were and then into Danny's office behind him.

"I'm pissed," Danny said speaking first and with a tone that reflected the mood.

Patrick, Joey and Marky stood silent thinking perhaps Danny knew about the murder of the cops by their prostitutes the night before.

"Did you hear me?" Danny asked.

"Heard you, boss," Patrick answered smartly. "What's up?" He clearly didn't want to give away anything until he could hear what Danny was talking about

"Another horse died up at Aqueduct. Just found out this morning from one of the handlers up there. What the hell is going on? That's four this year," he explained knowing these men would not have any answers but needing to vent to someone.

"One of yours, boss?" Joey asked Danny then looked at Patrick with a bit of relief on his face.

"No, thankfully. Not this time. One of the others in the same barn. Going to ask Doc Mason about his thoughts if I can ever get him on the phone."

Patrick chimed in. "I'm sure they're doing the best they can to see what's going on. Our money return has been good on some of those horses. Father Ralph's contact up there seems to have a lock sometimes. Lately they've been a little light on the number of races we can score on. But that should change for the better soon."

"Don't know his trick, but he sure can pick a race," Danny said then changed subjects. "What do we have today?"

———

CHAPTER 28

SUNSHINE STATE

The problem with bad news is that it doesn't stay put in any one place. Fred Rockwell's aggressive reporter's story about the governor's ties to the Big Seven and organized crime didn't stay in the corner office at the capitol in Providence. Danny controlled all the booze movement in this area, but as in all things political, a bad story could put a dent in or even end that operation. Then there was the question of the photographs they had of Fred. It could be a dirty business, and everyone knew that going in. Thomas Pike had pocketed his payoff and escaped to Florida, now living under another name with his 100 thousand. One of his favorite hangouts was the marina in St. Petersburg on Tampa Bay. It had a bar, and it was where he kept his small, 21-foot fishing boat. Fishing had been a passion since his childhood in Warwick, Rhode Island. Living in this part of Florida gave him fishing weather twelve months a year. A creature of habit, Thomas would typically start his day with coffee at a shop near his rented house. Then he would walk to the marina to fiddle with the boat and hang around with friends. All of them knew him as Frank Thomason, not Thomas Pike.

"Heading out today, Frank?" asked one of the young dock hands who also helped with the fueling of boats. "Looks like it's a little choppy out in the bay."

Thomas had just walked onto the dock. "Not today, Perry. Just going to clean her up a bit."

The dock hand went about his business as Thomas boarded his fishing boat. It was mostly an open boat with a center driving console. Under the console, there were a couple of compartments where he kept some tools and fishing tackle. It was also where he had a waterproof box. Reaching down into the bottom compartment, he felt around for the box, then pulled it out. He opened the box just to make sure its contents were still safe and dry. The ledger they had found with the body of the Bristol Gang member up north months ago was one of four that existed going back to the start of prohibition eleven years earlier when Governor Peter Baker was still the Mayor of Warwick, Rhode Island. His connections to the rackets had started well before he became the state's chief executive. Baker, Owney and Big Bill Dwyer knew of the existence of these other ledgers. Danny suspected they existed, but he had never seen them. Back then, he was just coming up. Each contained payouts and notes about those who were players and who were the enemies. They also had the actual signatures and initials of each man as they recorded the movement of money back during the early days of Volstead. In some sense they were Pike's get out of jail free card and, in fact, were keeping him alive. Before he had left for his forced, handsomely paid exile, he had let the governor know the ledgers existed and would be forever hidden away unless something happened to him. Thomas Pike had two brothers and told both where he would be living and under what name. He instructed his siblings on what to do should anything happen to him, where to get the ledgers and to whom they should bring them.

Thomas had mixed feelings about talking to the press. He knew the governor would do just about anything to keep this story out of the papers. Not to mention the Big Seven's reaction if they knew a story would be out there saying they had the governor in their stable of local and state officials on the payroll.

"How's it going, Frank?" asked a younger man who was walking down the dock. Thomas hadn't seen him before. His internal radar was up and running as he tried to assess this stranger who called him by his alias name.

"Good, thanks," Thomas replied, quickly pushing the box back into the storage compartment.

"Catch anything yet?" asked the tall, blond man who looked to be around thirty. He had pasty skin and clearly had not been in the Florida sun for long.

"Yesterday. Just cleaning today," Thomas replied in a friendly tone.

"Dave Doyle," the man said as he extended his hand across to the former chief of staff. "I do some charter work next door on the *Gifted Marie*," he continued while pointing to the next dock over. The *Gifted Marie* was an older charter fishing boat that looked like it could use some time in the yards for a refit.

"Nice to meet you. How's business been?" Thomas asked, still with his guard up.

"Quiet. Waiting for the tourists and snowbirds to come back," Dave explained. "Great looking boat."

"Thanks," Thomas said.

"Well, you take care, Frank," Dave said as he pulled his sunglasses down from where they had been resting on his head. "See you around the docks."

"You bet," Thomas said as Dave walked away. Something wasn't right in Thomas' gut about this guy.

Shrugging it off, there was work to be done on the boat of which Thomas completed about two hours later. He felt like an iced tea and sandwich now that it was coming up to lunchtime. Thomas really wanted a beer, but that would have to wait until later when some of the local speak's opened for business. Just down from the marina was a small restaurant and grocery combo called the Variety Store. Thomas decided to walk over and take a break. He went up the stairs to the entrance and sat at the counter. Marina workers, vacationers and some locals kept the little place busy most of the year.

He ordered a B.L.T. and tea. A few minutes later the dock hand from the Marina showed up looking for some grub after a busy morning. He took a seat just down from Thomas.

"Hi, Perry," Thomas started. "Busy morning?"

"Hey, Frank. You said it. Just crazy. Repairs and more repairs," said the younger dock hand of around twenty with dirty blond hair and a bit of a sunburn.

Thomas took a bite of his sandwich after the waitress delivered it. It had been his favorite sandwich since childhood back in New England. The waitress went to Perry to take his order next. Once he ordered, she headed for the kitchen to get some drinks.

Thomas looked over at Perry. "That guy from the *Gifted Marie* seems kind of nice. He stopped by as I was cleaning this morning."

The waitress returned with a lemonade for Perry, then went back to the other side of the counter. He took a sip, then spoke. "Eddie is a nice guy."

As soon as Perry said that, Thomas felt a knot in his stomach. "Eddie? He said his name was Dave. He said he owned that boat."

Perry took another sip of lemonade. "Maybe Eddie sold it, but I saw the old man on it yesterday. Don't know a Dave. There's only one name on the vessel documentation for *Gifted Marie*. Eddie's run that boat for years."

Thomas suddenly wasn't hungry. He waved to get the waitress' attention and gestured that he would like the check. "Oh, maybe the guy was mistaken, or maybe I got it wrong. Have you seen him around the docks before?"

The waitress returned with Perry's sandwich. He took a bite and paused for a second. Then he spoke. "I just saw him today before you got there. He was walking along the docks then stopped and chatted with you. I didn't pay much attention."

Thomas looked at the check, pulled out three coins and left them next to his plate. He looked over at Perry. "Thanks, my friend. By the way, if you see that Dave guy around again, can you let me know?"

Perry thought that was a little strange but assured Thomas that he would keep an eye out and tell him if Dave returned.

Thomas left the restaurant and started walking back toward the marina where his car was parked. He looked back over his shoulder a couple of times. He wondered if he was being paranoid. Was he just bring overly cautious? He got into his car and headed back to his house.

———

The best thing about having his blood pressure checked was that Ted Connelly could use the exam room in the Brockton, Massachusetts doctor's office. His family doctor knew what he did for a living and was always glad to accommodate the G-Man. The doctor felt he was doing something to contribute to the well-being of society by helping out his law enforcement patient.

"You're good to go, Ted. Keep the salt low, and you should have no problem. I'll send in your friend," the good doctor said. Ted waited about a minute or two, then the door opened and Patrick walked in closing it behind him.

"They're onto your little warehouse drop next week on the South Shore," Ted started right in. "You need to reschedule or relocate it."

Patrick thought about this for a few seconds. "What the fuck are you talking about?"

"We have good intel that you guys are planning a warehouse drop next week or the week after," Ted insisted.

"We're not doing warehouse drops anymore. Too risky. We're using bigger trucks to stage and move product. You've got some bad information, Agent Connelly," Patrick said, then continued. "Is that it? I don't want to be seen here or with you. You've completely wasted my afternoon driving all the way up here. Don't reach out unless you have some good intel."

Surprised, Ted looked at Patrick. "I don't unless I have good info and it's only to help you shitheads. Fuck you. Next time I'll just forget it."

"We're the shitheads who put money in your pocket. Lots of it. Careful not to bite the hand that feeds you. Wait a few minutes before leaving, too," Patrick said then walked out the door.

Ted followed a few minutes later and got into his government issued Ford. Something wasn't right about that intel, he thought as he cranked the engine. He backed out of the parking space next to the building then headed back north toward Boston.

A few minutes later, Special Agent Robbie Boone got out of his car parked across the street and went into the doctor's office. He wanted to have a conversation with the good doc, but it had nothing to do with his health.

They worked on creating new names and identities with the help of the Special Agent Davis. They knew once the exchange was made, they would have about a week's head start to their new life before Owney Madden and others with the Big Seven were brought down. Arizona was where Sally and Kevin told the FBI they were headed once they hit the road. What the FBI didn't know was that they both wanted Florida as their final destination. Kevin gave them a Phoenix address where the two would live temporarily and made no mention that the plan was to move after staying maybe three months out west. Each knew the risks involved with this disappearing act and wanted the first few months to have a number of different moves. Kevin also knew that this was a good strategy. Owney was due back by Friday. Their plan was to meet with the FBI Thursday, exchange the ledgers and affidavits, sign with a notary that what they said in the paperwork was true then be on their way with new names and lives. Special Agent Kent Davis insisted that the final meet up not be at One Police Plaza or at the Federal Building in Manhattan. He wanted to make sure they would not be followed or watched. Sally and Kevin appreciated his abundance of caution. The meeting was set for noon on Friday at a farm just across the Hudson River in New Jersey. That would put them on the road heading away from New York and their former lives with the Big Seven. Kevin had taken about twenty thousand dollars in cash that he had been skimming here and there off the top and put it inside a special compartment in his large suitcase. They finished packing and sipped some of Owney's whiskey talking about just where in Florida they would eventually like to settle.

———

CHAPTER 29

WIN, PLACE & SHOW

It was just after the fifth race of the day at Aqueduct, and Doc Mason was checking on a horse that had come in sixth place and seemed to be struggling. Eli was holding the reins. The odds on the horse had him as the favorite, and plenty of money was lost when he didn't even show.

"Hold him still, Eli," Doc said. "I'm going to give him another vitamin shot."

"That's the second today, isn't it? Didn't we give him one this morning before the race?"

"Yeah, that was a vitamin and booster," said the large animal vet. This horse belonged to a wealthy insurance man who lived on Long Island. The horse started kicking. "Easy, boy."

Minutes later, four men approached the stall in the barn. Doc Mason had his head on the other side of the horse and didn't see them.

"Are you Doctor Paul Mason?" the booming voice said as the four entered the stable stall.

"I am," Doc Mason said from the other side of the horse. "Who's asking?"

"NYPD Detective Hal Robinson. We have a warrant for your arrest."

That got the doctor's attention, and he stood up and walked to the other side of the thoroughbred. "What are you talking about?" Doc asked the lead detective.

"Eli, you do the honors," said the detective.

Eli turned to the doctor and pulled out a set of handcuffs he had on his belt under his shirt. "You're under arrest, Doc, for a number of charges including animal endangerment, conspiracy, fraud and more." He clicked on the cuffs without any problem.

Shocked, the doctor looked at Eli. "You're a cop?"

"Yes, and this is my boss and three other NYPD undercover officers. We've been watching you for months and testing some of your 'vitamin' shots. Those were meant to slow these horses down and ended up killing a few of them," Eli spelled out to the shocked vet.

"Secure the horse, Eli. We've got the doctor," Robinson ordered as he took the handcuffed prisoner by the arm.

A few minutes later, the horse was in his stall, and the police walked the doctor out of the stable to a waiting car. Members of the press had been tipped off, and a few flash bulbs exploded in his face as the officers placed him in the black 1928 Packard police car. Detective Robinson didn't like the press and wasn't going to wait around to cause more commotion than they already had. The chief of detectives was the one who had wanted the press there.

The police cars sped off through the back gate of Aqueduct on the way to a Queens substation in a cloud of dust. There was a lot to discuss with the good doctor.

———

181 miles north of Aqueduct, the phone rang in the rectory. Usually at this hour, it was someone calling Father Ralph about a parishioner who may be sick or dying. In this case, it was neither.

"Hello," answered Father Ralph.

"We have a big problem," the voice on the other side of the party line replied.

"Rudy?" Father Ralph asked just to confirm the guy calling was who he thought it was.

"Yeah, Father, we have a big problem, and we need to talk tonight. Not over the phone. These party lines have ears," Rudy replied in a tone that told Father Ralph something definitely was up.

"Come right over. I'll turn the light on."

Thirty minutes later, Rudy House and Todd Ellis appeared at the rectory door. It was about ten o'clock at night. Things were quiet and calm outside. Father Ralph answered the bell and invited the two men inside.

"What's all the hubbub about?" asked Father Ralph who had been rolling that question around in his head since they had hung up the phone about a half hour before.

"Your veterinarian friend is sitting in a police station in Queens," Todd said. Father Ralph had never really explained his system and how he picked the races, but these two were connected with the Big Seven, and after some investigating, it was easy to put the pieces together. They were not sure but suspected something was crooked with the vet and the winning or losing horses each month. Danny had started looking into the reason his horse, along with others, had died. Something wasn't adding up in his gut. Owney had a few people on the arm at Aqueduct, and they started sniffing around. They hadn't told Danny just yet, but let Rudy and Todd knew the vet was Father Ralph's connection to the races, and they were sharing in the profits of the scam. Owney planned on letting Danny know when he had more concrete evidence of just what it was they were doing. The arrest pretty much let the cat out of the bag, and with the connections the Big Seven had inside the NYPD, they now knew it all.

"Cops say your doctor pal was drugging the horses to slow them down, and a few have died over the last year," Todd said.

Father Ralph let this sink in for a minute before responding. "Do you boys want a drink?"

Todd looked at Rudy. "A drink? Did you hear what we've been saying?"

Father made himself a shorty with the whisky he had hidden. "I heard you," he said while making the drink.

"And just how long do you think it's going to take before they find out who the vet's been working with?" Rudy asked.

"How do we know he'll talk?" Father asked knowing the answer.

"He'll talk. Believe me. He'll sing like a blue jay," Todd said. "He'll talk about you then---"

"---about you guys and your operation," Father interrupted.

"Maybe I will have a drink," Rudy said with a bit of levity in his voice as he walked over and took a glass out of the kitchen cabinet.

The three men sat silently for a few minutes. The light was low in the kitchen as they thought about what had happened and what to do next.

"You've got a bigger problem, Father," Todd said finally breaking the awkward silence.

"The Church?" Father asked.

"Bigger than that," Todd continued.

"The Bishop?" Father asked again.

"Bigger than that," Todd continued.

Father Ralph sat silent.

"The Big Seven and, in particular, Danny. It was one of his horses that died at the hands of Doc Mason as a result your little scheme. He loved that horse and he's vowed to get to the bottom of what killed it. Typically, he doesn't take this kind of news well."

Suddenly Father Ralph felt a knot in his stomach. He knew who the Big Seven were and what they were capable of. He did business with them but always thought of them as a partner, not an adversary.

"That was an accident," Father said to his two guests. Now all three were drinking whisky.

"Doesn't matter, padre. The horse is dead. Danny will soon know the doc did it, and you were part of the deal. Might want to take a vacation someplace," Rudy injected into the conversation.

"Why are you telling me then? You work for these people," Father asked.

"Call it a gift, Father. We know what you've done for the community in spite of your nasty side business. Next time we come, it might be under different circumstances," Rudy said.

The men finished the bottle, and Father Ralph let them out the door into the calm night. Thoughts in his head were spinning around and more than a little confusing. Father Ralph worked to stay calm as he pondered what to do next.

———

It was rare that all three ships were in port at the same time. Captain Rick St. Pierre had some work to be done on the *Black Duck* including new belts for the engines that pushed her thought the rough waters off the Canadian and New England coasts. The *Goose* and the *Gander* were also in for some minor work. Each crew was caught up on deliveries and movements for the week. The land-based aircraft also took some of the load off of them. Even in summer, the chilly Canadian maritime air was blowing on this early morning in the Port of Miquelon on the small French island just off Nova Scotia known for smuggling whisky. Seagulls played in the wind making their trademark sound which echoed off the old brightly colored buildings.

Two men approached one of the deck hands who was replacing a line on the dock.

"Captain?" one of the men asked. He was large and had a Canadian accent. The other didn't talk.

"Up in the wheelhouse," said the deckhand while pointing up. "Feel free to go on up."

The men boarded the ship and made their way forward to the wheelhouse where Rick was working on some navigational charts. Coffee was brewing, and the smell hit the men as they walked from the cold into the warmth of the navigational space.

"Captain?" said the same man.

"Can I help you?" Captain Rick said not knowing these guys and wondering why his deck hand allowed them on board without asking. Rick always kept a pistol in the second drawer of the plot table which was in the back of the wheelhouse. The location of that gun was now very much on his mind.

"My name is Martini, like the drink. Some friends in Chicago asked us to drop by and inquire about a colleague who may have been on board your vessel not too long ago. His name is Tony O'Shea. He worked for your boss."

Rick shook the man's hand as he started talking. Then Rick backed a bit toward the navigational table where he knew the loaded firearm waited. Sipping on his coffee, he measured his words before speaking them.

"We haven't had a Tony O'Shea on the crew. Once in a while we get some help from the shore-based support, but I don't remember a guy by that name. You sure you have the right boat? Or maybe he went by another name?" Rick answered.

The men looked around the wheelhouse a bit before Mr. Martini replied. "You would have remembered him. He may have come aboard with some of the people who run your booze in New England. Kind of a young guy, stood about---"

Rick interrupted. "I don't know who you're talking about, Mr. Martini. You might want to try some of the other boats. I can also speak for the *Goose* and the *Gander* which are part of our little fleet."

Clearly this was going nowhere for the men from Chicago or wherever they were from.

"Is that all you fella's want?" Rick asked in a nice tone that also told them they were done. "Sorry you came all the way out here on a wild goose chase."

Mr. Martini offered his hand once again. "We're just being thorough for our friends in Chicago. We're thorough people. Thanks for your time. Let's go, Andy."

With that the two men left the wheelhouse and made their way off the boat. Rick waved to his deck hand who was now going to get a little bit of his bottom chewed by the boss for letting these guys on board without asking. Who they were was still a mystery, but Rick had a good idea and would let Danny and Owney know by wire that they had stopped by for a visit asking about Tony.

———

CHAPTER 30

ON THE RUN

She had only one suitcase and he had two. He wanted to make love one more time in Owney's bed before the two left the New York City brownstone and headed to the meeting place in Jersey. It was sort of like Kevin's middle finger to his soon to be ex-boss. Sally decided they didn't have time, and the couple would have to settle for a drink of Owney's whisky to toast to their new future away from this life and city.

The car had been tuned and fueled just a day before. The roads were busy heading out of the city on this early Friday morning. Dew was glistening off the trees and lawns as the landscape transformed from urban jungle to Jersey countryside. The weather was bright, and so was their future, Keven thought as he drove to the rendezvous point.

The farm was well off the main road as Kevin drove the 1927 Duesenberg Model X Boattail Roadster. Driving this car was the second middle finger to Owney. Kevin insisted they take the Duesenberg because that was the favorite vehicle of the boss. Sally had driven it a few times, but Kevin had never had the pleasure. It was Owney's special car, and no one touched it. His animosity toward Owney had started a few years back when he was looked down upon as just a worker bee. Eventually

Kevin would work himself up in the organization, but he was always jealous of everything Owney had. Jealous about the amounts of money the Big Seven made compared to what he was paid. Jealous about the love life Owney had with Sally and the girls on the side. Jealous about not getting credit where credit was due when it came to ideas Kevin brought to the table like using faster rum runners. Owney had an empire, or at least part of one, and Kevin was not even a stock holder. Just a worker. All that would change today as he walked away with the boss's wife, plenty of money and left enough evidence in the ledgers to give the FBI and Bureau of Prohibition plenty to lock him up with.

As the small dirt road narrowed, they approached the entrance to the farm which was gated. The gate had been left open. Agent Davis of the FBI had used this farm for other clandestine meetings in the past and liked that fact it was well away from public view. Kevin and Sally expected Special Agent Kent Davis and one other as a witness to the papers they would sign. The Black Ford "G-ride" was sitting next to the old barn with no men in sight.

Parking the Duesenberg behind the Ford next to the barn, the two got out of the car. The air was heavy and cool. The only sound was some blue jays playing in a nearby tree.

"I guess they're in the barn," Sally said. Kevin closed his door and started walking toward her. "Don't forget the ledgers."

Surprised by his own forgetfulness, he returned to the car and reached behind the seat for the pot of gold the FBI would use to charge Owney and other members of the Big Seven within the days and weeks to come.

Catching up with Sally, they both walked around to the front of the barn which had no door. Just inside stood Special Agent Kent Davis with another man Kevin didn't recognize. Kevin figured it was one of the Bureau's lawyers that Davis had said he would be bringing along.

"Good to see you two," Agent Davis said in a bit of a sarcastic tone. "I was afraid you would skip out on me."

Kevin looked at Sally then back at Agent Davis. "We have a deal, and I keep my word,"

The wind started to blow a bit, and a slight chill filled the air as Sally looked over to Special Agent Davis. "Let's get this done. I want to get the hell out of here."

"This is what you came for," Kevin said handing over the ledgers wrapped in red string.

Agent Davis took the ledgers from Kevin's hands and opened one up. Indeed, it was a treasure of notes, signatures, payoffs and more.

"Now what do we have to sign?" Kevin asked. The man with Agent Davis hadn't said a word yet. "Do you have the affidavit?" Kevin asked looking at the man in the black suit with no name. Kevin looked back at Agent Davis. "Do you have it? I want to get the hell out of here and on the road."

At that moment a loud, but familiar voice came booming into the barn from the opposite side from they were standing. "I have it."

Kevin's face turned white as snow as he actually felt a little light head-ed. He instantly recognized the voice.

"I have it." The voice boomed for a second time, but this time he could see the shadow of the man walking toward them from the back of the dark barn.

Kevin couldn't speak. He looked over at Sally. Then at Special Agent Davis.

The man approached Kevin and got right up close to his ear and gently whispered into it. "I have it."

"Owney!" Kevin managed to say. That was just about all he could say at the moment now that the reality of the situation started to sink in.

"Sally?" Kevin said looking over to his lover.

"Don't look at her," Owney said looking into Kevin's eyes. "Good job, by the way," he said to his wife.

"Sally?" Kevin repeated now with a questioning tone in his desperate voice. "What the fuck?"

The man Kevin didn't recognize was part of Big Bill Dwyer's crew.

Owney walked over to Special Agent Davis and gestured toward the man in the black suit Kevin had believed was a lawyer. Looking at Davis he spoke. "Keno here has your money. He also has two cases of our best Canadian to put in your car."

Owney had driven with Keno, and they were parked well out of sight before Kevin and Sally arrived.

"Now, what are we going to do with this piece of shit," Owney said pointing to Kevin. Keno pulled out a gun and pointed it at Kevin. Owney walked to the back of the barn where minutes before he had been hiding out waiting for the appropriate moment. He returned with a large rope with a noose tied to the end. He then reached into his coat pocket and pulled out a set of handcuffs. "You do the honors," Owney said to his wife tossing the cuffs to her. She grabbed Kevin's right arm, pulled it behind his back and cuffed the wrist before doing the same to the left arm. It was futile for him to resist.

"You're part of this, too?" Kevin asked looking over at Agent Davis.

"I have to make a living," Davis said with a wink of the eye toward Owney.

Owney took the rope and threw it to Big Keno as he was known with Dwyer's crew. Keno threw it over the closest beam about ten feet above them.

With Agent Davis, Sally and Owney looking on, Keno put the noose around Kevin's neck. Then he pulled just a bit to tighten it.

Owney walked over to Kevin and looked him in the eye. "Did you really think you were going to get away with this? Have I not talked about loyalty and what it means to me? This is going to be a lesson not only to you but to anyone else in this organization who is disloyal."

Kevin was silent. He looked over at Sally who managed a cruel smile.

Keno tied his end of the rope to an old farm crank used to lift and move hay. Then he looked at Owney.

"Goodbye, Kevin, and fuck you," Owney said coldly. With that, Keno started cranking until Kevin's neck was stretched backward, then jerkily pulled his body upward until his feet left the ground as his eyes rolled left and stopped blinking leaving a death stare Owney wished his whole crew could see.

The lifeless body swung as the chilly breeze rushed in and out of the barn off the surrounding hills.

"Keno's got this," Owney said to Sally knowing that Dwyer's man would dispose of the traitor after they left. "Let's go. I'm starved and want to get something to eat."

———

Humidity and Florida go hand in hand, but they're always worse in the summer. Jesse knew that when he took a week of vacation time and headed south to interview his key witness before completing the article which could finish the sitting governor of Rhode Island.

With almost five weeks of vacation on the books, Jesse felt this was time well spent. Plus, any excuse to go to Florida was a good excuse as far as he was concerned, even though it took a good two to three days to get there by car. Around the world, good journalists were starting to respect the award named after Joseph Pulitzer established thirteen years earlier in 1917, and many hoped their work would be deemed worthy of this honor. This was clearly in the back of Jesse's mind when driving south and working on such a big story, but awards were not his main motivation. Getting to the bottom of corruption was.

He had told only his family and the city editor at the paper that he was making another trip south. The city editor and he had collaborated quite a bit on background for this story, and they were also good friends. Very intentionally, he didn't want the rest of the newsroom to know what he was up to. Reporters are very protective of their stories and never want anyone getting the jump on them. The workflow in the newsroom was always busy. Fred Rockwell didn't sit in on all the editorial meetings, but he did make it a point to walk through the newsroom to chat with the troops. When Fred asked where Jesse was, the city editor confided in the boss about the trip and suggested that this story of Jesse's could blow the roof off the State House. Fred agreed and continued his walk stopping next at the sports desk.

Twenty minutes later, Fred was back upstairs in his office where he was about to go over the next quarter's budget. First, though, he picked up the phone. "Johnston 25433," he said to the operator who connected all calls. The operators were instructed to disconnect themselves from the line after the ringing started. The phone rang five times before being picked up. "We may have a little problem with our friend in Florida," Fred said in a quiet tone.

———

Two days later in Boston, Special Agent Ted Connelly was sitting at his desk when he looked at his phone messages. One of them said "Al would like to get coffee with you." He took that one, stuck it in his pocket, stood up and put on his sport coat. Then he walked over to the squad secretary who took the calls and acted like a gatekeeper for the agents.

"I'm going to run and get a coffee. You want one, Emma?" he asked the young 25-year-old sitting at an old wooden desk with cigarette burn marks all over it.

"No, thanks, Ted."

It was late morning, and things would be rather slow at the coffee shop after the typical morning rush he thought as he exited the door onto Scollay Plaza and a chilly late summer wind blowing off the harbor.

Minutes later he entered the coffee shop, and, as suspected, there were only a couple of people at the counter. The waiter at the far end of the counter refreshing a customer's coffee looked over and saw him enter.

Ted took a seat in the middle of the counter where there were no other patrons within listening distance. The waiter reached for a fresh coffee cup and saucer stacked on the shelf behind him and brought it over to Ted.

"Coffee?" he asked.

"Sure." Ted answered.

The waiter poured a cup and looked up and down the counter and around the shop to see if anyone was in ear shot. Thankfully, it was a quiet moment.

"You've got a problem," the man started to tell Ted. "You've been fin-gered, and they're going to arrest you."

At that moment, another customer in a nearby booth looked over to-ward Ted and the waiter asking for a refill.

"I've got you," the waiter said in a raised voice so the man in the booth and everyone else could hear. He grabbed his coffee pot and walked over to the man in the booth giving him a refill. Then he returned to stand in front of Ted still sitting at the counter trying to understand what was going on.

"Did you hear what I said?" the waiter asked again in a hushed tone.

"I heard you. What are you talking about?" Ted asked, still not sure what was going on. Was this some sort of trap? Had the Big Seven turned on him?

"We've got one of the Boston federal operators on the arm, and they heard a conversation between your boss and a guy named," he paused to pull out a piece of paper and read the name. "Agent Robbie Boone. This Agent Boone has been investigating, and they're going to pinch you. Needless to say, that would be big a problem for us."

Ted let that sink in as the waiter left him for another couple of minutes to attend to other customers. It dawned on Ted just then that the infor-mation about the warehouse raid he had given Patrick seemed to be false. Patrick said they were not using warehouses. Ted was finding it hard to tell who was telling the truth. The waiter returned.

"You need to get out of there. Time to retire before they retire you to Walpole while taking along some of our people."

Ted sat quietly, his thoughts swirling. Typically, this waiter never talk-ed to him. There were only notes back and forth. Clearly someone with the Big Seven wanted Ted to get this information as fast as possible.

"How long?" Ted asked. "When will they move?"

"No telling. They're probably building a case. Could be today, tomor-row or next month," said the waiter.

Ted took a sip of his now cool coffee. Then looked up and into the waiter's eyes.

"You speak for Patrick or Danny?" he asked.

"I do. This is what they told me to tell you."

"Thanks for the coffee," Ted said politely. With that he got up off the stool and headed for the door of the coffee shop. The waiter went back to his customers knowing he had passed the information along and done his job.

CHAPTER 31

THE CHASE

It didn't take long for Danny to get the word that his horse, along with others, had been fatally drugged by the crooked vet at Aqueduct. The arrest in New York made the papers, and one of Big Bill Dwyer's cop informants gave him the inside scoop. Dwyer called Danny personally to tell him what was going on. He also told him that the track's vet had not been working alone and had given up the name of a priest in Massachusetts who was his partner. The odd thing was that it was part of Danny's own gambling racket profiting from the scam, along with others in the Big Seven. He had no idea this was the trick the priest had been using to pick the races. As a lover of horses, this didn't sit well with him. The other bosses left it up to him whether to do anything with this information. Danny knew it was only a matter of time until law enforcement would track down and arrest the priest as well. Confession may be good for the soul, but for the Big Seven, it would be an embarrassment not to mention put a sizable dent in their gambling operation. Danny sat at his desk and picked up the phone to call Patrick.

———

The drive took two full days down U.S. 1 then across to Florida's west coast on roads that were often almost impassable for his 1927 Ford. Jesse always brought two extra tires on these road trips along with food and water. For summer, the sun was strong and reflecting off of Tampa Bay directly into his eyes as he waited at the park where they said they would meet up.

It was a little after lunch when the car approached with a cloud of dust trailing behind it down the dirt road. The rustic park was almost empty seeing that it was a Tuesday, and most people were working.

The car rolled up and stopped. The door opened and Thomas Pike stepped out wearing sunglasses and a hat. Jesse wasn't sure if they were for sun protection or to hide.

"How are you, my friend?" Jesse started as he approached the car to shake the hand of his best source.

"I'm not your friend. I'm just a guy trying to clear his name and live a life of peace away from the corruption back home," he said.

The two shook hands.

"I've got a little situation," Thomas said.

"Same here. You go first." Jesse replied.

"What do you have?" Thomas asked now with his curiosity piqued. "You came a long way, so I'm sure it's more important."

Jesse pulled out a cigarette and lit it. Then he looked at Pike. "A lot of people are going to be upset when this story comes out in the papers. Not just the governor. There are powerful people who may get hurt by this story. You need to make sure you're safe down here, and no one knows where you are."

Thomas looked at Jesse with a disgusted smirk on his face and shook his head. "Fuck me. I knew this was a bad idea to talk to you. Goddamn it," he said with a clear angry tone. "I guess I can't ask you to kill the story."

"It's too big now. My editor knows, and some of the people I've been interviewing are getting the idea."

Thomas walked a few steps away to smoke and think for a moment. He turned and walked back toward Jesse. "My situation is that a guy has been around asking about me at a few of the places I hang out. He approached me on the dock and said he was another boat owner which was bogus. My sixth sense said it was a weird encounter. Now some people have said he's been asking questions at other places."

Jesse thought this over for a few moments then spoke. "You could be in danger. The Big Seven have a pretty good footprint in South Florida. If they've found out you've been talking to me and that a story is coming out, that's a cause for concern."

"'Cause for concern?'" Thomas said in a mocking tone. "'Cause for concern?' Yeah, you don't know these people. Especially Madden and Dwyer. The New York crowd."

Thomas was silent for a few minutes. The sound of seagulls filled the air and he longed for his days growing up on Rhode Island's south shore.

Jesse broke the awkward silence. "You're pretty well hidden down here, Thomas."

Thomas looked in his eyes and put his index finger on Jesse's chest. "Who the fuck do you think put me here with this life and money? It wasn't the Feds!" he said in a scary, dark tone. "They know where I am and how to get to me."

Jesse took out his notebook. "I'd like to go over some of the story and timeline if you don't mind."

Thomas threw his cigarette to the ground and put it out with his foot. "Marina, tomorrow at noon. We can talk then." He paused. "If I show up. I've given you quite a lot." Then he got into his car, started it up and pulled away as the tires spun dirt back into the face of Jesse who was just standing there still not sure what had just transpired.

———

Twelve hundred miles north, Ted Connelly was back in his office in Boston. He never kept anything around that connected him to the Big Seven. Mostly it was money for information. That was it. The new car, house on the Cape and other goodies had started to draw the attention of his fellow law enforcement brothers, but in particular, the folks in Internal Affairs. Ted now felt the entire Bureau of Prohibition may have knowledge of his extracurricular activities. He wondered if he was being too paranoid. James Warren made an excuse three times that day to walk close enough to his desk to see what he was doing. That, in and of itself, was odd. Now he had a clue as to why.

"Hi, Ted," Sergeant Jeff Howard called out as he walked down the row of desks in the office. "Got a minute?"

Ted's stomach started to rumble. He couldn't just walk out of there right now.

"Yeah, Jeff. What's up?" he answered trying to act as normal as possible. Smoke was filling the squad room as agents worked at their desks with the occasional sound of a phone ringing in the background.

"That warehouse raid is on for the morning. The one James briefed. We're going to take down one of the Big Seven's stashes. It's close hold. Only you and a few other guys know about it, and we're going in with just a few people," he whispered on the down low.

Ted's training and background knew there was something wrong with this. He decided to probe a bit. "Eric joining us?"

His partner Eric was always involved in raids. Always.

"No Eric this time. He's off sick today, and we won't need him for this tomorrow. Oh, and mums the word on this one. Even here on the inside. Just be ready to leave at 0500."

Ted acknowledged his supervisor as Jeff walked away. It was time for Ted to call it a day, so he packed up his briefcase with more than the usual stuff he would take home. In the back of his mind, he knew this might be the last time he would sit at that desk. Ted had a stop to make on the way home. He needed to go to the bank before it closed.

—————

CHAPTER 32

PAYBACK

The whisky was flowing nicely on this Friday night, and most of the mill workers were descending down the stairs to the Central Avenue speakeasy in the basement of a small grocery store just a few doors from St. Cecelia's Catholic Church. Technically this place was a "secret," but walking by, everyone could smell the cigarette smoke coming from the basement windows that circled the bottom of the building. Even some of the off-duty Pawtucket policeman were in the house washing away their troubles after a long work week.

Marky was in the back room counting up cash that had come in the night before when they delivered ten cases of liquor to another speak' over the Massachusetts state line in South Attleboro.

"There's a guy looking for you at the bar," Lynn the barmaid said when she cracked the old wooden door open. "He asked for Patrick first. I told him he wasn't here, but you were."

"Be right out," Marky said. Lynn retreated back to the bar as Marky put away the money in a green velvet cash bag and left it on the desk. This was one of many company speak's in Danny's territory. Before he went out to the noisy and crowded bar, he made sure his Colt .38 was tucked in the small of his back and loaded.

A few minutes later, he came out from the back and approached the bar looking over at Lynn. She, in turn, looked toward a man sitting close to the end and nodded her head toward him. Marky made his way over to the man, walking up behind him.

"Who's looking for me?" Marky said to the man who had a black top-coat on. Instantly Marky thought it was far too warm at this time of year for that kind of coat.

"I'm looking for someone who might know where Tony O'Shea is," the man said trying to keep his voice low but still be heard over the Friday night crowd noise.

"Who's asking?" Marky said.

"A friend."

"He did some work for us a few months back, but we haven't seen him in a while," Marky answered. "What's your name?"

"Carl."

Marky had a feeling this guy was from Chicago.

"I'm supposed to find Tony," Carl said.

"Well, buddy, I don't know where Tony is," Marky replied then paused. He continued with a more sarcastic tone. "If that's his real name. But I have no idea. Maybe you should file a police report."

"Can we talk in private?" Carl asked. "I have something to tell Danny."

Marky looked over at Lynn who was serving whisky at the crowded bar. Then he looked back at Carl. "Come with me," he said to the visitor.

Carl got off his stool and followed Marky to the door that led to the back of the house. Lynn watched from the bar and didn't have a good feeling seeing the two of them head to the back alone.

Once the door shut behind them Marky spoke. "What do you want me to tell Danny?"

"I have something for him. A gift from some business associates," Carl said as he reached into his overcoat and pulled out a gift-wrapped box.

Marky had moved his right hand toward the small of his back where the Colt was hidden, just in case. When he saw the gift box, he relaxed a bit and took the same hand forward to receive the package. The noise of the speakeasy was in the background along with the smell of booze and smoke.

As Carl put the package in Marky's hand, he used his other hand to grab Marky's arm. All at once, the force of Carl's right hand with the gift box lunged into Marky's stomach and a five-inch chef's knife ripped through the box, through Marky's shirt and into his body. Carl pulled the knife out and repeated. On his third stab and with the knife in Marky's stomach, Carl pulled up and cut almost all the way to the base of the throat. Blood was spilling out on the floor as Marky's shocked face began to turn pale and the astonished look in his eyes transitioned from life to death.

Out front, Lynn continued to serve drinks at the bar as her helper worked the floor. The speakeasy usually had three people working the bar and floor, but the third hadn't yet showed up. Marky's job that night was to keep an eye on things and move the cash.

In the back room, Carl took off his coat, now soaked with blood, and wiped his shoes with it. He then pulled out a playing card from the jacket pocket and inserted it into Marky's mouth. Finished, he took the velvet sack of cash and threw the coat over Marky's body.

Walking out the door and closing it behind him, Carl went over to the bar.

"He said he doesn't want to be disturbed. I'm taking this back to Danny," he showed the green cash bag to Lynn who nodded. Except for not knowing exactly who he was, she was used to these sorts of comings and goings. Carl walked out the front door and into a waiting '28 Packard.

226

"Hi, Frank," the dockmaster said to Thomas as he approached from the parking lot. "Your pal is down waiting on the boat. I put that box you gave me in my locker."

Thomas looked down the dock and saw Jesse standing next to his boat. The bright Florida sun was starting to heat up the day. "Thanks, Perry. Keep it until either I take it back or that guy down there, Jesse, asks for it. Only give it to one of us."

He handed a five-dollar bill to the dockhand then quickly started down to the boat. As he approached, he saw the guy from a couple of days ago sitting inside the vessel. "Your friend Doyle here wants to go for a boat ride," Jesse said nervously. It became clear as Thomas approached the slip where his boat was tied that this guy Dave Doyle wasn't there on a social call. He had on a life jacket and his hand tucked inside held a loaded pistol. Jesse looked at Thomas then back at Doyle.

"Let's get going," Doyle ordered the two. "Come on, time's wasting."

The wind blew across the bay and into the marina bringing the morning to life. Thomas got into the boat and started the engine. The boat was backed into the slip. He looked up to Jesse still standing on the dock. "Stay up there and get ready to release the lines." Jesse did as he was told. "She's got to warm for a minute."

Dave Doyle sat toward the front of the boat facing back to watch the men. His gun was now more visible. The helm was near the back on a center console. Dave was clearly not at ease on the water. In fact, he had almost no experience on boats or on the water for that matter. He had one job to do today and then was going to the train station to start the long journey back to New England. "Let's go, damn it," he said to Thomas.

Thomas looked up at Jesse on the dock. He reached back to the fuel line that fed the engine from the tank. It was close to the floor of the boat and out of Dave's field of vision from the bow. He pulled it out of the removeable tank knowing the engine would run for maybe three minutes with whatever was left in the line and motor. "Release the lines and wait until I tell you to hop on."

Jesse untied the forward line and threw it into the boat and then went to loosen the aft line. The boat was now free from the dock. Thomas looked up at Jesse as he stood at the helm. In one motion, he took his right hand and pushed the engine throttle all the way forward to wide open then dove off the back. The boat immediately launched like a rocket out of the slip headed out into Tampa Bay with Dave on the front. Jesse immediately kneeled down on the dock to help Thomas climb out of the water. Dave was struggling to regain his balance and appeared to have dropped his gun in the confusion.

"They not only don't want this story to run; they want to kill you," Jesse said.

"Us, asshole. Us. They want to kill us both. Do you think that guy was just after me?"

Jesse let that sink in for a moment then spoke. "We have to get out of here. He's going to figure out how to drive that boat and be back."

"He'll have to row for a little while because it's going to run out of gas. Let's go."

Thomas and Jesse ran to the parking lot. Thomas told Perry who came running toward them that the boat had been stolen and that he should call the police immediately. That, he figured, would slow down Dave or whatever the guy's real name was.

Father Ralph went over to the school where Sister Judy Ann was teaching after he put a suitcase in his car which was parked on the street behind the classroom building. Since before the sun came, up he had been planning his departure and packing his civilian clothes. He didn't have the heart to tell her what was going on, but he needed to tell her something. After climbing the three sets of stairs, he walked into the school's third floor hallway. Father Ralph always recognized the smell inside the building since it was the same as when he had been a student himself there years ago.

One child came out of a classroom and walked by him on the way to the stairs. "Good morning, Father," the second grader said.

"Good morning," he said. As Father Ralph approached Sister Judy Ann's classroom, he looked out of one of the windows and saw a couple of local police officers talking to one of the groundskeepers who was pointing them to the rectory. He knew he had to get out of there fast or risk going to jail. He opened the door to her classroom and she stopped teaching as she saw him standing there.

"Hi, Father Ralph," she said with an upbeat tone. "Say hello, boys and girls." The kids all said hi as Sister walked to where he was standing. "What's wrong?" She could tell instantly that there was something on his mind. She also wondered why he was wearing street clothes on a weekday.

"I've got to go. Not sure when I'll be back." he said while backing away from the door into the hallway. She stood in the doorway with a lost look on her face. They looked at each other for what seemed like an eternity, but in reality, it was only a few seconds.

"I love you," he said in a very low, almost whisper of a voice.

She was silent as the kids looked on and wondered what was happening. Father Ralph looked at her one more time. He knew he couldn't give her a kiss there in public and in front of the students. He mouthed the words one more time. "I love you." Then in an instant he walked away headed quickly for the back staircase.

A couple of buildings over, the police knocked on the door of the rectory. They seemed in no hurry. They knocked again.

Father Ralph ran down the back staircase of the classroom building and out the emergency exit side door to his car waiting next to the curb. He grabbed the old gray jacket in the front seat and quickly put it on along with the hat he pulled out of his closet earlier in the day while packing.

The car started on the first try, and Father Ralph pulled away on the old dirt road that ran behind the school building. A few minutes later he was rolling down State Road 152 headed toward U.S. Route 1 north as his eyes filled with tears.

Back at the church and school, the local police officers and one FBI agent were moving from building to building on the campus looking for him.

"Have you seen Father Ralph?" one police officer asked a custodian. Most of the church community knew him well, and one of the officers was even a parishioner.

"Not for a while," the man replied while moving down the first-floor hall with a large broom. The policemen repeated this to no avail. Finally, they made it to the third floor and Sister Judy Ann's classroom. She opened the door and couldn't hold back the surprised look on her face.

"Have you seen Father Ralph," one of the policemen asked. She recognized the man from church but didn't know his name. The other two she had never seen before. She didn't know what this was all about. Things were spinning around in her head.

"Saw him this morning," she said not giving an exact time. At this point she had moved out into the hallway so that the kids couldn't hear what this was all about. She was very protective of the children. "Why are you looking for him? Is everything okay?"

"We have a warrant for his arrest out of New York State. Other than that, I can't comment," the officer said.

"Arrest?"

"Yes, Sister. We need to know where he is. Do you have any idea?"

"Not at all." This was the truth. Yes, she had seen Father Ralph just a little before they showed up at her door, but she had no idea where he went. Now her curiosity was kicking in. "Why do you want to arrest him?"

"Again, we can't comment on this investigation. If you know where he is and are holding back, you could also be charged," the FBI agent replied.

Her eyes opened wide at that news. "I would tell you if I knew. Clearly, I don't lie," she said while adjusting the veil to her nun's habit.

The police officers and FBI agent seemed taken aback and wouldn't press the issue with this Religious Sister of Mercy. "Thank you, Sister. If he makes contact with you or anyone else here at the school, please call us right away."

All three officers left the floor and building. They returned to the rectory and went inside after the custodian opened the door with the master key. Armed with a warrant to search his home, they did just that. There was nothing out of the ordinary except for what looked like some pretty high-end art work. Whatever this priest had done with the crooked veterinarian in New York, there was no sign of it here. The law men left and headed back to the police station.

With a thirty minute or so lead, Father Ralph was continuing to head north on U.S. Route 1.

Three hours later, two other men showed up at the church looking for Father Ralph. Sister Judy Ann saw them talking to one of the other teachers. These men looked somewhat familiar, and she thought she may have seen them in the past during soup kitchen. They didn't look like homeless, though. Once they walked away and got into a car, she walked over and asked her friend if they were policemen like earlier in the day.

"No, they said they were business associates," the teacher said. "Was Father Ralph part of another business? One of their names was Todd."

———

CHAPTER 33

BOTTOM LINE

The three men met again in Charlestown at Danny's farm. He enjoyed hosting the other bosses rather than take the train or drive all the way down to New York City. On those trips, he would always work in some time at Aqueduct.

The large farmhouse had a long porch on the back with comfortable chairs and a view of the six large paddocks that seemed to go on for miles. Horses grazed while goats kept the grass short. Late summer also brought out the mosquitos.

"How's that drink, Owney?" Danny asked.

"Perfect. Unlike your troubles with the Drucci organization. You know Capone has a piece of that, don't you?" Owney answered with a tone indicating that this was not a social call.

"They started taking over my territory in Western Mass and the Albany area of New York State. All of a sudden, our product was out and their product was in. We've been over this. They were costing me money, and I pushed back," Danny said defending himself and his operation.

Big Bill Dwyer chimed in. "We know, Danny. And I agree with you. That was your territory. This pissing match is costing money, and now it's cost us some soldiers, may they rest in peace."

Danny took a sip of his whisky. He was a hot-headed Irishman and more than a little set in his ways. Prohibition had made him rich and powerful. It had made them all rich and powerful. They knew it would come to an end soon and needed to plan for what would come after liquor was legal again. The Big Seven wanted to make nice with Chicago knowing business deals, both legal and otherwise, were in the future.

"How about a sit down?" Owney offered. "Let's meet halfway in Pittsburgh and make the peace."

Danny thought about that for a minute. He had lost one of his trusted lieutenants. There has been bloodshed on both sides. He had almost lost his own life. Pulling out a Cuban cigar, he lit it and took a large puff. While exhaling smoke he said, "Set it up."

Owney and Big Bill nodded their heads in agreement. There was just too much money in this and their other future ventures.

"We should invite the North Enders too," Danny offered. "Why not? We've been playing nice lately. Wouldn't hurt to sort all of this out."

Big Bill agreed. "Good idea. Boston is key for our future. They've got a nice chunk of business up there not to mention some judges and cops. I thought the Irish were big in Boston, and now the Italians have a good footprint."

Owney spoke next. "We thought it was the North End Gang who took those shots at you before you found out it was Chicago."

At that moment a woman came out of the house with some sandwiches and placed them on a table. She left as quickly as she had come. The men each took a sandwich.

"This is nice living, Danny," Big Bill said changing the subject to a more enjoyable one.

"Thank you, Bill. I like the room out here and having the horses around," Danny replied.

"I know you didn't have anything to do with the business of the dead horses at Aqueduct, but that was fucked up. Yes, we all made some money on the races, but that doctor was out of control. And the fact that it was the idea of a priest or partner or whatever. Jesus, Danny," Big Bill said.

Danny took another sip of his drink and a bite of the sandwich before continuing. The wind was blowing warm air across the farm, and the smell of manure would occasionally mix in. "That's being taken care of. Sad to see those horses wasted like that, including one of mine."

The men finished their sandwiches and would soon be headed to Providence where Patrick had prepared a fine night on the town along with some ladies from their operation in Blackstone Valley. Danny got up to go to the bathroom, still using his cane occasionally. He always kept the cane within reach, and each man sitting on that porch knew there was a .410 shotgun shell in the disguised gun's chamber at all times. The other Big Seven bosses liked the cane gun so much, each man had commissioned one from the same Belgian gunsmith and had them shipped across the Atlantic.

———

The sea was running around two feet just twelve miles off Groton, Connecticut where the *Black Duck* and the *Gander* offloaded 100 barrels each of Canadian whisky to the rum runners. A stiff south breeze was blowing, and the smell of diesel was washing over choppy waters. The maritime limit of the Coast Guard and U.S. Treasury had been extended from three to twelve miles five years earlier in the hope that the larger jurisdiction would put a bigger dent into smuggling operations. It didn't.

Captain Rick St. Pierre yelled down to the men on the first small boat tied along the port side to move faster. There was something amiss about this crew he thought as he supervised the offload. Of the four smaller rum runners, he hadn't seen this boat or these people before. Crews were all vetted by Big Bill's people on shore, and they were paid well. Occasionally, a prohibition agent would sneak into the operation only to be flushed out or paid off.

"Stay on your own vessel," Captain Rick yelled down to one of the four men on the first smaller boat who had decided to climb aboard the *Black Duck*. This was not typical protocol. It was also dangerous as the two boats rocked in the waves occasionally hitting each other's bumpers. Alarm bells starting going off in his head. The other three rum runners and crews were busy aft loading the barrels. Most were not paying attention to these guys.

In a flash of a second, the man who boarded *Black Duck* pulled out a Thompson submachine gun and pointed it up at Rick standing outside the pilot house. "Department of the Treasury, federal agents, you're all under arrest," the man yelled as his other three crew members pulled out weapons and produced badges.

Instantly crew members in the boat tied up just aft of the one the agents pulled out their own weapons, aimed and shot the G-man standing on the deck of the *Black Duck,* killing him instantly.

All of a sudden, the other three federal agents started firing back at the boats tied to the *Black Duck*'s aft section. Over on the *Gander* about a hundred hundred yards away, crews were now all producing weapons and firing.

Rick ducked into the pilot house and pulled out his pistol. He emerged and fired back at the agents still in the first boat. They returned fire hitting him in his shoulder knocking him back into the pilot house and to the floor.

It seemed like bullets were flying everywhere as the rum runner crews fired at the agents. Some were hitting the *Black Duck* putting small holes in the wooden hull.

"Untie us," one of the rum runner crew members yelled to a deck hand ducking by the rail on the *Black Duck*. He quickly jumped up and untied the smaller boat. They backed away from the *Black Duck* still firing at the agents in the boat secured to the front end. The pitch of the waves had picked up, and shots landed all around their targets as the boats rode the choppy ocean and the sea spray soaked everyone and everything.

Now an additional rum runner that had earlier been tied to the *Gander* was speeding toward the *Black Duck* with two men holding Tommys. As they closed, the shots began to find their targets. First one, then two and finally three agents were shot down. Rick, along with three other rum runners had been hit by bullets, one fatally.

In a moment the shooting stopped, and all that could be heard were the engines and the sound of the waves crashing together and against the boats. Four federal prohibition agents were dead along with one rum runner. Rick tied a towel around his shoulder and was holding pressure on it with his good arm and looking at the mess that had been made of the *Black Duck*. Through his pain, he was trying to assess their current situation.

"Get down below and check for leaks," he ordered his first officer, Jim, who was still shaken from the gunfight. "Grab their guns," he ordered another crew member pointing to the dead agents.

Both men did what they were told. By now all the small rum runner boats were untied from the *Black Duck* and the *Gander*. They took up a defense posture circling should another attack come. The rum runners were heavily loaded with barrels of whisky. "We're good. Head for shore," ordered Rick to the lead rum runner.

"This guy is alive," Little Tim, one of Big Bill Dwyer's crew yelled up to Rick.

"Bring him up on deck then untie that boat," Rick yelled back to the crew. The smell of gunpowder was starting to disperse as the winds picked up. From below, first officer Jim Studley returned with a report.

"We're taking on a small amount of water from bullet holes, but I've got Stan working on them. Should be okay. What do you want to do with him?" Jim said to Rick who clearly was in pain. The wounded agent had two bullets in his body. One in his arm the other in his leg.

Rick didn't suffer fools gladly. "Tie his feet to the forward anchor. Let him swing in the wind and the sea for a while," he ordered taking a page from the pirates of years past. Little Tim and one other crew member dragged the agent to the front of the boat as Jim looked after Rick's wound in the wheelhouse.

Using the rope that just hours ago secured barrels of Canadian whisky to the forward deck, the wounded agent's feet were tied to the large, black iron anchor. Then, as the agent's body hung upside down from the anchor, Rick ordered the smaller rum runner the Feds arrived in to be set on fire and released to drift away from the *Black Duck*.

"Let's get the hell out of here," Rick said to Jim.

"With pleasure," Jim said now at the helm and pushing the throttle forward.

"Zero five five," Rick ordered. "Make for Block Island."

The *Black Duck* picked up speed slowly as the seas also continued to build. The *Gander* did the same following about a thousand yards behind. Hanging upside down from the front anchor, the wounded agent smashed forward against the waves and then back against the solid oak of the forecastle. It didn't take long until any life left in him was gone as the battered body continued to be ripped apart by the force of the water and ship colliding.

Marge Connelly was standing in the kitchen when Ted arrived back at his house. He had close to five thousand dollars cash with him and was about to explain to his wife why they had to leave right away. For a minute, Ted thought perhaps she had been drinking. Then he looked at her hands that were covered in blood.

"What the fuck, Marge?" he managed to say once he collected himself. She was silent. He walked a few more feet into the kitchen and saw the body of Lenny Asquino lying next to the kitchen table. His pants were pulled down to his ankles, and a knife was still in his hand. Asquino had been a soldier for the North End Gang who also did business with Ted. Like he did with the Big Seven, Ted would sell information to North End members when they came asking or if he had some good intel to help them out. Neither they nor the Big Seven cared who Ted did business with, as long as his information was good and he didn't sell them out. The money for information side hustle had been profitable, but now it was time for Ted to retire, and this dead body had just put a big wrench into his plans.

"Marge?" he yelled to snap her out of what looked like shock.

"He tried to kill me, Ted," she said. "He was looking for you then decided to try to have his way with me when I said you were gone for the day."

"Holy shit," he said.

"He pulled me close and dropped his pants. I struggled to get away, and I thought it was actually working. I grabbed the knife from the sink. He came at me again trying to get the knife from my hand, but I kicked him then stuck it in his belly." Marge sounded strangely emotionless. "He looked surprised. I pulled it out and did it again. And again, until he was dead," she said beginning to sob, the realization of what had happened setting in. The smell of blood started to fill the room.

Ted was due to report the next morning at 5:00 a.m. Leaving now, he would have an eleven-hour head start before they realized he was gone.

"Get yourself together, Marge. I want you to wash your hands, go upstairs and pack very quickly for a few months away. We are leaving in fifteen minutes and taking the new car," he said calmly.

"I'm sorry I've got us into this mess," she said sadly while she started washing blood off her hands. A few minutes later she went upstairs and started packing not knowing that was just one of their problems. Ted knew the FBI and Bureau of Prohibition would be all over his house in the morning when he didn't show up to the office or for the bogus take down James was touting. Now, in addition, the North End Gang would also be looking for him thinking he killed their guy. Ted had an idea where to go and hide out, but he also knew the clock was ticking.

———

CHAPTER 34

CABIN FEVER

Sister Judy Ann had been to Vermont a few times with Father Ralph on occasional summer weekends, which for them, would be a Friday and Saturday. Five or six hours of driving each way would give them plenty of time together while exploring western New England. With fall about to kick off, the roads leading from Massachusetts to Vermont were often busy. Not so on this day; they were fine.

She started out heading north after lunch on the day after Father Ralph disappeared. It was a quiet Thursday, and with Friday off from school, Sister had until Monday morning to return to the church and school. Racing the sun, she drove the church's four door 1926 Chevrolet Series V Superior toward her destination as fast as the car would go. Thinking ahead, she had brought along an extra can of gas, now sitting on the back floor should she not find a gas station or worse, get lost. The downside was the gas smell from an occasional drop or two coming out as the car bounced along on some of the older roads with little or no pavement.

After almost five hours of driving, she shifted into low gear to make it up the steep, narrow road to the lake. The leaves on the Vermont trees had just started changing but had not yet fallen. The dirt road was soft in some places thanks to heavy rains that had been more on than off lately. The small, one-bedroom cabin sat on a lake, and it had a half-mile driveway cutting through the thick woods from the main road. As she turned into the path, her heart started beating faster seeing fresh tire tracks. Her hunch was starting to pay off. The skinny dirt driveway wound left, then right, then left again before allowing a view of the small wooden cabin. As it came into view, she saw Father Ralph's car sitting just outside and smoke coming from the single chimney. It had been a while since she had seen the cabin, but it looked just as it did in the past. She pulled her car up behind his. There wasn't enough room to park side by side.

Upon opening the door, the smell of Vermont pine rushed to greet her along with the chilly northeast wind famous in that part of the state known as the Northeast Kingdom. She instantly recognized the smell which was actually the reason Father Ralph and his family had built the place.

Sister Judy Ann walked up to the cabin door and knocked. No response. She knocked again. No response. Now she was starting to worry. The door was not locked, so she cracked it and looked in.

"Ralph," she said. Nothing in response. The fire was starting to burn out in the fireplace. She stepped inside. "Ralph?" she said again. Still nothing. The cabin was literally two rooms. The main room included the fireplace, living area and little kitchen toward the back. The bedroom was to the left and had a back door to the outside. She was afraid to look into the other room. The door leading to the bedroom was cracked open enough to peek inside. Slowly walking up to the door, she knocked on it causing it to open a little further with the classic creaking sound coming from the old, rusty hinges. Sister Judy Ann slowly and cautiously stuck her head into the room terrified she would find something bad. Then she saw it. The back door leading from the bedroom to the outside was wide open. The shadow of a man moving around could be seen from where she was now standing in the bedroom. As she approached the door, the chilly Vermont air swept in blowing the veil of her habit. The shadow suddenly disappeared. Strange, she thought as she walked through the back doorway into the outside.

"Jesus, Mary and Joseph," were the words she heard in a very familiar voice.

She quickly turned to see Father Ralph standing with his back pressed up against the cabin wall and a pistol in his right hand.

"Ralph!" she yelled.

"What are you doing here, Sister?" he said now starting to breathe normally after what had clearly been a scare for him. It was too late to hide the gun. He stuck it in his belt and walked over to her where she stood, and they embraced. One part of him was sorry she had come all this way, especially under the circumstances, while the other part was excited to see her.

"The cops are looking for you! So are some other men that have been by the soup kitchen in the past. What's going on, Ralph?" she asked now wanting the complete truth as to why he was there.

He looked down at the ground, then went over to pick up a couple of logs. "Come in and we can talk," he offered pointing to the door that she had just come out of.

"You're in trouble. I want to help," she said not even knowing the situation.

"Yes, I'm in a bit of trouble, but it's nothing you can help with," he started while putting the new logs on the fire after they walked into the living area. A bottle of wine sat half empty on the little table. It was real wine, not the weak stuff allowed by the Volstead Act with almost no alcohol. She knew he had some connections to get wine and occasional whisky brought to the rectory. Father Ralph took another wine glass from the shelf in the tiny kitchen area and filled it. "Here," he said handing her the glass.

She sat on the small couch across from him. He was seated on an old, brown leather chair closer to the fire.

"Let me start from the beginning," he said before taking a sip of his wine. "This old friend of mine is a large animal vet down in New York and works for two of the largest horse race tracks in the state. I wanted to raise money for the poor, and a little for myself, to be truthful. He had this idea about fixing the races, and we bet on them. All he had to do is give the horses, except the ones we wanted to win, a little sedative or something before whatever race we were betting on. It was brilliant, but--" he paused and actually choked up a bit. Sister Judy Ann sat silent. He continued. "I didn't know those horses would die. I would have never gone into this with Paul Mason. Never. Jesus, they're pissed, too."

She tried to understand what he was saying but didn't know the complete story. "'They?' Who's pissed?" she asked.

"That guy Todd, the Bristol Gang, the Big Seven. They're all the same really," he answered in a soft tone. "One of the horses that died was owned by a guy named Danny Walsh, the Big Seven boss of New England."

"Boss of New England? What the hell is that?" she asked now curious.

"They're the booze runners. The bootleggers. Speakeasy operators. The racket," he answered. "And they're pissed."

She took a bigger sip of her wine and then poured more into the glass. "Why were the cops there?"

"They arrested Paul. I'm sure he gave me up. That's why they came to the school," Father Ralph answered.

"Who were the other guys? I think one of them was named Todd, now that you mention it."

"The Big Seven. They probably want their money. Or worse. If the bosses know I was the other player in the horserace scam, I'm a dead man. And you can't stay here if that's the case. They'll kill you, too. These are not nice people, Judy," he continued explaining.

The fire crackled in the background. If it weren't for the current situation, this would have been a very romantic setting.

She listened to his story, and for some odd reason, she could sympathize with him because his intentions had been to help those less fortunate. Yes, he had profited from this scheme as well. Yes, that was a sin. But she knew there may have been some good coming from the bad. The dead horses, on the other hand, were another matter.

"Where the hell did you get a gun?" she asked changing the subject slightly.

"I've had it since I was a kid," he said. "Never actually thought I would need it. Used to shoot cans out behind the old school in Rumford."

The two sat silent for a few minutes. The fire crackled. The wind blew outside, and some of the cool, mountain air sneaked through the cracks in the logs that made up the old cabin.

Father Ralph moved to the couch and sat next to her. Her face in the light of the fire was too much for him. He reached over and kissed her on the mouth. She didn't object or back away. She had known deep down that this day might arrive. What she didn't know was the more than un-usual circumstances that would surround it. But at the moment, both had passion in their eyes. She almost ripped his shirt off as he moved his hand up her leg under the habit that represented the religion she was committed to.

"Ralph, no," Judy's voice was husky, but determined. "I'm pretty sure I've been in love with you for as long as I can remember, but we just can't. Not like this."

Ralph pulled away with a sigh. Their service to God would always be a part of their lives, but now they had entered a new chapter, and each knew it would be as part of the laity. "We've got a lot to figure out. You're right, as always."

"What's that noise?" Sister Judy Ann asked as she looked up and out toward the front of the cabin where there was a single window. It was get-ting dark.

"I didn't hear anything," Ralph said not wanting this moment in time to end.

She sat up and took a sip of her wine. He did the same.

"There it is again," she said, and this time he heard it, too. The sound came from the woods just outside the front door and to the left of the driveway.

"Stay here," he said while quickly straightening his pants and shirt. Ralph walked toward the window to take a look outside. Surely, they couldn't have found him here, he thought with dread. Then again, he was more scared of the Big Seven than the Feds.

Looking back down the driveway, he could see another car parked about 100 yards away. Instantly his stomach turned. He knew they had company. Ralph went back to the coffee table next to the couch and picked up his pistol. "Get up! Hurry and go in the bedroom, and lock the back door. Stay out of sight," he whispered. She did what he said immediately.

Ralph looked back out the window carefully to see what kind of a car it was. The sun had just set, and dusk was quickly turning into night. The smell of the fire was now diminishing for lack of fresh wood. The car was too far away for him to read the license plate on the front, but from what he saw, Ralph figured it to be a "G."

Judy Ann peeked out of the bedroom after a few endless minutes looking for more instructions.

Ralph walked back to where she was standing and whispered. "There's a car down the driveway. We're not alone. Looks like a 'G,'" he said. "I'm going to check it out," he said.

"No! You should stay right here," she said concerned now for his safety should he leave the cabin.

"It's probably nothing. Have a seat and sip your wine," he ordered. Then Ralph slowly opened the front door with one hand and his old Colt .25 caliber pistol in the other. Darkness was quickly overtaking the cabin and the surrounding woods. He had no lantern to guide him. There was some light, though, from the window of the cabin, and he knew this property like the back of his hand. He walked down the short dirt path toward where his car and Judy's were parked. Ralph thought he saw a lantern light in the distance, but it was hard to judge given the darkness. Sister Judy remained back inside the cabin. The darkness now enveloped the new arrival's car down the driveway, and he couldn't see it at all any more. All around him was complete silence except for some crickets chirping. A loud noise came from the bushes just a few feet away and to the right of the cars startling Father Ralph. His heart raced. Just then he could see the eyes and antlers of a young buck. The deer's head turned and its eyes stared at Ralph for what seemed to be an eternity. Finally, the deer jumped through the bushes and hopped away into the woods.

Almost in the same instant, before he could turn his attention back to the additional car in the driveway, he felt a cold sensation on the back of his skull. Then he heard the telltale sound of a hammer being pulled back on a gun. It was now pitch dark, and cooler winds started blowing through the woods.

"Don't move an inch," the voice in the darkness said quietly and calmly. Ralph figured he was a dead man and said a quick prayer closing his eyes. The cold hand of the man standing behind took the gun out of Ralph's hand. Almost at the same time, the man in the dark violently yanked him around to look at his face. At that moment both men were in shock.

"Fuck me," screamed the guy who now had Ralph's arm pulled behind his back, clearly from law enforcement training.

"Holy shit! I could have shot you," Ralph said almost wanting to vomit right then and there from the stress.

The man released Ralph's hand and tried to catch his breath while backing away.

"Ralph!!!" he said.

"Ted!!!" Ralph said.

The two brothers then embraced as tears started to flow for both men, now happy to see each other.

"Marge," Ted yelled into the darkness of the driveway. "Marge, come on out."

A minute later Marge walked down the driveway with a small gas lantern in one hand and a completely shocked expression as she saw her brother-in-law the priest standing there.

Ralph yelled back toward the cabin. "Judy...look who's---"

"Is that Ted?" she interrupted in a yell from the other side of the cabin door.

Pointing back to the cabin, Ted took charge. "Come on, let's get inside, everyone."

Ralph entered the cabin and immediately took three fresh logs off the pile near the door, adding them to the dying fire.

The women were laughing at this crazy, unplanned reunion. Ted took the lantern Marge had and returned to his car about halfway down the driveway to move it closer. Then he came back inside carrying three bottles.

"You're breaking the law," Ralph joked as he pointed to the two bottles of whisky and one Scotch.

Ted opened the first bottle as Ralph went to the small kitchen to get four small glasses. They didn't match, but no one cared. "Three fingers for each," Ted said has he poured.

All four people took a glass and looked at each other.

"To hiding in the woods," Ted said with a bit of a sarcastic tone while raising his glass.

They each had a few sips of the whisky as the fire now crackled loudly from the fresh wood while illuminating the cabin brighter than it had been.

"What do you mean hiding?" Ralph asked breaking the silence.

"It's a long story. I'm in a bit of trouble," he paused. "We're in a bit of trouble, actually," Ted continued pointing at Marge. He went on to explain the payoffs he'd taken and that his boss had set up a bogus raid in order to trap him knowing that Ted would leak the details about the fake raid to the Big Seven. Then he explained the murder in their kitchen of the North End Gang member.

Ralph and Judy Ann were in more than a bit of shock trying to digest all of this information at once. Then it was Ralph's turn.

"I've got a confession to make as well," Ralph started. He explained the scam with the horses, the money they were making fixing races and the fact that some of the thoroughbreds had accidentally died in the process, including one owned by a Big Seven boss. Judy Ann hadn't heard the whole story laid out this way, and she also had to try to process this information as well as her newly acknowledged feelings for Ralph.

"The Feds and the Big Seven are after us," Ralph said. "That's why I came up here to the cabin. Then Judy came looking for me. We'll be here at least for a couple of days until we can head to Canada."

Ted couldn't resist the irony of the moment and took a sip of his whisky before giving his current state of affairs. "The Feds and The North End Gang are after us," he admitted. "Looks like Canada will be a new home for all of us. That's if we can get there alive and not arrested."

In spite of their predicament, Judy Ann smiled at Ralph's use of the word "we."

CHAPTER 35

TROPICAL HEAT

It took about 45 minutes to arrive at Thomas' rented house. He and Jesse parked the car in the driveway and walked up to the front door. Thomas was getting out his key when Jesse pushed the door open with his finger.

"Forget the key," Jesse said. "They've already been here." Ever the good reporter, Jesse took out his notebook.

"Oh no," Thomas said walking into his house where everything was turned upside down. "Oh no."

"What were they looking for, Thomas?" Jesse asked knowing that people don't do this type of ransacking unless they were after something specific.

Thomas sat down at the kitchen table after picking up one of the overturned chairs. Then he looked at Jesse. "That guy would have killed us both if he, or they, had found what they were looking for."

That knowledge gave Jesse pause. He knew he had a big story about the bootleggers, the rackets and the governor. What he didn't know was that his best source had some goods on them, too.

"Ledgers?" Jesse asked figuring it was the only thing that the Big Seven, the governor or whoever would be looking for. Yes, they wanted to kill the story, but more importantly, they wanted those books back containing all the incriminating evidence hand written inside along with other documentation.

"Yeah. How'd you know?" Thomas asked.

"Good guess. Most people have an insurance policy. If they found them, yours has officially expired," Jesse replied.

Thomas picked around the mess for a bit looking for a few things. The money he had from the golden parachute, however, was safely tucked away in a few different banks.

"We need to go," Jesse said. Thomas knew that as well. The man on the boat would be back to shore soon, pissed, and no doubt he would return here first.

"You're right," Thomas answered. "That guy will kill us both if he gets those books."

"He'll kill you. I'm just a reporter," Jesse replied with a lighter tone to bring a little levity to the conversation.

Thomas looked at him, walked over and put his index finger into the reporter's chest. "They want that story dead. I'm not the only one that could end up with cement shoes at the bottom of Tampa Bay."

Jesse had to think about that for a few minutes. Come to think of it, how did the governor's office or the Big Seven know he was down there, and was it just a coincidence that this guy had come looking for them both? The gunman clearly knew both of their names. Only two people from the newsroom had any knowledge that he was in Florida.

"As long as the books are safe, they won't touch you," Jesse offered. "Are they safe?"

"For now, unless this guy finds them. I gave them to Perry the dock hand at the marina to hide and told him only I or you could take them back," Thomas said.

Jesse thought about that for a few minutes as Thomas finished picking out the things he wanted to take. "Jesus, let's hope Perry knows how valuable those books are!"

"Or not," Thomas said. "If he knew how valuable they were to these people, he might even try to sell them back for a lot of money. Either way, there's a target on both of our heads."

The men left the house and got into Jesse's car. The older Ford took a few moments to start which added more stress to the situation. Finally, it did. "Where to?" Jesse asked.

"Back to the marina first," Thomas answered.

"The marina! Are you crazy?" Jesse exclaimed.

"It's the last place he'll look for us. We'll make sure he's not around, get the books and head north. I have an idea," Thomas said.

———

The weather in Pawtucket was cloudy, and a taste of fall was in the air as the morning coffee crowd squeezed into the Modern Diner to start another week. For most of the clientele, after they had breakfast it was off to the factories that made up this industrial city just north of the capital, Providence.

The smell of brewing coffee and burning cigarettes hit Patrick as he entered the restaurant looking for the newspaper editor. Toward the middle, he could see the back of Fred Rockwell's head occupying a booth. As part of standard operating practice after Marky's murder, Patrick had Joey Cardin with him. Joey stood close to the door watching everyone in the place while Patrick made his way to the booth.

"You promised me nothing was going to happen to my people," Fred started with an ugly tone.

"What are you talking about?" Patrick answered.

"We have people in Florida. We have a sister newspaper in Tampa. I let you people know Jesse was going there as a courtesy. So that you know about the story he's working on. Not to hurt him. I don't care about Pike, but you can't touch one of my reporters," lectured Fred.

A waitress approached. "Coffee?"

"Yes, please, two sugars," Patrick said staring into Fred's eyes without looking at the waitress.

She quickly disappeared. Patrick spoke. "I don't know what you're talking about, Fred. You have a very active imagination."

"Fuck you, Patrick," Fred replied in a low, hostile tone. "I know about you people. If anything happens to him, the story he's working on will end up on the front page with three-inch headlines immediately."

The waitress returned as Patrick sat back and she put the hot coffee in front of him. The sound of clanking dishes filled the air along with the smell of breakfast. She retreated after the coffee was served.

"Again, we pay you to help keep a lid on bad stories that may create problems for our little operation." Patrick said as he reached into his coat pocket and pulled out an envelope filled with cash. "And you've been good, Freddy. Really good. There's a little bonus in it this month for you."

Fred took the envelope from the table and tucked it away inside of his coat.

The two men sat silent for a few minutes as they sipped their coffee.

"How's Linda doing?" Patrick asked. "She's such a nice dame."

Fred's stomach began to turn with that question. The last thing he wanted was to get her involved in his little side hustle. He also knew about the pictures they had of him.

"Forget Linda," Fred said sternly. "This is just business between you and me."

Patrick calmly sipped his coffee as Joey looked on from the doorway keeping an eye on any possible problems that could arise. Joey knew Fred was a newspaper man and no real physical threat. What he didn't comprehend was how much of an existential threat he was. Patrick, Danny and the other bosses of the Big Seven did, though.

"Just do your job, Fred. Say hi to that fine-looking doll, Linda," Patrick said before taking a final sip of his coffee, getting up and walking toward the door. Seconds later, he and Joey got into their car and headed to meet Danny.

CHAPTER 36

CONNECTIONS

The entire Bureau of Prohibition Boston office was buzzing about Ted, his wife and the murder that had taken place at his home. James Warren had issued arrest warrants for both Ted and his wife, Marge. He called an urgent meeting the morning after the murder was discovered with the squad and said it was their number one priority to find the fugitives now on the run.

Special Agent Eric Thompson was still in shock over the news that his partner was selling information to the bootleggers. Not just the Big Seven, but the North End Gang as well. And murder? Could his partner commit murder? These were the questions rolling around his head as James called him into his office.

"You know Connelly better than anyone in this squad. Where is he?" James asked in his usual condescending tone and getting right to the point.

"What the hell are you talking about, James? I resent the implication that I know where he is. I don't. We don't socialize. Ted was my partner, yes. He was a loner and went home after every shift or out to his house on the Cape," Eric said in a clearly angry tone. He didn't like his boss's accusation that he might have knowledge of Ted's plans or whereabouts.

"Yeah, we had Falmouth P.D. check the Cape house, and it was empty, but they have a unit watching the place," James said to him while looking out the window. "Anything you might know, we need to know."

"If he's not there or at their family cabin, I have no idea where he is. Who knows how long a head start he's had? At least 24 hours," Eric said to his boss.

James turned around and looked at Eric. "What family cabin?"

"Ted shares an old family cabin up in Vermont with his brother, the priest. He's mentioned it once or twice," Eric told James who clearly didn't know about this place.

"Are you fucking kidding me?" James asked in a hostile, sarcastic tone. He picked up the phone. "Back Bay 29934," he told the operator who connected him with the Internal Affairs Division two floors above him. "Robbie, one of my guys just told me he's got a place in Vermont."

———

They watched the marina office from across the street for about 45 minutes. His boat was back, but it was clearly parked at another dock. Someone must have helped Doyle return. There was no sign of his car. A few minutes later, Perry came out of the office and filled a jug with water from one of the hoses on the first dock. Everything looked normal. Jesse was in the driver's seat with the engine running, should they need to make a fast getaway, as Thomas got out and cautiously made his way to the marina office.

Perry returned to the office just as Thomas was about to open the door. They met and shook hands.

"Hi, Frank. Hey, what happened with that guy getting stuck on your boat? We finally had to send someone out there to tow him back. He was like three or four miles out."

"Don't worry about him. He had the wrong boat," Thomas said to Perry who still knew him by his alias, Frank. "You have that box for me?"

The two men walked into the office as Perry went behind the counter and pulled out the box Thomas had given him for safe keeping.

"Got it right here," Perry said with a smile. The skinny college age dock hand was proud he had done his friend a favor and wondered what was so important inside. "You got booze in there, don't you Frank?"

In spite of all that was happening, Thomas couldn't help but chuckle at his young friend as he gave him a ten-dollar bill as thanks. Then he asked to make a phone call and for Perry to step out of the room for a minute.

Returning to the car with the box, Thomas kept a sharp lookout for any signs of Doyle.

"Let's get out of here," he told Jesse while climbing into the Model A still clutching the box like it was a life preserver. In some sense, it was.

The two sped off with a cloud of dust trailing the black Ford.

———

About 36 hours later, 1,453 miles north just outside St. Johnsbury, Vermont, before the sun came across the horizon, a squad of G-men closed in on the small cabin in the woods. With them were a couple of the men from the Boston office including Ted's supervisor, James Warren. The others were from the Burlington Field Office of the F.B.I.

They surrounded the cabin which had no light emanating from the one window in front. A couple of agents also watched over the car in the driveway.

Special Agent Gary Goldman, better known to his pals in the Bureau as the "Real G-Man," led the squad and quietly approached the back door. With men watching the front, Goldman wanted to approach from the rear thinking that they could still be sleeping in the bedroom. The dim light of the American Eveready Company's newly invented battery powered flashlight with its tungsten filament bulb illuminated the door. The chill of the Vermont early morning could be felt through the long, black trench coats the men were wearing.

"Ready?" Goldman whispered looking across at the other two men standing on either side. Both nodded in the affirmative. "Go," he said as they breached the door entering the bedroom of the small cabin.

"Federal agents," he yelled into the darkness. Simultaneously, the men at the front door did the same. Once inside, using their flashlights, they found two lanterns and lit them.

"We're clear," James Warren said to Goldman as they met in the middle of the living room still high from the adrenaline rush of the raid.

Goldman looked over at his other men now entering the cabin. One told him the car was also clear and empty.

"Shit," he said out loud as everyone else said the same to themselves.

———

Upstate New York was still in a state of confusion as to who controlled that territory. Owney and Big Bill really didn't care. They had plenty of territory from New England down to the Bahamas. It was Danny who still wanted to control that part of the Empire State. With the Volstead Act getting ready to be repealed, he knew that the more territory he controlled, the better it would be in the post-Volstead world of legal liquor. Profits were going to drop as prices clearly would do the same. He wanted to make sure he made up for that with volume. There was no argument about Vermont and the rest of New England. That was Danny's and the Big Seven's.

Lake George was just north of the town of Glens Falls. Chicago controlled the flow of booze to many of the speakeasys around the lake and the small towns like Queensbury.

One of the larger Chicago-supplied speakeasys in Glens Falls and two others in Queensbury were raided by the Bureau of Prohibition after a tip about the operation was leaked to them. Thousands of gallons of liquor were confiscated and destroyed. All three were out of business and their staffs arrested. The press was also tipped off by the same informant who told the Feds. The story ended up in all the newspapers across the state.

One of the newspaper men getting the story scoop was from Albany, and he was allowed to take and publish exclusive pictures of the raid.

Sources were always kept confidential. It was an unwritten rule for reporters, part of their unwritten constitution.

The Albany reporter received high praise from his editors for the front-page story. They also gave him two extra days off in addition to the weekend for all his hard work and digging. He took the train from Albany to Chicago with his wife and checked into the elegant Warwick Allerton Hotel on the North Side.

"10th floor Mr. Livingston," the front desk clerk said handing him the key to the three-room suite. "And this was left for you." The desk clerk handed him an envelope that was in the mailbox associated with his room. He unbuttoned his overcoat and put the envelope securely in the inside pocket. He could feel it was a large amount of cash.

"Compliments of Mr. Drucci and Mr. Capone," the man said in a quiet whisper after looking around to see if anyone else could hear them.

The reporter reached into his pants pocket and pulled out a piece of paper folded in half. He slid it across the top of the counter to the clerk and then walked away without saying a word.

The clerk opened the folded piece of paper, read it and put it in his back pocket.

The paper had three words written on it. "Big Seven Danny."

———

CHAPTER 37

FAMILY

The report Patrick made to Danny about his meeting with Fred Rockwell, the newspaper situation and the possible story didn't sit well. Danny still had pain from the bullet wound and used his cane gun walking stick more often than not. News like this made his back feel worse, though he didn't know why. Danny knew Owney and Big Bill would not be pleased and may take drastic action to head off any story that could expose their operation and connections to government officials. This newspaper problem was happening in Danny's territory, and he figured the money and blackmail photos of the editor would have keep a lid on it. Patrick's information said otherwise. Now he would have to inform New York about what was going on, but Danny would wait for the right moment during their upcoming sit down in Pittsburgh. Nine hours on the train gave him plenty of time to prepare for the meeting and come up with a good way to break this news to Owney and Big Bill.

Pittsburgh was a growing industrial city providing steel to the rest of the country for the building boom that had going on until the stock market crash a year earlier in 1929. Steam poured from the many stacks rising above factories along the banks of the great Ohio and Allegheny Rivers.

The weather was chilly and leaves were turning as summer turned into fall. Even with prohibition in full swing, there were plenty of blind tigers and speakeasys around the great steel city. The supply of booze came from Canada via Detroit, and the flow was controlled mostly by Chicago. Pittsburgh also had plenty of home-grown distilling operations and local breweries adding to the supply and the level of corruption.

The fire station located in the Polish Hill neighborhood looked like any other with fire trucks at the ready and men hanging around waiting for the next emergency. The house next door also looked like a typical Pittsburgh two-family. What most people knew, but didn't admit, was that the two properties shared a common basement. Between the house and the fire station, the basement was large, and years earlier someone had realized it was the perfect place for a speakeasy. The entrance was through the kitchen of the house. People came in using the side kitchen door, met the bouncer and, if approved, used the basement stairs to enter. There was also a secret entrance at the fire station that some higher end patrons like politicians and wealthy businessmen used. The fire station end of the speakeasy was separated from the rest of the nightclub by a wall, door and its own bouncer. Owney, Big Bill and Danny came in through the fire station entrance and were quickly escorted to a corner table where two people from Chicago sat.

Owney and the others had known for quite a while that the North Side Gang had lost most of its influence in Chicago after their assassination attempt against Capone failed and they were forced to make the peace. Drucci's partner, Bugs Moran, wanted to continue the war against Capone but knew it was better for business to end the fighting. Capone consolidated power and controlled most of the underworld activities in the Windy City including running booze, prostitution and gambling.

"Look who the fuck they let into this dump," said Jack "Machine Gun" McGurn when he saw Owney walk in and walk toward their table. "Oh, and this asshole too," he continued pointing to Danny in a joking manner. McGurn knew Big Bill, but not as well as Owney and Danny.

All the men shook hands with a hug and kiss on the cheek. It was understood that nobody would take weapons to a high level sit down.

"Drinks for everyone," Jack ordered long time bar tender, Connie Burr. "Whatever they want, it's on the house."

This speakeasy was owned and operated by Chicago, so Jack McGurn could do just about anything he wanted. He represented Capone.

Owney took off his overcoat and put it on the table next to the one they were sitting at. The lights were low and smoke filled the air along with the sound of music emanating from the more public side of the speakeasy separated by the wall.

"How's Al?" Owney asked.

"Ready to do business," Jack replied coldly. "This is Jerry Martini, and before you ask, that's his real name," he said introducing the man with him who was mainly his traveling companion and muscle if needed. Jack didn't like to waste time. He also wasn't too fond of taking a train all the way to Pittsburgh for a sit down. He felt the Big Seven guys should have come to Chicago out of respect for Capone. Growing up as a boxer, Jack still liked a good fight and to jab. "We heard *Black Duck* got all shot up by the Feds."

Danny didn't like Jack, or anyone for that matter, with the Chicago organizations. "We heard in the papers your Lake George speak's were busted pretty good," he replied.

Jack looked at Danny and took a sip of his drink. Then he spoke in an even angrier monotone. "Somebody tipped them off." He paused for a few seconds, then continued. "Tell me something, does that guy Marky still work for you guys? How's he doing?" Jack said knowing that would infuriate his counterpart sitting across the table.

Owney could see where this was going right away and stepped in. "We're here to iron out territory and distribution. We've got an agreement and want to make sure it sticks. We also want to make peace."

Danny and Jack stared at each other without saying a word. Big Bill also jumped into the conversation. "Upstate New York seems to be causing all the problems between us. I thought that was settled," he said.

"And western Mass," Danny said still glaring at Jack.

"We don't supply western Mass, Danny. That's yours," Jack explained while sipping his whisky. "We don't touch it."

"Bullshit, Jack," Danny barked. "Bullshit."

Both men were known to be hot heads. Owney and Big Bill knew that.

"This is from Al. We don't and won't touch Western Mass or any part of New England. You stay out of New York State, Pennsylvania and our other territories. It's that simple," Jack said almost like he was lecturing a high school class.

"And a complete ceasefire?" Owney asked. Never at a sit down would one family or organization accuse the other of violence or revenge even though both knew it was happening.

Jack took another sip of his whisky then spoke. "And a complete ceasefire."

Owney stood up and reached across to shake Jack's hand. Jack stood and came around the table to shake hands and both men embraced and kissed each other on the cheek. In theory, all seven members of the Big Seven would have a say, but it was clearly understood that Owney, Big Bill and Danny were senior and made deals on behalf of them all.

Jack then offered his hand to Danny sitting across from him. Danny sat motionless for a few seconds that seemed like a week to the others. They needed peace between the organizations, and Danny was one of the key players. Except for the music low in the background, the room was quiet. Danny looked at Owney and Big Bill then back to Jack. He picked up his glass and took a long sip of whisky then placed it down on the table. Danny then stood up and extended his hand to shake Jack's. The two shook hands then sat back down. They didn't embrace.

"Connie," Jack yelled loudly across the room breaking the tension. "What do you have to feed some hungry train travelers?"

She brought out some food as the men sat, drank and told stories for another few hours just like they were old friends. Finally, Jack took his leave heading for the train station and the midnight Silver Star to Chicago. Owney, Big Bill and Danny would be staying the night before heading back east in the morning. As they were about to leave, Danny took Owney aside.

"You need to know about a problem we might have with a newspaper story in Providence," he explained. "A reporter is poking around the business we have with the governor and a couple of our judges from what I understand. Got this from an editor we have on the arm at the *Journal*. It's one of his reporters."

Owney had enjoyed a few drinks that evening but was sober enough to answer his friend and partner.

"Danny, my boy," Owney said while putting his arm on Danny's shoulder. "That's not going to be a problem."

Danny was perplexed. "You know about this reporter?" he asked now truly surprised. He knew Owney was tied in with the governor and other Rhode Island officials but wondered how he had found out about this particular story. Danny thought he was the only one with a newspaper insider on the payroll.

"Danny, my boy," Owney said again. "Not going to be a problem. Now let's get the hell out of here."

———

U. S. Route 5 had been completed just about four years earlier in 1926. That was where Joey Cardin was driving as he entered the small town of Newport, Vermont. Most people came to Newport on vacation while spending time on Lake Memphremagog. Others used it as a gas stop on the way into Canada. The town was just ten miles from the border. Joey was betting on the latter. He and his partner, Johnny Howell, were sitting in the parking lot of one of the larger gas stations and grocery stores. Johnny was new to the crew and had been recruited by Joey who had now moved up after Marky's death. They were there on Patrick's hunch. He had told them this would be the likely route north for someone headed to Canada from where the Connelly cabin was located.

"This is a waste of time," Joey said doubting Patrick's thinking. Joey and Johnny had already gone by the cabin on the drive up and found it empty. They noticed the tracks in the dirt driveway when they were there. "Someone was at the cabin. If it was Connelly, he's gone. If it was the priest, he's gone, too."

Johnny didn't say much. He was the new guy. The two sat at the gas station for a couple of hours. They decided to get out of the car and go into the grocery store in search of sandwiches likely sold at the lunch counter. After the sandwiches were made, Joey paid the tab then started walking toward the front of the store. In an instant, Joey stopped in his tracks and put his arm out for Johnny to do the same. Johnny didn't know what was happening.

"North End? Way up here?" Joey questioned almost to himself. "What the fuck?"

"What?" Johnny asked sounding like a new student.

"See that guy getting gas in the Rugby?" Joey asked his new sidekick pointing to the Durant Motor Company Model R Rugby sedan at the pump.

"Yeah, so?"

"Boston guy. North End. Name is Dario, I think," Joey explained while trying to figure out in his head what this guy was doing way up here. The man finished paying the attendant for the gas and pulled forward but not out of the parking lot. There was a light rain, almost a mist in the chilly Vermont air. Joey saw the gas attendant coming back to the grocery building to dry off. *Perfect timing*, he thought. When the young man, pretty much a kid, entered the building, he walked toward the checkout counter where another employee was standing. Joey handed the bag with the sandwiches to Johnny then walked over to where the two men were talking.

"Excuse me," Joey said clearly interrupting their conversation.

"Can I help you?" the grocery checkout guy asked.

"Do you know that guy?" Joey said pointing to the man still sitting in the running car now parked closer to the tree line.

"You a G?" the young man asked. "We're legal here. No booze."

Joey couldn't help but chuckle that this guy would think of him as a G-man.

"No, not at all. Just from Boston, and that looked like an old friend," Joey said.

"Well, yeah, that's Mr. Simpson from Boston. He and his friend Dario have been here for a couple of days. Not sure what they're doing. We figure they're looking for someone. Thought he was a 'G,' too, but no," explained the cashier.

Joey thanked them and returned to his partner standing a few aisles away in order to fill him in. North End Gang in this part of Vermont looking for someone who may be headed to Canada? *Sounds all too familiar*, he thought.

Not three minutes later, the kid from the gas pump came over as Joey and Johnny watched the two guys sitting in the car across the way. "Now that's a real G-man," the kid said proudly while pointing to a government owned and registered Model A pulling up to the opposite pump.

"Shit!" Johnny said. Joey thought the same thing. At first, they figured the two G-men to be Bureau of Prohibition and working the border crossing not far away. Then just a few minutes into the Feds' car getting fueled up, Joey recognized Father Ralph's sedan drive by with four people inside headed north. "Jesus, what are the odds?" he said to his partner while grabbing him by the arm. "Come on, that's them."

The two men walked quickly out to their car on the side of the building. They didn't want to alert the G-men or the guys from Boston, but it was too late. The Boston crew had good eyes and started to pull away in pursuit headed north on U.S. 5.

"Fuck me," Joey said while quickly putting the car in gear. He pulled out and also headed north on U.S. 5 toward the Canadian border. The one thing he couldn't do was go over the border with two Tommys sitting loaded in the trunk. Up ahead he could see the back of the 1927 Essex Super 6 the Boston crew was driving. "Did the Feds follow?"

Johnny kept an eye out the back window. "Nope. Don't think so. They were still getting gas."

Both vehicles sped north toward Canada with the Boston crew closing on Father Ralph's car.

"Are you kidding me?" Joey yelled as he looked ahead and saw Dario hanging out of the passenger window with his Tommy in hand. The next thing everyone could hear was the sound of machine gun fire. Instantly Father Ralph's car swerved from side to side avoiding direct hits while creating a giant cloud of dust from the edges of the road. U.S. 5 in this part of Vermont was a bit bumpy in places. It was not easy for the Boston crew to get a good shot. Again, the rat-a-tat-tat sound of a Thompson firing could be heard as Joey stepped on the gas to get closer.

Father Ralph could handle himself in the driver's seat. He crossed back and forth on the road to avoid the bullets from the car pursuing them. "Keep your heads down," he yelled to the ladies in the back seat. Ted reached under his seat and pulled out his Colt .45, stuck half his body out the window to get a good shot and squeezed off a few rounds.

"Christ," Dario said ducking back into the car to reload. "Get closer."

The Boston car closed in on Father Ralph's. Dario once again leaned far out the window with his Tommy and fired off another burst. One of the bullets smashed through the rear window of Father Ralph's car finding the back of Marge's head splattering blood and brain matter across the car. Sister Judy Ann screamed. Father Ralph swerved again to avoid more bullets.

Ted took aim at the driver of the pursuing Boston car and pulled his trigger again and again. Instantly he could see the front windshield turn dark red and the car swerve sharply to the right. Its tires found the edge of the road flipping the heavy vehicle over onto its side. From what Ted could see, the guy with the Tommy who had been halfway out the window was crushed by the car while the driver had a bullet in his face.

Father Ralph sped off as fast as he could go. Ted looked back as Marge's lifeless body slumped onto the back floor. Sister Judy Ann had her rosary out and in her hand because that was all she could do for Ted's wife at this point.

Just a few miles back, the Feds and local police were headed to the car wreck and would have to figure out what happened before continuing to look for them. A few minutes later, Ted slowed his car as they approached a street that intersected U.S. 5.

"I think this is it," he said to his brother who was now weeping for his dead wife. Father Ralph looked to the left and right. Putting the car in gear, he took a left and started down a small, poorly paved road.

"Are you sure about this, Ralph?" Ted said trying to focus on the task at hand and not his loss. "Are you sure?"

"I think so," he answered. "We were just kids last time we were up this far."

The car bounced down the road which started to narrow to where the pavement finally ended. With the light rain picking up, the dirt road was starting to get muddy. Downshifting, Father Ralph slowed but continued. He knew the Feds would be on their tail. He figured they would be headed a few more miles straight to the border to look for them.

"Is that it?" Ted yelled.

"Please Lord," Sister Judy said also looking through the front window of the shot-up car. Father Ralph's plan would work if everything was in place. One thing missing and they would all either end up in jail or dead.

Father Ralph slowed the car down. His brother stuck his head out the window to see better. Just ahead he could see Lake Memphremagog. It was a calm, overcast day and the lake reflected the color of the changing leaves. In other circumstances, this would be a beautiful place to visit and stay awhile. Ted recognized it from his childhood.

Father Ralph stopped the car as the road came to an end in a small, dirt parking lot. There was a 1927 Peerless four door sedan sitting on the side near a boat landing. A man quickly got out and ran over to Father Ralph's car.

"Ralph, oh my God!"

Ted reached back into his memory and childhood now recognizing the man helping Sister Judy out of the back seat.

"Burt, you're literally a life saver," Father Ralph said. He looked over at Ted. "You remember Burt LaFrance, don't you?"

"Holy shit, yeah." Ted said. "It's been a long time."

"Was this your wife?" he asked Ted. "She'll have to stay here," Burt said coldly as he looked at Marge's body in the back seat. Ted wanted to take her but knew his childhood friend was right. They were headed to Canada, and the first thing a Mountie would do would be to arrest them if they were carrying a dead body, and then a full investigation would follow.

"We've got to go," Father Ralph said collecting his two suitcases out of the trunk. "Everything set?"

"Right this way," Burt said and led the three through a winding path in the woods that led to an opening where a Hacker Belle Isle Bear Cat boat was tied to an old dock. Ted was more than impressed with his little brother the priest. All three climbed aboard the wooden power boat which was fully fueled. Father Ralph opened one of his suitcases and pulled out a large amount of cash, handing it to Burt.

"There's a little extra in there for the trouble of ditching the car," he said to his childhood friend. "Unfortunately, no more sure thing bets at Aqueduct. I'm out of business."

Burt chuckled. "You've got a good three to four hours of daylight left and should make Georgeville with no problem. It's around 22 to 25 miles north. My guy will pick up the boat there and have a car for you," he explained.

Lake Memphremagog was a favorite among those who wanted to cross into Canada without going by land and dealing with border check points. The lake was shared by both countries and perfect for those who could afford a boat charter. In this case, Father Ralph would pay for the use of one with his old buddy's help.

"Thank you, Burt," Ted said. "We owe you."

"No, you don't. Ralph took care of that part," Burt said holding up the bag he put his money in. Ted had to smile.

"Take care of Marge for me," Ted said to Burt before taking a seat next to Sister Judy in the boat. Burt just nodded and waved. It was all Ted could do for her at this point, but he trusted Burt to take care of her remains properly.

Ralph backed the boat and turned it north pushing the throttle forward to pick up speed. Ted got up and stood next to him while watching the dock, his dead wife and his past slowly disappear to the south. Canada and a new life awaited all three just a few miles north.

"I don't even want to know how you did this or how you paid for it," Ted yelled over the sound of the wind and the engine as they moved through the calm lake water.

"Burt owed me a favor," Father Ralph yelled back.

"What does he do now?" Ted asked curious to at least know that much.

"He's police chief back there in Newport."

Ted was silent for the rest of the boat trip and glad he wasn't the only crooked cop in America.

———

CHAPTER 38

TRUSTED SOURCES

Jacksonville was always muggy this time of the year when fall was in the air. The north Florida city was starting to flourish with industry and had a busy port given its easy access to the Atlantic Ocean.

Jesse and Thomas had been driving for hours and wanted to stop for a break. The sun was still out, but dusk was approaching. Thomas suggested they spend the night just south of Jacksonville at a motel on U.S. Route 1. Their plan was that Thomas would agree to return to Rhode Island and be an explosive source for Jesse's story after seeking protection from the state Attorney General.

Using a fake name, Thomas checked in while Jesse sat in the car. In short time he returned to with two keys. The Evergreen Motel was not very busy seeing that it was in the middle of the week, and the snow birds from the northeast had not invaded just yet. Jesse was not familiar with the area. On trips to interview his number one source, he would take U.S. 301 down the center of Florida toward the Sunshine State's west coast.

"105 & 106," Thomas said to Jesse. "Let's eat first. I know a good seafood place not too far from here."

Both men were hungry. Thomas got back into the driver's seat and they headed south toward the waterfront.

Twenty minutes later a marina appeared with tall palm trees blowing in the wind while a scent of low tide filled the air. A small restaurant stood just across from the marina called Mario's Seafood. Thomas pulled into the parking lot, and the two men got out of the car.

"Well damn," Thomas said pointing to the marina.

"What is it?" Jesse asked. In his mind was how their last visit to a marina ended and whether that guy named Doyle was still looking for them.

Thomas pointed to a boat tied up at the end of the longest dock. It was a rather large vessel with several men washing the deck. "I know those guys and that boat."

Jesse looked toward where he was pointing and squinted in the setting sun. "How do you know them?"

"From Tampa. Let's say hi." Thomas said as he started across the street and walked toward the marina.

Jesse was hungry but went along with the quick visit idea. The two men walked onto the dock and about fifty yards out to the end where the boat was secured. Jesse figured it was a fishing boat. He didn't see many lines or nets, but it looked like it. *Definitely an ocean-going boat,* he thought as they approached.

"Thomas Pike," the man in the wheelhouse yelled out. "What the hell are you doing here?"

Thomas looked up. "Captain," he yelled. "Permission to come aboard?"

"Of course. I thought you were retired down in Tampa. What brings you here?"

Jesse followed Thomas across the brow onto the deck of the boat. The captain came out of the wheelhouse and down the steps to the deck to meet his friend.

"This is Jesse Young," Thomas said introducing his traveling companion.

The captain and Jesse shook hands.

"How the hell are you, my friend?" asked the captain looking over at Thomas.

"Doing well. Sort of retired," Thomas answered.

"Sort of?" the captain asked.

Thomas looked at Jesse and winked. "Long story. How about a drink? I'm sure you have some booze on this thing."

"Down below, come on," the captain said to his visitors. The other men that were on deck had already gone below.

"You first," Thomas said to Jesse extending his hand pointing to the stairs leading below deck.

Jesse ducked his head and walked down the stairs into the belly of the ship. He couldn't miss the smell of old wood and what he thought was whisky. Once below, he saw the two of the men who had been on deck. It didn't look like they had anything to drink except for what might have been in a few of the barrels sitting on the other side of the hold. On the wall Jesse saw a typical life ring hanging on a hook with rope.

"*Black Duck*, is that the name of the boat?" Jesse asked pointing to the ring with the words on it.

"It is," answered Captain Rick St. Pierre.

One of the deck hands was standing behind Jesse and put a .32 caliber revolver to his head pulling the trigger. Instantly the reporter's body crumpled to the floor. Three more shots to the chest made sure that this was the end of the story, literally.

"We still have a deal, right?" Thomas said to Captain Rick St. Pierre.

"We do. Go back to your life in Tampa or wherever it is. Owney sent this for you with thanks," Rick said while handing a small bag to Thomas. Thomas took the bag and, without saying a word, climbed back up to the deck and walked off the *Black Duck*. The box with the ledgers was still in his possession but would not see the light of day.

An hour later the *Black Duck* sailed out of the little marina and turned north heading back to Canada for another run.

CHAPTER 39

(two years later)

DINNER PLANS

The morning was quiet on Ives Street just down from Brown University where Danny was waking up. Of his three Rhode Island residences, he used this one the least but enjoyed the location being so close to the East Side. His head was spinning from the long night before. He was expecting Patrick and his attorney who wanted to talk about the settlement he had made with the IRS five years earlier. The sound of a trolley could be heard down the street picking up passengers headed downtown. Making his way to the small kitchen, he put on a pot of coffee then took a quick shower hoping it would cleanse the now almost legal booze from his system.

As he dried off in the bathroom, a knock at the door echoed through the apartment.

"Come in, Patrick," he yelled. "Be out in a minute."

Patrick and Sal, the attorney, made themselves at home. For Patrick, these meetings were routine. He went into the kitchen and poured three cups of coffee from the freshly made pot. Just the smell of the brewing coffee helped all three men adjust to the early hour.

"Sal, how are you?" Danny said in a booming voice walking into the kitchen half-dressed and wiping his hair dry with a towel.

"Good, Danny. Booze is almost legal again, and the IRS is still pissed at you for not paying enough," Sal said with a bit of a chuckle in his voice.

"Fuck 'em. Water under the bridge. We settled that back in 1928. I've been a good boy paying my fair share since," Danny said in a half proud and half sarcastic tone.

"Sure, you have, boss," Patrick said also with a sarcastic inflection. It was estimated that when the IRS had sued him, he was making around 700 to 750 thousand a year. They settled for less than 300 thousand. Clearly, he was making even more than that now, but the cost of doing business, including payoffs and bribe money, had also risen.

"They're going to come back at you again," Sal said with a more serious tone now. "After repeal, you're going to have to figure out a way to declare less income while putting the extra funds in safer places."

Patrick had a plan for this as did Danny. They were planning on investing in more real estate and stocks as the country slowly recovered from the crash and subsequent depression. And horses. Danny still loved horses, the pricier the better.

"We'll take care of it, Sal. We've got a plan in place for a portfolio of legit businesses," Patrick said.

Danny took a sip of his coffee. "You worry too much, Sal."

The three men continued their conversation for a while longer before Sal took his leave. He and Patrick had come in separate cars.

"Drop me at the office. Then I want you to go over and make sure the locations for the retail stores are solid," Danny ordered Patrick. "Broadway in Pawtucket and Central Falls will be first and second after repeal. My younger brothers will run those on the up and up."

Patrick sipped his coffee and nodded his acknowledgment of the daily orders. Danny had learned over the past few years that he had to diversify his portfolio of businesses and bring on legitimate enterprises. The Big Seven's plan was to continue after prohibition in the rackets and underworld black markets along with influence peddling and protection.

Danny would run his territory with these money makers while at the same time building retail liquor outlets and buying real estate. Now a major player, Danny was still a thorn in the side of Capone's former cohorts in Chicago and the North End Gang in Boston which continued to expand their families and influence. Capone himself had been in prison for two years, and his crime was one familiar to Danny: tax evasion.

The two men left the apartment headed for the office just a few miles away on Broad Street on the south side of Providence.

"We still on for dinner tonight?" Patrick asked as Danny got out of the black Ford at the curb.

"Yeah, Bank Cafe at seven," Danny replied then closed the door and went into the building to start his day.

Patrick then pulled out and headed on his way. Three cars behind Patrick, another black Ford pulled into a parking spot on the street with a view of the building Danny had just entered. The men in that car would now wait and watch.

———

Warwick was one of the larger cities in the smallest state in the union, Rhode Island. Pawtuxet Village was a sleepy little neighborhood where many Irish Americans made their homes.

The Bank Cafe was a small place but a favorite of Danny and his crew. He had taken Owney and Big Bill there a few times along with other Big Seven associates. Tonight Patrick, Joey and four other business cronies from the speakeasys they managed on Cape Cod were being treated after a good month of earning in January.

"We have had a good start to the year," Joey announced to the others sitting around the table. "Salute," he said raising his glass as did the others in a toast to prosperity during prohibition. The irony that they were drinking their own illegal product was never lost on this bunch. As was tradition, the mangers of the Cape Cod speakeasys, which had made exceptional profits in December and January, were part of this dinner at the

Bank Cafe. They had brought Danny $40,000 cash in a brown paper bag. Clearly, the past two months had been *very* strong.

The men ate dinner and sipped whisky until around 9 p.m. Danny was still tired from the night before. His plan was to head back to Providence for the night before going to the farm in Charlestown the next morning. Danny was rich, and he never forgot the little people, making many cash contributions to churches, schools and other organizations which, in this second-hand way, also benefited from the Volstead Act.

"You want me to follow you home, boss?" Patrick asked as they were leaving the cafe.

"I'm good," Danny said.

"You sure?" Patrick questioned, knowing in his gut the boss should always have

some protection muscle around. It was standard operating procedure.

"No, you go home to that wife, and I'll see you in the morning," Danny answered.

Deep inside, Patrick still felt he should follow the boss, but it was getting late, and he wanted to see the kids before they went to sleep.

"Okay, see you in the morning." Patrick said to Danny who was about to get in his car.

Patrick started his car and drove by Danny's as he headed out of the parking lot.

He looked over at Danny and waved. Danny waved back at him. That was the last time the two would ever see each other.

———

Patrick arrived at the office the next day along with the rest of the small staff. As the morning wore on, it became evident that everyone was there except Danny. No phone call. No note. Nothing. Patrick called a meeting, and throughout the day members of the crew searched for Danny at all of his residences. Calls were made to Owney in New York. Nothing.

A few days later, a ransom note arrived demanding $40,000. Danny's crew along with his brothers Joseph and William drove up to Boston with the 40 grand and dropped it at the required location. Then they waited for Danny's return. It never came. Danny Walsh was never seen again.

EPILOGUE

For months and years after Danny's disappearance, his crew along with the Big Seven searched for answers. Like many high-profile mob hits, this mystery went unsolved. Tensions between disputed territories continued with other organized crime organizations such as the emerging Italian families in Boston and Capone's gang in Chicago even after its leader went to prison. It was an unwritten rule that when someone of Danny's status went missing, a silent yet clear message was received by all the families and organizations.

During prohibition and especially the last three years leading up to the repeal of the Volstead Act in 1933, Owney "The Killer" Madden, "Big Bill" Dwyer and Danny Walsh built an empire becoming one of the United States' largest bootlegging operations. The Big Seven, also known as the Combine, controlled much of the movement of liquor on the east coast along with other illegal activities such as gambling, prostitution and extortion. They were tied into and did business with other famous names like Joseph Kennedy and Al Capone.

Over the decades that followed Danny's disappearance, whenever human remains were found in this part of the country, authorities would check the bones against his dental records. This was also the case in 2016. The remains found on his former property in Charlestown, Rhode Island that year proved to be those of someone else.

The mystery of Danny Walsh's disappearance remains just that to this day--a mystery.

AUTHOR'S NOTE

Danny Walsh was my great uncle. He and his brothers, including my grandfather William Walsh, Sr., were instrumental during this colorful period in our country's history. I did not know Danny as his disappearance happened a few years before the birth of my father. I did spend many years growing up hearing stories about Danny's life, adventures and his infamous kidnapping from my grandfather who was reportedly part of the squad who delivered the ransom payment. My grandfather started selling legal liquor the day after prohibition ended. He held the first liquor license issued in the State of Rhode Island. It was license number 00001.

This story and most of its characters are fictional, built around a few actual individuals as well as some true case history of their sometimes-ruthless business. It's dedicated to my father William Walsh, Jr. who carried on the liquor business until he retired and sold Walsh's Liquor, Inc. He said he always wanted to write a book about these colorful relatives from the 1920s. We both agreed a good fictional tale could be crafted. This one is for you, Dad.

———————

CPSIA information can be obtained
at www.ICGtesting.com
Printed in the USA
LVHW040028200819
628263LV00022B/1755/P